Early Praise for *Aberrations*

"Under Przekop's artful care, narcolepsy and gay identity receive humorous, humanizing treatment, creating a novel that lingers in the consciousness with passion and compassion. *Aberrations* exposes the myth of the straight and narrow path. It is a tale filled with ghosts that ultimately invites us to celebrate life and to embrace fully the hand that we are dealt."

—Lars Clausen, award-winning author of *Straight Into Gay America: My Unicycle Journey for Equal Rights*

"Contrast and the chasm that results—contrast as sure as that between a clear, cloudless sky and impending storm clouds—is what drives Angel, the main character of Przekop's engrossing first novel. The contrast between awake and asleep. Between guilt and innocence. Between right and wrong. Between mother and father.

One of the threads that Przekop weaves effortlessly throughout the book is a series of photographs, the significance of which unfolds and presents itself in a myriad of ways to both Angel and those most important to her. We're gripped by the journey that Angel takes and her discovery of that exquisite moment before the shutter is clicked and its potential to show us so much of ourselves. We discover along with her that we determine our own composition and like life, it's what we choose to see that brings about the most stunning results."

—Teresa Lauer, psychotherapist/rape recovery expert, author of *The Truth about Rape* and *Hours of Torture, Years of Silence: My Soul was the Scene of the Crime*

"Penelope Przekop has not only accurately captured the hallmark symptoms of narcolepsy and their presentation, she has also created a character that is both self-aware and self-accepting of her disorder and the way it has shaped her life and decisions."

—Narcolepsy Network, a national nonprofit narcolepsy support organization

"Based on my extensive 38-year-career with the Houston Police Department, Przekop's tale of secrets and shame accurately conveys both the short- and long-term impact of violent crime. Przekop's well-written novel, which vividly demonstrates the effect rape can have on the victim as well as the extended family, is authentic and insightful. As a result, *Aberrations*' main character, Angel, experiences a thought-provoking struggle with her own selfishness, deceit, and apathy. Przekop successfully shows us how violence can twist reality in ways we never imagined."
—Johnny E. Neely, security consultant, retired police officer/detective, Houston Police Department

"*Aberrations* is alternatingly stormy, stark, and poignant—contemporary Southern fiction at its finest. From the first page, Penelope Przekop plunges readers soul-deep, gifting them with the intriguingly flawed character of Angel Duet. In perfectly executed stages of intensity and revelation, Przekop shares Angel's exhumation of dark personal tragedies, that even while held in secret, indelibly shaped the woman she'd become. *Aberrations* is an authentically told story of rebirth through the discovery of truth, and of the acceptance of peace—and love—in the aftermath of life's cruelest betrayals."
—Kim Lenox, author of *Night Falls Darkly*

"Penelope Przekop's *Aberrations* is one of the best novels I've read in a long time. She writes as if she's been a best-selling author for years. She's created a stunning page-turner packed with emotion and beautiful storytelling. I can't wait to read her next novel!"
—Kelly Jameson, author of the suspense-thriller *Dead On*

Aberrations

Published by Emerald Book Company
4425 South Mo Pac Expwy, Suite 600,
Austin, TX 78735

For ordering information or special discounts for bulk purchases, please contact Emerald Book Company at: 4425 South Mo Pac Expwy, Suite 600, Austin, TX 78735, (512) 891-6100.

Design and composition by Greenleaf Book Group LLC

Publisher's Cataloging-In-Publication Data
(Prepared by The Donohue Group, Inc.)

Przekop, Penelope.
    Aberrations : a novel / Penelope Przekop. -- 1st ed.

    p. ; cm.

    ISBN: 978-1-934572-03-0

    1. Young women--United States--Fiction. 2. Fathers and daughters--United States--Fiction. 3. Family secrets--United States--Fiction. 4. Narcolepsy--Fiction. 5. Domestic fiction, American. I. Title.

PS3616.R94 A24 2008
813/.6   2008927639

Printed in the United States of America on acid-free paper

11 10 09 08 07   10 9 8 7 6 5 4 3 2 1

First Edition

Aberrations

a novel

Penelope Przekop

EMERALD
BOOK CO.
A Division of Greenleaf Book Group LLC

Aberration (ab-*uh*-**rey**-*shuhn*):

1. the act of departing from the right, normal, or usual course
2. the act of deviating from the ordinary, usual, or normal type
3. deviation from truth or moral rectitude
4. mental irregularity or disorder, especially of a minor or temporary nature; lapse from a sound mental state
5. *Astronomy.* Apparent displacement of a heavenly body, owing to the motion of the earth in its orbit
6. *Optics.* Any disturbance of the rays of a pencil of light such that they can no longer be brought to a sharp focus or form a clear image
7. *Photography.* A defect in a camera lens or lens system, due to flaws in design, material, or construction that can distort the image

Source: aberration. Dictionary.com. Dictionary.com Unabridged (v 1.1). Random House, Inc.

http://dictionary.reference.com/browse/aberration
(accessed: June 11, 2007).

LOCAL POLICE NEWS

SARASOTA — A 22-year-old woman was sexually assaulted on Nov. 25. The incident took place on Siesta Key. The woman described one assailant as approximately six feet in height with brown hair and a mustache. The second assailant was also described as approximately six feet in height, but with broad shoulders, blond hair, and distinguishing freckles on his face and arms. The two men were last seen running down Lands End Lane on Siesta Key at approximately 9:30 p.m. on the night of the crime. The victim suffered a broken leg and nose, numerous superficial knife wounds to the arms and chest, and a concussion. The victim remains in stable condition at Sarasota General Hospital. The Sarasota Police Department is offering a reward for information leading to an arrest.

☑ angel

My father is a liar. He claimed to name me Angel the day my mother died. He said it was because God sent me to save him, but as the years passed he shriveled up anyway into a wad of sadness and self-pity. The lies he told about her death became my foundation—they were the kind that anchor little girls when they don't have a mother.

He gave me a story.

Before I began the real search for my mother, I was lonely. All I had was the liar, who, based on my meager experience, seemed to be doing the best he could. After all, he taught me to love the wide-open distance surrounding us, and sometimes that space made me feel as if I could actually fly. The cotton fields made it seem possible more than anything. Sometimes when he gazed up into the blue-sea sky, my father cried. The more he cried, the less I cried, but no matter what degree of strength I gained, the cotton fields stirred something in me. Each time I felt that rousing beat of my heart, I thought I understood his tall tale. See, my mother, Betty Lou, had loved fields, and my father, filled with a grief so rich it turned generous, showed me all her favorites. He took me onto private property, and even to the top of a high-rise building erected on the very spot where she had stretched out across the grass, searching for shapes in the clouds. She photographed them—it was her passion—or so the story went.

Only later I found out I had to create my own story. Ironically, it began in a giant bug-infested cotton field, surrounded by cows, at the LSU Agricultural Center. For several years, I'd worked a few hours a week at the hospital near our home, which was convenient and a good way to make a few bucks, keep as active as possible, and seem normal. It was perfect, filled with a variety of healthcare professionals, lots of capable hands to catch me if I fell. The situation changed, though, in the spring of my junior year, when my neurologist decided to increase my medication, hoping to propel me through my last year of college.

He winked, saying, "It might actually make you hyper," which sounded interesting. I didn't think I'd ever been hyper.

Imagine a hyper turtle. I was a turtle. So on his advice, and my father's strong support, I took a full-time summer job at the Ag Center. They hoped the nature of the work and the sunshine, along with the new regimen, would somehow give my body a jump-start. As they discussed the possibilities, I imagined I'd be like the turtle I found in our yard as a kid. I'd painted its back white in hope of finding it again. I worried that they'd need to tag me so I could be found at the end of the summer. As the doctor scribbled down my new prescription, my father just smiled like he had for the last twenty years, kind of sad but hopeful. I smiled back, guessing that the turtle with the white back was dead now.

So I ended up in a field of my own, and it was there I met Tim and Kimmy.

Thrown together on the first day of work, we seemed an unlikely threesome. College appeared to be our only connection. Tim was a small-boned guy who, despite his lack of muscle, was tough enough to make us think he was strong, and Kimmy, older than Tim and me by several years, was tall, soft, and rounded with very few edges. Tim struck me as a know-it-all, and she seemed to know very little considering her age. She had puppy-dog eyes. Later I realized just how perfect we were for each other; in fact, our dynamic set my story in motion, and if it wasn't for that, I might still be asleep.

From the beginning, they could see I was both tired and wired, a combination that would make anyone curious. I tried to hide it, but dull eyes, drooping lids, and slurred words followed by drug-induced hyperactive behavior (a hyper turtle) are hard to hide, even for the most skilled of my kind. I'd been trying to mask my narcolepsy for almost ten years. I had some great tricks, but being with Tim and Kimmy for eight hours a day, five days a week, presented a new challenge. I'd never considered being open about it. I hadn't once stopped to think that other people might have afflictions or issues to hide that equaled mine. Things like not ever knowing what to say, or being insecure, or having bad teeth, a wife, fat parents, or being gay or ugly or unloved. In the end, I really just wanted everyone to leave me alone. I wanted to sleep.

I certainly didn't think Tim or Kimmy had anything to hide until, for some odd reason, Kimmy told me she was a virgin. Her confession came at me out of the blue, like looking up into the sky to find a giant horse or house or snail floating, perfectly shaped by billowing clouds, both plump and narrow-striped. And just like seeing a cloud take recognizable form, Kimmy gave me a little wondrous shock. She told me her secret about two weeks into the summer. During a lunch break, she was rambling on and on about her life, and Tim had wandered off to pee. It popped out of the drone, the blue, and there I was staring at the cloud.

Later, as I mulled over why in the world she would tell me such a thing, sweat dribbled down the side of my neck and down my back. I was hotter than I'd ever been. My backside pointed toward that beautiful Betty Lou space, and although my mouth wasn't close enough to touch the dirt, I could taste it. It was particularly humid that day and my jeans clung to my legs in a gross, heavy way. The Ag Center had a rule against its summer employees wearing shorts. The pesticides we were studying might seep into our skin and harm us at some basic level not yet understood. I pulled a handful of weeds from the brittle ground, and three bugs scurried away. I thought it odd—they weren't supposed to be there. I'd just spent the last half-hour teasing all the insects out of my designated section. The only explanation was that they'd crawled up from farther below, deeper than I'd been instructed to dig.

I spat to keep a bug from flying in my mouth. My head hurt. The way I was bent at the waist to avoid plopping my knees into the dirt wasn't helping. I kept trying to remain clean in what was basically a huge pile of dirt. I squatted low instead, and for a moment wondered what it might feel like to give in and roll in the dirt. It reminded me of Betty Lou and I imagined her under the dirt, beneath a frozen pond, swimming on her back, breath held, hands to the ice. I touched the ground, palms down, fingers widely spread. I scratched at it as if to make contact, to pull her out, but when I lifted my hands, I had nothing. So I searched the sky instead. Moments earlier it had been clear and blue but now clouds were rolling overhead. In Louisiana, everything can change within minutes.

"Why are you so strung out all the time?" Tim asked. "Are you on drugs?" He liked to talk and shock.

I didn't answer.

"Ignore me if you want, but I know it when I see it. You cleared those bugs before I even got my gear set up."

I straightened up, ready to confess. "I have narcolepsy, okay?"

"What's that?" asked Kimmy, genuinely interested.

"It's a sleepin' disorder," I said, pulling weeds again. "It's no big deal."

"Yeah, I think I've heard of that," said Tim. "It's like you're just goin' about your business, livin' your life, and Boom! You fall." He fell limp into the dirt, drama-queen fashion. Kimmy and I watched a brown cloud swirl around him until he disappeared. Then, from out of the dust, "How does that make you hyper? You *look* tired. I don't get it."

"Sometimes the medicine I take makes me hyper. I really don't wanna talk about it," I said, as nicely as I could.

"So you mean you don't normally shake your head and wave your hands around like that every time you talk?"

My head started to shake harder. Before I could answer, the sky rumbled.

"Never mind," Tim said, tossing a handful of weeds over his shoulder. "Alleluia! Let's go." He ran in a girlish way to the driver's side of the dirty pickup that brought us daily to what seemed the most deserted spot in the center. We had strict orders to head indoors at the first sign of thunder and lightning, which often turned out to be a refreshing break.

"You drive," I said, climbing into the other side. I scooted toward him, making room for Kimmy. She squeezed in, slamming the door against her leg. Tall and big-boned, she didn't seem to belong in a cotton field any more than I did. She was a sad girl. Actually, she wasn't a girl. She was twenty-six, but now I knew she was a virgin and, in my opinion, that made her a girl. And I knew it made her sad. She told me so. Her sweet, lonely face told me, too. It bore the knowledge of feeling big and being plain. But I thought she was appealing. She was normal, average, and ordinary, exactly what I wanted to be.

"Why don't we just wait it out?" she said. "Half the time we hear thunder, drive back, and nothin' happens."

As they stared at me from either side, it struck me that there was something else sad about her, something more than what she'd told me and how she looked. I saw it in Tim, too, but couldn't figure out exactly what it was or where it came from. Besides the fact that we were all in college, this nameless feeling was the thing we had in common. Despite the virgin white cotton and clouds, we were in a soiled place. None of us were gritty enough for it. We were each soft and swollen, bruised in our own way.

My foot started tapping and wouldn't stop.

Finally Tim said, "I like ridin' back. All those bumps feel good, real good, if you know what I mean."

Kimmy looked embarrassed.

It began to rain and I wondered if we should have gone in. The water ran down the windows of the truck, blocking our view. After thirty minutes of it, I began to fear we might sink, and the field that promised liberation would trap us. "We should have gone in," I said. "I think your idea was good, Kimmy, but it's not gonna dry up quick this time."

"We're gonna get stuck," Tim said, twisting around, searching for a way out. "Crap. In another thirty minutes, this is gonna be part of the frickin' Red River."

"Relax," Kimmy said. "All we can do now is wait and see what happens." She had a knack for calming Tim. "Just take a deep breath and pray for patience."

My foot tapped harder.

Tim's eyes rolled. "Well, we might as well get to know each other a little better then," he said. "Let's play this game I know. Each person has to tell a secret."

"We already know each other," I said. Kimmy looked worried and I decided she'd better start praying a little more.

"Not really," Tim said. "I don't know anythang personal about either of y'all, except now I know Angel has narco-whatever-shit. All we do out here is talk about nothin'."

These were the moments I hated most. The ones when I felt cornered into becoming a closer friend. The atmosphere condoned it and they wanted it. The close space. The rain. It's not that people weren't interesting to me. They were, but I always seemed to focus on their weaknesses, their self-centeredness, and their undeniable march toward death. When you have a dead mother, you're closer to death than most. And you know they're close, too. Every time I began to see a potential friend's life rounding out around me, I realized how small a dot I was upon it. I was too small to matter and, subsequently, too small to make the required effort. My attitude was selfish, but the piece necessary for unselfishness was the piece I couldn't find. My lack of that mysterious element enabled me, time after time, to refocus on the smallness. Their insignificance. My worthlessness. Everything appeared petty without the piece I called *mother*. Mother, I'd finally concluded, was something soft and warm, accepting and positive. The thing I'd never had.

Of course there was my father, who should have made me feel better but didn't. He and I were a team always coming up one player short. We sat together on the sidelines, holding hands. "Trust me, my life ain't that excitin'," I said, finally.

"Sure it is," Tim said, turning on the radio.

The ancient truck only had an AM dial, and Maurice Williams and the Zodiacs' whining oldie, "Stay," swirled around us like a plea for unity I didn't want. "Did you ever fall asleep durin' sex?" Tim asked. "You know, right at that *Xanadu* moment?"

"Oh my God," Kimmy said, reaching over me to slap at Tim. "What is wrong with you?"

Tim ignored her, singing, "Why don't you stay-ay-ay? Just a little bit longer . . ."

"No comment," I said, knowing they were both waiting for an answer.

"See, I knew it," Tim said, grinning. "She has some weird stuff goin' on with that narco shit."

"Will you grow up already?" Kimmy asked. She tried to turn down the music, but Tim pushed her hand away.

"Patience," he said, waving his finger in front of my face.

"What about you?" I asked Tim, trying not to shake my head. "You're the one who's dyin' to tell a secret." He wouldn't have suggested the game if he didn't want to talk. Despite his complaint, he was the one who most often brought up the subject of nothing.

"Okay, if you really wanna know. My secret is . . . The secret is . . ." His tone changed and I looked at Kimmy. My thick ponytail hit Tim in the face. "Oh, forget it," he said.

"What's the secret?" I asked, head shaking, hands gesturing.

"I cain't."

"Why not?" asked Kimmy.

"Stay, a little bit longer," the DJ said, saving Tim, who looked relieved. "Straight to us from 1960. What a year, what a song! In fact, Maurice Williams committed a crime when he made that song so dad-gum short," he said, his voice small and far away. "A mere one minute, thirty-seven seconds. So, let's hear it again. Let's stay . . . just a little bit longer, here on WYZE, where old is gold." And it began all over again.

"Just tell us the crappy secret," I said, feeling guilty already for being a jerk. "You started the stupid game. We didn't even wanna play."

He turned and looked at us with a face we hadn't seen, and then opened the door. Rain splashed into the truck, drenching him and me. Kimmy scooted closer to the opposite door, trying to keep dry.

I grabbed his wet shirt to keep him in the truck. "What the hell are you doin'?"

He gave in easily and closed the door. He folded his dripping arms over the steering wheel and buried his head between them. "I'm gay," he said, his voice muffled.

Kimmy sat up ultra-straight, shoving me closer to Tim. "Oh my God," she whispered. Tim's head shot up, and I moved back closer to her. See, we lived in the Bible Belt where, even in the late '80s, gay was hidden like a sin. Children never saw it—it came to us in whispers.

"Kimmy, aren't you breakin' one of the Ten Commandments?" Tim said. "Thou shalt not judge."

I thought he might be crying. "Is this serious?" I asked. His clouded eyes told me it was, and I realized that he was already feeling the pain of our rejection. I could see that he'd felt it before, and the depth of his sadness became clear.

"I've been wantin' to tell. I like to get it out of the way so I don't have to worry about it."

"But how can you be gay when you're only twenty?" I asked, feeling the dichotomy of our southern innocence, a confusing mix of public Bible Belt purity and bull-riding heterosexuality behind closed doors. We were taught to ask such questions, even when we already knew the answers. It kept the buckle closed.

"What does that have to do with anythang?" he asked.

"I don't know. I just . . . never met anybody who was."

"I'm not gonna judge," Kimmy finally spoke. "I'm a virgin. That's my secret, I guess. Angel knows, but I thought that maybe it would make you feel better if I told you. I don't even know what it's like."

"I already told my secret. I have narcolepsy."

"That's no secret," Tim said. "Surely you got somethin' else."

"No," I lied.

My father taught me well.

The winds changed, and rain slapped the windshield. I sat in the uncomfortable silence between them, trying to grasp how Kimmy could fully understand herself without having come to terms with her sexuality and how neither of us had realized Tim was gay. They'd just suckered me in to knowing them better, and I wondered if I could pass through the friendship developing between them without having to participate. I could almost see Kimmy's prayers floating in the air, sealing us together. The song ended for the second time as the rain weakened. We could all see again, just enough to know we were stuck.

* * *

After a tractor dragged us from the muddy field, I watched Tim drive away. "Don't you think that was strange, him tellin' us he's gay?" I said, turning to Kimmy.

"I think he's the kinda person who has to be known."

"I don't get it," I said, knowing I was the kind who had to hide.

"Well, I don't necessarily agree with the way he acts, but at least he wanted to be honest. I think he felt like a liar all this time." She suddenly seemed smarter than she looked, and I wondered if I had misjudged her.

"But wouldn't it be better to keep stuff like that to himself? I always thought he was the one who liked talkin' about nothin'."

"Yeah," she said, shrugging a shoulder. "Maybe he always talked like that because what he really wanted to say was so serious."

"Well, it's odd. I mean, I don't feel compelled to go around volunteerin' the details of my sexual exploits."

"I don't think he wanted to do that. It wasn't about anybody else. Just him."

"Well, I wish he hadn't told me. Now I'm gonna feel funny around him."

"Do you feel that way around me, 'cause I'm a virgin?" she asked without looking at me, because she was embarrassed. I knew what she meant, but it was only an issue because *she* felt funny about it. I realize that now; people create their own issues.

"At least bein' a virgin is somethin' I'm used to," I said to make her feel better even though I was a little uncomfortable. With men, the weirdness always turned into a sexual feeling, a sudden awareness of my body. With women, it just made me feel isolated.

"I guess you'll just have to get used to him."

"What do you really think about it?" I asked.

"I'm not gonna judge," she said, opening her car door. It was time to go.

"Because you're a virgin?"

"No, because I'm human."

"You mean because everybody makes mistakes and stuff like that?"

But she didn't hear. Waving at me to hurry and get in the car, she stared through the window as if looking into a foreign world. Mine.

* * *

By the time I got home that day, everything had changed. "What are you doin' here?" I asked Carla, who stood in our hallway with fabric swatches and a wallpaper book in her arms.

"You're late," she said. "We already ate dinner." I followed her into the dining room where, amidst their dirty dishes and my clean place setting, Carla's Persian, Bippy, lay in a fluffy heap.

I pushed past her, making my way into the den and then to the kitchen. "Where is he?" I asked as if she'd done something with my father.

"He ran out for champagne." She smiled. "We're celebratin'."

"What did you do with Betty Lou's pictures?" I stared at the faded squares on the foyer wall where Betty Lou had displayed her cloud photographs, all twenty-two. She hadn't hung them in a row like most people would, or even in two rows. Instead, she creatively placed them in an abstract pattern, magically allowing me to see the same sky.

They'd been hanging there for years and I couldn't imagine beginning each day without that view. It was all I had left of her.

"I put 'em away," Carla said, as if discussing the china or heavy winter coats we rarely used.

"What's your cat doin' here?" I suddenly felt tired and realized that without the aid of that familiar lethargic dip my narcolepsy offered, I'd lose control. "What are you celebratin'?"

She dumped the decorating mess on the table. "I'm movin' in with you and your dad. He was gonna tell you at dinner."

"He wouldn't let you move in here without askin' me first."

"Well, too bad. I'm already in." She moved in front of me in her cool, confident way, blocking my view of the empty wall. Bippy followed close behind, rubbing my legs on his way. I took a deep breath and prayed for patience like Kimmy always suggested. I knew she'd be gone the minute my father saw the empty wall. "Where are my clouds?" I asked again.

"I think you and those pictures could use a little time apart. Trust me, it's for the best."

"What's wrong with you?" Even after a tense year and a half of putting up with her, it was the boldest tone I'd used. "I don't appreciate you rearrangin' my life."

She walked over and grabbed my shoulders. Her nails dug in, and just as if she'd opened a hole, the last bit of energy I had drained. Her chunkiness overwhelmed me, but I didn't struggle. Instead, she held me like a girl holds her doll, her strength coming from a place I didn't understand. "Your daddy taught you that 'A is for Betty Lou,' 'B is for Betty Lou,' and 'C is for Betty Lou.' The whole thang's sad, and I'm tellin' you, it's time to go back to kindergarten and relearn your ABCs." She was choking me, perfume stinging my eyes. All the while I kept thinking, *Where is he?*

"You both need to relearn a few thangs, because he loves me, whether you like it or not, and because I'm not leavin'. And I'm also not prepared to live in a goddamn shrine." She winked.

I didn't cry. "You're just jealous."

I never cried.

"I'm more mature than that." She let me go and bent down to pet Bippy. "I don't need to be jealous of someone who died over twenty years ago."

"She was his one true love." I moved closer to the wall, searching for a ghost. I felt childish.

"Have you ever been in love, Angel?"

She didn't give me time to answer, but even so, I wasn't sure.

"I didn't think so. Why don't you call me in ten or twelve years and we'll discuss love."

"You've never been married," I said. "Don't you ever wonder why?"

"I'm thirty-seven years old, and trust me, I know a lot more about love than you do." She smiled again. Bippy froze and then slithered toward the front door. My father was home.

"Sorry I couldn't pick you up," he said to me as he strolled past the complete set of faded squares to kiss Carla's forehead. "Why did it take you so long?"

My head began to shake despite the fact that my medication had worn off hours ago. "We got stuck in the mud. By the time they got a tractor to pull us out, it was already six. Kimmy gave me a ride, but she had to run an errand first." As he listened, he looked at the empty wall. No reaction. He seemed to have lost his sight. "I slept all the way," I said, realizing we'd both lost something.

* * *

For twenty-plus years, my father said he was destined to be part of a duet (the two of us) and nothing more. For as long as I could speak, I reminded him that Duet was just our last name, nothing more. He said, "It's ironic."

But after he met Carla, I wondered whether what he'd said was true, and if so, where that left me.

"Does Carla ever ask about Betty Lou?" I'd asked him the previous summer as we sat on the edge of the pool in our backyard, feet splashing.

"It doesn't really concern her," he said, staring into the water. "She doesn't care about the past, and I like that about her."

"That's why I *don't* like her. She's cold."

"Carla has good and bad points just like everybody."

"Not like Betty Lou."

He stood up. "I can't dwell on your mother, not anymore. You should be happy about that."

"But I still need you to answer my questions," I said, holding my hand over my eyes to block the sun. "There's stuff I gotta know."

"There's nothin' to say."

"It's not fair," I said.

He pulled me up then and hugged me, patting my back harder than he should. "It wasn't fair from the beginnin'. We just have to move on."

☑ baby

The moon was low and large. The Groves Community Hospital waited for me at the end of two long rows of weeping willows. It was the smallest hospital in town, known for its outpatient procedures and elective surgeries. The emergency room was small, seeing a steady flow of patients during the day but few in the evening hours.

The one-story brick building faced me like carnal pleasure on Sunday, a day when fundamental religious rules and southern preachers wearing black would gasp and choke on such desire. But the doctor (my secret) wore white, and I wasn't particularly religious anyway. At least, not like Carla and her Baptist friends. She went to church every Sunday, but in a desperate attempt to snare my father, she chose to live with him in sin on the days that fell between. Her southern yuppie friends conveniently looked the other way, proclaiming that God worked in mysterious ways. Caught between the world in which they were raised and the one slapping them in the face, it was their only option.

The Groves was a good place for me to work because it was within walking distance of our home. There was a shortcut, a narrow road intersecting the street running between the trees. I stood at the crossroads trying to get past my fear. I felt it every time, but I'd developed an extraordinary ability to squelch stress, just as I avoided full-bellied laughter and gut-wrenching pain. Narcolepsy stole such moments from me. In order to stay awake, I'd learned to walk through life asleep, believing I had the best sort of existence. Life without emotion. Now, I know that pain, joy, life, and the tears they create all intertwine. Without the strength of one, the others crumble, their combined power no longer able to fill you up. And then you're a ghost, simply moving among the living, feeling empty and shallow.

Lacking the energy to run, I crept down the road toward the hospital. The swaying arms of the willows skimmed my hair, dirtying me. The smell of pine was overwhelming, and I stopped to suck it in. The willow trees had no smell; instead, they baked in the piney scent saturating the hospital and Shreveport and Louisiana and the entire South, for that matter. The crickets cried as if burning in the soupy air.

I finally reached the far side of the field of dying grass between the hospital and the barbed-wire fence marking the property line. Popping up here and there, fields seemed to mark my life, making me believe I was in the right place at the right time. That was my religion, the seed planted on the day my mother died and I was born. Our foyer wall made it grow. Betty Lou's wall of clouds, and her, lying on those spacious fields my father showed me through his tears. I couldn't shake it, even when it didn't make sense. As with Christianity, it was a story that required faith.

With that thought in mind, I relied on my energy reserve to bolt across the yellow grass toward the back of the hospital. I checked the windows along the side of the building for people. Racing past, I saw two or three heads lying on pillows inside the rooms that were lighted. For some reason, their indistinguishable faces always assured me that I should run while I could toward whatever waited or toward those who were willing to wait. In these rare moments, I didn't care who saw me.

The patients didn't know me, and my weekend co-workers didn't talk to me much more than the work required, but I'd heard the snickering and seen their eyes as I fell asleep, my head flopping over, and as

I woke. They didn't realize I'd known Mac before he was the new ER doctor, and before he was married. He never laughed, rolled his eyes, or whispered that I was lazy or irresponsible. He thought of me when he saved lives. And when he held his wife's potentially shattered life in his arms, he remembered me. The sheer breadth of his chest assured me that we could both fit into his world. I did feel badly for his wife. I wasn't cruel, just lonely. I guessed that was also why he did it—why he cheated. He'd only been married for a few months, so I assumed he'd made a mistake. I wondered what he saw in me. I knew he didn't love me. Maybe I thought his fascination for my narcolepsy would blossom into fascination for me. Fact is, I tried not to think about it too deeply for fear of what I might decide. Loneliness makes people do things others won't. So I kept running through the dark, dead field, believing that someday I'd find the arms of *mother*.

That was the promise of my father's story, my religion.

When I made it to the back of the hospital, I knocked four times on the last window and then bent over, trying to catch my breath. Within moments, I spotted Mac creeping toward me. He'd walked off the worn path connecting the ER to the hospital's left wing in an attempt to surprise me. I thought it odd, knowing he fully under-stood my hatred of heart-jumping, head-flopping surprises. Before I could react, his arms were around me, lifting me off the ground in a single scoop.

"Put me down," I said, struggling a little.

"I wanted to catch you before you conked out," he said, walking with his chest out, shoulders back.

My head began to drop but I jerked it up. "Who said I was gonna conk out?"

"Trust me. I'm a doctor." He carried me through the steel backdoor and into the room assigned to him for the night. No one saw us; we were slick that way. We shared a mutual disrespect for order and commitment and rules. But we weren't bad people. At least, I didn't think so.

"You don't know jack about narcolepsy."

He lowered me onto the high hospital bed. "Who does?"

I sat up, and he held my face in his large hands, still dusty from his powdered gloves, and kissed me. "I love your eyes," he said, letting go before I was ready.

"I know all about it, and I wasn't gonna conk out," I said. "I was tryin' to catch my breath."

He winked. "That's what all the narcos say."

I kissed him hard then, just because he possessed the ability to make me laugh without laughter. I wondered if that was *happiness*.

"You look tired," he said, heading for the bathroom. "I told you not to take that cotton-pickin' job. Don't ask for my advice if you're not gonna take it. I gave you my medical opinion."

"So did my neurologist, and we don't pick cotton!" I yelled, rolling my eyes.

I listened while he washed up. The sound of running water and his habitual whistling made me tired again and I fell back, my head landing on his fat pillow. Then he was by my side, undressing me as if I belonged to him. "So what's up in la-la land?" he said, moving his hands into my shirt. He kissed my neck and I knew he didn't care if I answered or not. It was always like that.

"Carla took our cloud photographs down, the ones I told you about."

He tugged at my shorts. "She's an ass."

I wasn't sure if he remembered. "She's weird. She said she's thinkin' about givin' 'em back, but not all at once. Her exact words were, 'I may be willin' to part with one a month, no more, no less,'" I said, doing my best imitation. "Like we were involved in some kind of legal negotiation."

"Like I said, she's an ass." He pulled off his scrub shirt and snuggled next to me. "Remember when we first met, and Carla had just started workin' with your dad?"

I shook my head.

"Well, one time I was out with some friends and I saw her. She was drunk, and from what I could tell, she was alone. She's not much older than I am, you know."

"How come you never told me this?"

"My wife knows her sister," he said.

Silence.

I felt like an idiot. I didn't realize Mac knew his wife back then. I assumed he met her during his intern year away. I thought his out-of-state training was the reason he'd stopped calling me. Either way, he'd dumped me. The fact that he picked me right back up as soon as he got the chance didn't make me feel any better.

"I felt a little sorry for her." He smiled. "She wanted me."

"She's actually ten years older than you and she's an ass, remember?"

"Yeah, well, she wanted it," he said, hugging me as if I was a tool created to help him hug himself. "They all do." He winked.

"I'm sure," I said, knowing it was true. "She thinks I'm gonna start suckin' up just to get my pictures back. She acts like I'm twelve years old. You'd think she'd realize that most people my age are out on their own, away at college anyway," I said, aware of my shaking head. "She cain't be too stupid if she's a lawyer, right?"

"Well, maybe you will."

"I cain't. At least not until I finish school," I said. "I still need my dad. I cain't even drive." It sounded pathetic.

"I wasn't talkin' about movin' out." He pulled my legs up around him, burying his face in my breasts. "You might suck up to her, I mean."

I stared at the ceiling. It was made out of those spongy, plastic squares. Not real. "I'll get the pictures."

"Why is your dad puttin' up with her crap, anyway?"

"I'll get 'em back," I said.

"Do you think she has 'em at her house or at their office? You could snoop around." He didn't know Carla had moved in with us. Raising his head, he stared up at me with honest eyes. "Who knows what secrets lurk behind closed doors at the esteemed office of Franklin, Duet & Mercer?"

"It wouldn't work," I said, shaking my head. "Twenty-five or thirty people work there. And the security's tight, you know, being downtown and all."

"Maybe I can help," he said. "I always wanted to be a spy. I'd be a good James Bond, don't you think?"

"Yeah." He was better looking than all the 007's combined and probably just as smart. I wondered if that's what kept me interested. I stared into his nearly black eyes and stopped thinking. Truth is, sometimes we do a thing for no apparent reason, even when we think we shouldn't, because our gut tells us what we need. Like eating ice cream when you're hungry. Maybe you need calcium. Sometimes you find out the reason later, but sometimes you never do.

"Why don't you just ask your dad about it?"

The phone rang, saving me from a painful thought. "Shit," he said. "I guarantee it's some welfare mom bringin' her kid in with a cold."

"But it's summer."

"You think that matters?" He sat up, running his fingers through his hair while the phone continued to ring. "Shit!"

I wondered if someone might be dying.

"They always decide to drag 'em in here at ten o'clock . . . just when I'm about to . . ." But rather than finish, he picked up the phone, staring at me. "Yeah? What's up?"

"DOA," he said, dropping the receiver into its cradle. "Dead on arrival, over eighty-five. Shouldn't take long."

"But what about the family?"

"No family. Just take a nap and I'll be back."

Then he was gone and I was asleep. When my eyes opened again, it was dark except for the wide beam of light coming from the bathroom. I tried to move but couldn't. A familiar narcoleptic dream had taken over.

A tall woman stood at the end of the bed. She was older than me by several years, with a real life, a husband, perfect hair, and bright, rested eyes. Her laughter shook the bed, but my body only swayed from side to side. Involuntary. I watched her breathe the air I needed. She moved toward me and her shrill laughter stopped. Praying to the God I hoped was real, I tried to concentrate on taking a breath. I willed my arms to move, to grab something, but they rested limp at my sides. I called for Mac, but couldn't hear my own voice.

"He's not comin' back," the woman said. "You're an idiot. Nobody comes back for idiots. Or babies." She slapped me and dribble rolled down my chin. "You cain't even roll over." I tried to lick the blood away, but couldn't taste it. It was gone. She was gone, too, but her suffocating perfume lingered. She'd gone to confront Mac, giving me a way out.

I grabbed my clothes from the floor, putting them on as I fled. I slithered through the steel door leading outside and ran around the corner of the hospital, but then stopped, realizing I'd chosen the path next to the windows instead of on the far side of the field. A woman, propped up in her hospital bed with a book in hand, was only three feet from where I stood outside. I sank to the ground and cried into my hands until the lady's light went out. When I touched the field of dead grass, it turned my hands muddy.

"Angel," Mac called through the darkness. "What are you doin'?" I didn't answer. Sitting next to me, he wiped my face with his white lab coat. "You're all dirty."

"I saw your wife," I said, unable to hide my humiliation. "She hit me."

"She's out of town. You had a dream, but this is real." The cricket air pushed me onto the ground in a lethargic slump as Mac's voice washed over me in waves that seemed as if they could take me somewhere. I wanted him to take me somewhere. "Don't cry. It's just me." But I wasn't crying because of his wife. I'd lived with narcolepsy long enough to know she wasn't real. I cried because my dreams were invading my life, making it less real. It was a symptom of my narcolepsy, and it was getting worse. I couldn't erase the reality of it. She'd hit me and laughed at me. Looking past Mac into the darkness, I wondered if Betty Lou had ever searched the night sky for clouds. The few that hung above us were disappearing like her. All I felt was Carla's crushing presence. Like an unexpected change in the weather, she'd engulfed us.

"I want my pictures back," I whispered as he stroked my dirty hair.

"You'll get 'em," he said. "Don't worry." He rubbed my humped back. "She even said she was gonna give 'em back."

"I know you think I'm silly," I said, finally wiping the tears away, "gettin' so upset over a bunch of stupid pictures."

"They're not stupid. When my dad died, I took all his tools out of our garage and put 'em in my bedroom. I had these shelves that filled up a whole wall." He paused and stared at the barbed-wire fence. "My dad built 'em. I took all my books down and put his tools up there, lined 'em all up. My mom watched me carry 'em in the house and she never said a word. I still have 'em. I don't use 'em, but I'll never get rid of 'em," he said, shaking his head. "It's not stupid."

"You're lucky you had the chance to watch your dad work," I said, finally knowing Mac *had* remembered the clouds. He *had* come back for me. Although his wife had only been a dream, I knew she'd say those very words if she knew about me, if she knew me.

"He made all our furniture with his own hands."

"I was the last thang my mother made."

"But you *were* there," he said, holding me now in a warm, spoon-like snuggle, his large body surrounding my smaller one like a womb, a fortress, or just a good place to hide. He didn't care that we were lying on the ground beneath a sick woman's window. He seemed to understand that we were lying in a sanctuary.

☑ candy

Tim's sweaty face peered through a row of prickly cotton plants. "I hope you know I have no idea what the hell you're talkin' about. What's cataplexy?" He'd been asking questions for the last couple of weeks. Usually, Kimmy distracted him by bringing up his deviant social life. She knew it was his favorite subject. Since his confession, he'd volunteered just about every unwanted detail. Recently, he'd begun an in-depth account of his high school social activities. His best friends had all been girls, which didn't surprise us. I remembered a couple of guys in my high school class who seemed to share his interests, and when I mentioned them, Tim said they were probably gay. Still, I found it hard to believe.

Kimmy also knew how much I hated discussing my nonexistent social life. But this time, she wasn't around to rescue me.

Although I didn't want to answer Tim's questions, he seemed to have a genuine interest, which counted for something. But I was tired of squelching the curiosity of those who listened with charming, honest intensity, but then failed to handle the reality. It made me wonder if I'd explained my condition poorly, if I'd misled them into thinking it was glamorous. I'd explained narcolepsy to tons of people: friends, potential boyfriends, teachers, and acquaintances.

"It's a sudden loss of muscle control," is how I would always begin, feeling cornered, "while remaining conscious. It's as if your body's faintin' but you're not." Then I'd go on to explain that not all narcoleptics have attacks of cataplexy. The main measurable symptom of narcolepsy is that a person passes into REM sleep, the stage in which you dream, at an unusually fast rate. Normal people don't get to REM until forty-five minutes or an hour after falling asleep. For me, it takes less than two minutes. And cataplexy is associated with REM sleep. During that stage of sleep, people—all people—have a sort of sleep paralysis. A narcoleptic can fall asleep in mid-sentence, but when they have an attack of cataplexy, they experience the sleep paralysis while awake.

Tim's forehead wrinkled, creating an unnatural frown as I provided my dry, rehearsed explanation. I'd seen the look before.

"I get paralyzed because I'm hittin' REM too fast. It usually happens when I'm laughin' really hard, or if I'm upset about somethin' or angry. I just conk out; that's what I call it."

"Or durin' those *Xanadu* moments?" he asked, grinning like a ten-year-old. The summer sun had bleached his hair white. It stuck to his sweaty head, reminding me of Dennis the Menace.

"Why do you act like that?" I asked, staring at him until he was uncomfortable.

"I'm just tryin' to cheer you up. You take it so seriously—your narco-whatever-shit, I mean. I've never even seen you laugh very hard."

"And now you know why. Narcolepsy is a serious problem." I sat down. I didn't care about getting dirty anymore. "You'd understand if you'd had to live with it as long as I have."

At thirteen, I fell from my bicycle during a major attack of cataplexy, crashing onto the concrete driveway. My body softened and crumpled, my leg broke, and the bone popped through my skin, changing my life. I screamed for help, but my father could only hear a pathetic mumble. We learned later this was a symptom of cataplexy.

"It's a medical problem, but it's not a *real* problem," he said. "I think it makes you more interestin', like being gay makes me interestin'."

"Don't kid yourself."

"I guess I deserved that," he said, looking tired and twenty again. His arms hung rigid as he walked back to his designated area, putting the plants between us.

We worked in silence for nearly half an hour, but then he came back. He stood close behind me, looking down. "What?" I asked without looking up. I felt like a bitch.

"Why do you hate me?"

"I don't hate you."

"Yes, you do. Because I told you the truth . . . about my life, I mean."

His blunt approach, like an innocent child's, embarrassed me. It forced the truth, though, and I had no choice but to forgive. "I didn't ask you about that, you know, and besides, I don't hate you."

"So we're friends then?"

Silence.

"Kimmy said you're too tired to have friends, but you don't usually seem all that tired to me."

"Do you tell Kimmy everythang I say?"

"This is the most you've ever said."

I stopped and held my head in my hands. "It's not easy," I said, trying to focus on the hair between my fingers. "I take medication durin' the day, but just because I don't act tired doesn't mean I'm not. After a zillion people tell you you're lazy or call you a big slug, you learn to hide it."

I watched his face turn earnest again. It always happened when his sadness surfaced, but this time I knew he'd seen mine. I could feel it, as if his honesty had seeped in and found what I was hiding. "So what else do you wanna know?" I asked, realizing he'd suckered me again. "Come on, ask me anythang."

"Is it hereditary? Did you get it from somebody in your family?"

"My neurologist says it's likely, but it hasn't been proven yet. My dad doesn't have it. My mother's dead, and I don't know her relatives. They live in Florida, I think."

"You should know your medical history. Kimmy's adopted and she said her parents went out of their way to find that shit out."

"It wouldn't make any difference," I said, shrugging my shoulders.

"I think bein' gay's hereditary. I have two gay cousins . . . a girl and a guy. They're comin' down this weekend. They live in Hope. That's where I'm from. Hope, Arkansas."

"If people really are born gay, I guess it's possible."

"You know, Angel, few people understand that either. It ain't no party, that's for sure."

"I know," I said, feeling hot and uncomfortable.

"Well, I don't see how you have time for anythang," he said, changing the subject. "You must sleep all the time."

"Well, I have no social life." Besides Mac, I thought. "I'm not allowed to drive. I work here durin' the week, and I work at the hospital from eleven to seven on Saturdays. I can walk there 'cause it's close to my house. My dad has to drop me here, or he gets a ride for me. And I sleep. That's my life, and if I wasn't workin', I'd just be sleepin' all the time."

"That stinks. You should go out with me tonight, with me and my cousins . . . if you think you can handle it."

"I don't think I can stay up that late," I said, shaking my head.

"Cain't you take a nap when you get home? Work up to it."

I stared at him.

"Give it a chance, for God's sake."

"Well, maybe I could do that, and then take my medicine. I usually don't take it at night, but I could try." I hadn't gone anywhere since Mac had showed up at the hospital. "Is Kimmy goin'?"

"She's pretty sick with a stomach virus or somethin'. I don't think she'll go but I'll call her when I get home."

"You'd have to come pick me up, and I won't be able to drink."

He waved his hand through the air in what seemed to me an odd salute. "We don't care about all that," he said. "Just promise you'll have an open mind." He stood perfectly still, as if waiting for me to return the salute. As if I now belonged to his organization, one that dictated how you should live and what choices you should make.

But knowing it wasn't really a salute, I shoved my fluttering hands beneath my dirt-covered knees instead and looked at a piece of cotton. I wished Kimmy hadn't stayed home sick.

* * *

As Tim and I stepped into his apartment, what I noticed first were the entwined manicured hands of two girls. Their ten fingernails were all one color, as if they'd recently shared the same pink bottle. Both girls looked soft and sweet, and seemed like childhood friends whose clinging playground hands had never parted.

Tim bolted toward his compact kitchen. In the few moments it took him to navigate through the small crowd packed into his living room, Samantha's heart-shaped face swelled in my mind. She was the one tiny friend whose hand had fit perfectly into mine.

"Hey, everybody," Tim said, ending my daydream. "This is Angel, my cotton-field friend." All five sets of eyes stared at me. "Don't worry, she promised to have a wide-open mind tonight." With that said, his friends inched toward me, smiling like children gathering around a new addition to the class. The girls with the pink fingernails continued to hold each other as they moved closer. I wondered if their toenails were pink, too.

Their mutual joy made me sad.

I'd always wanted to paint someone's nails. Once, when I was nine, I asked my dad to volunteer but he refused. The next day he stopped on his way home from work to buy two bottles of polish, one red and one pink. He still wouldn't let me near his nails, but he sat and watched while I painted mine.

"I'm so glad you came," Tim shouted from the kitchen. "Do you want somethin' to drink?"

"Do you have Diet Coke?"

"Oh, that's right, you cain't drink," he yelled, triggering a dark shift in at least half the eyes. "I forgot about your narco-whatever-shit."

"Narcolepsy," I muttered.

"Angel has a neurological disorder," he said, as if announcing I'd won the lottery. "So don't freak if she falls asleep or hits the floor while you're talkin' to her." He seemed to believe I'd won a prize and that they would all cheer and beg me to share it.

I stared at his beaming face, and then at his friends, smiling in what was, most certainly, a response to his joke.

Me.

Their unfamiliar faces eased closer until they seemed to be ganging up on me, as if they planned to steal my winnings and waste it all. Watching their mouths begin to speak, saying my name and asking questions, I feared that in the end I'd be left with nothing. I turned and walked back out the door, slamming it behind me.

Once outside, I froze, caught in a familiar sluggish moment between full awareness and cataplectic rigor.

The door opened behind me.

"What are you doin'?" Tim said, trying to grab my arm. "Stop doin' that."

I continued to pinch the inside of my leg, a technique that sometimes saved me from falling. I'd discovered that self-inflicted pain had value few people recognized. But Tim's grip tightened and my arm shot toward him. I grabbed his shoulder and held on. My face twitched. I tried to focus my rolling eyes on his face and we stood, my wobbling body leaning against his for several minutes until the feeling passed.

"I'm okay now," I finally said, realizing that he'd held me up, something few were willing to do. When faced with the overwhelming power of my dead weight, even the strongest and most determined stepped away, only to witness the crumbling humiliation that no degree of poise or charm could counteract. And then, eventually, they walked away.

"That was weird," he said. "You were really trippin'. Your eyes were totally white. The blue part went all up in your head."

"Well, the show's over, so get out of my way. I'm leavin'; I want you to take me home."

"So you're gonna run home to daddy and crawl back under the covers?" he called after me as I headed toward his car. "Maybe dream about havin' a good time instead of makin' it happen."

"That's exactly what I should do."

"Give me a reason."

"I came here tryin' to be nice to you, and the minute we walked in the door you turned into a little shit. No, actually you were just bein' yourself. I should have known better." Then I stopped, but only for a moment. "And because most of the time my dreams are better than reality, in ways you couldn't understand."

"That's bullshit. You're just mad because you're too weak to handle bein' different."

"Okay, blame it on me. It's all my fault."

"There's a million people out there who are just like everybody else," he said, following me across the parking lot. "And they're all borin', if you ask me."

"I don't like people starin' at me."

"Look at Kimmy. There are a lot of people like her, normal as all get out, but not really livin' any kind of special life. One day all those regular people are just gonna fall over dead, standin' in the exact place they started."

"That's not a very nice thang to say." But hearing him say it, I knew I'd rather die on the spot than die still standing on it tomorrow. "But I do know what you mean," I mumbled.

"See, you're startin' to admit it." He held his hand out as if to draw me back. "It's not that great to be just like everybody else."

My hands were trembling, and I couldn't seem to get a grip on his car door. "That's not what I meant."

"Look, my friends make very few judgments. Besides, it's not a crime to have somethin' wrong with your brain. You act like somebody died."

"Everybody makes judgments. And we're not the same," I said as my purse dropped to the pavement. I bent down, but instead of grabbing it and standing back up, I squatted there and stared at a piece of gum. Someone, tired of chewing, had spat it out next to Tim's back tire. "You've got a lot of friends, people like you. I'll never have that. And you didn't have the easiest time tellin' me and Kimmy that you're gay." I'd never stand at the center of five narcoleptic souls, clinging to each other, smiling. My kind were all asleep, depressed, or crazy already. "Don't forget about that."

The wind blew some of his fine white hair straight up. "Well, at least I tried," he said, with the ten-year-old eyes I'd seen in the cotton field. "Just come back. You might have fun."

His friends still had the same silly grins plastered over their gay faces, as if I'd never left. I wanted to run away again, but Tim took my arm, leading me toward the couch where the two girls now sat, curled up together like mother and child, or sisters, like something unfamiliar.

I knew right away, it was *mother*.

Then they kissed and their familial connection blew apart. I tried not to stare, but couldn't look away. I searched for *mother* until I was sure it was still there. It wound around them like a blanket, warm and safe. Protecting them from the pain men can inflict, and stroking their arms and hair with soft, buttery love.

"Relax, Timmy Logan," a singsong voice said from behind us. "I think right about now your friend Angel's mind is pretty wide open, all right." Flustered, I turned to face Scarlett, Tim's cousin, down from Hope. "They're in pretty mushy love, I guess," she said, shrugging. Then she leaned toward me, whispering in my ear, so close that I could feel her warm breath, "You'd think they'd choose to be a little more reserved, what with you bein' here and all."

I stepped away from her, shaking my head in agreement until I realized I was over doing it. "Your last name's not O'Hara or Butler, is it?" I finally asked, unable to think of anything better.

"No, just Logan, same as Timmy's. But my brother's name is Rhett."

"Are you serious?" I asked, but then worried she'd taken it the wrong way.

She smiled as if she had a secret. "I'm really glad you came back. You'll like the place we're goin'—The Blue Flower—although I'm sure it's a lot different than what you're used to. Just wait till you see *the* Blue Flower."

Too uncomfortable to ask what she meant, I chose to stay with the Scarlett O'Hara subject. "So I guess *Gone with the Wind* was your mother's favorite movie?"

"Actually, she read the book when she was a teenager. She loved it so much she named us all right off its pages. And our daddy didn't care either. My little sister's name is Tara."

I stared at her, surprised that a mother would name her children after such closely linked characters. I'd heard of people giving their children names that all began with the same letter, but this mother earmarked her kids for major teasing. I wondered how much their mother's fixation affected who they became. Scarlett was average in height, like me, but she had small bones and delicate features like Tim's. Her skin was pale like his, too, but her hair was almost black. And Rhett was tall and dark. Their mother's love seemed to have magically molded them into the physical embodiment of their namesakes.

"Tara's only sixteen," she said, "so she doesn't get to come down here with us all that much."

I would never have guessed that either Scarlett or Rhett were gay. I wondered about Tara. "How far is it to Hope?"

"Closer than you might think. Rhett and I go back and forth all the time. There's not a whole heck of a lot to do up there, you know." Her words were like music. "Your name's nice," she said, accentuating an already strong southern accent. "Now *there's* a book people around here love, you know." Her controlled speech indicated that she knew exactly what she was doing, heightening the musical quality of her voice. And as I watched her speak and listened, I wondered if her mother taught her the technique. "What's your last name, anyway?"

"Duet." I spoke as quick and sharp as I could, wishing I had a voice like hers, wondering if it was something Betty Lou could have taught me.

"That's cool. Your momma must have had a special reason for namin' you Angel. And just look how wonderful it all worked out. Because of your sleepin' problem, I mean. I bet when your momma tucked you in at night . . ." The tips of her fingers touched my arm. I could barely feel it. ". . . she told you to sleep like a little sweet angel."

"My dad named me," I said, feeling awkward.

Before she could ask why, I walked away, telling her I had to go to the bathroom. She knew something was wrong.

When I finally came out, Tim, Scarlett, Rhett, and their three friends were ready to leave. They were standing in a strange huddle, waiting for me. I wondered if they realized that I hadn't really used the bathroom; I was only hiding.

☑ decoy

Before we left for The Blue Flower, I told Tim there was a 99-percent chance that I'd fall asleep on the way. He and Scarlett both promised to keep me awake but failed. As we approached the place, Tim's blaring horn woke me. By the time I remembered where I was, he had stopped at a red light, providing an excellent view into the backseat of Rhett's car. The girls with the nails were all over each other, and their hands, now torn apart, moved as if desperate to find their way back together. Entwined in each other's hair, their fingers joined but then snapped away. Watching made me hot.

"They're gonna get us killed," Tim said, shaking his head. Scarlett leaned into the front seat, dangling her arms and face between us. We all watched as the taller of the two girls held a giant curl of the shorter one's dark hair. She twirled it around her finger and then pressed it into her lover's thick, messed-up hair. At the same time, she pushed the girl's head back against the passenger window and kissed her slowly and deeply.

Scarlett's face inched closer to mine, and I moved toward the door. She didn't look worried. In fact, she was smiling. "I think those girls should have just stayed home tonight," she said. "They should stay in Rhett's car while the rest of us go on in."

"I thought you weren't ashamed of bein' gay," I said to Tim, staring past Scarlett. I tried not to focus on her face.

"Well, I'm not willin' to flaunt it and risk gettin' the shit beat out of me by some redneck Baptist."

I looked down the street. "I guess there's a lot of religious people around here, huh?" But the place seemed deserted.

"Not as many as there are in Hope," said Scarlett, who managed to ease closer to me again. I wasn't sure if her movement was intentional or just a side effect of her touchy-feely personality. She'd touched me three times already. "Believe me, you don't wanna go there. Well, you might. I cain't imagine anybody ever wantin' to hurt a girl named Angel."

She obviously didn't know Carla Carr, attorney-at-law, or any of the others who'd passed in and out of my sleepy life, not giving a shit what my name was.

"Yeah, but if you're gay, you should stay the hell out of Hope, that's for sure," said Tim, honking again. "These morons think they're in frickin' New York City or somethin'."

The light turned green.

"It's ironic," he said, driving forward. "There ain't no hope for queers in Hope." He made a phony laugh. "It's always like that, you know. People who need it the most cain't get it."

"Everybody just wants what they cain't have," Scarlett said, sounding sad.

"Why didn't you go to school in Dallas or New Orleans?" I asked.

"I didn't wanna go too far." He grinned and whipped the car into an available space in front of The Blue Flower.

We sat in the car, waiting for Rhett and the others to find a spot.

I didn't know what to say.

"It's because Hope is where Momma is, right, Timmy?" Scarlett said, breaking the silence. "Timmy's momma is so sweet." She rubbed his head, and he seemed to enjoy it. I knew I'd fall asleep if she rubbed my head for any length of time. Just watching made me groggy. "Don't deny it, Timmy Logan. You cain't bear to be too far away from your mom."

"Hope the frickin' Pope," he said, brushing her hand away as if to pull himself out of a trance. "Get off it, Scar." Then he gave me that charitable look people make when they remember your mother's dead.

Scarlett's eyes widened. "Oh, Angel, you're not Catholic, are you?" she asked.

"No, are you?"

"Oh, my God, no. We're Baptist."

Silence.

Tim ran his hand through his hair. "I don't get how you can stay awake in school," he said, changing the subject. "I cain't barely stand it sometimes, and there's nothin' wrong with me."

"I eat and cross-stitch and draw. Whatever I can do to stay awake. Usually, I can fight it if I keep movin', especially if I'm medicated." I chose my words carefully, making an effort to be more open. But I knew that in the morning, I'd feel like part of a one-night stand. "I tape record a lot. And I get my books early and read as much as I can before the semester starts." I hated the sound of my voice. "I'm takin' a grad course in the fall. I have to write a paper and the professor gave me the topic ahead of time. I've been workin' on it all summer, when I have time."

"They're lettin' you take a graduate course?"

"The history of science," I said, aware of my bobbing chin. "I'm a history major. I plan to get a master's degree, and maybe a PhD, if I can stay awake for it." My hands began to gesture in a way that seemed necessary to keep the words coming. "My neurologist thinks the amount of education I get will dictate the amount of control I have over my professional life." I glanced at Tim and Scarlett self-consciously. They looked bored. "I think I might like to teach."

Scarlett giggled.

"That way, I can lecture for an hour here and there, and take naps in between."

"They do have a lot of office hours," Tim said. "What's your paper on?"

"It's called, The Evolution of Darwin's Theory."

"That's really catchy," said Scarlett, her expressive eyes flying toward me through the dark. "Do you like to write?" Her head shook and mine moved along with hers, up and down, up and down, until I wanted to grab my own or grab hers to make them both stop.

"I almost majored in English," I said, feeling as if I was falling from an alcoholic's wagon. I'd managed to keep my distance from people for a long time, but I couldn't resist the lure of their friendship. "But I love studyin' the lives of real people, the decisions they made and why. The paths they forged. How they affected the overall scheme of thangs or how the scheme affected them. When I'm readin' about real people, especially people who are gone now, it's almost as if, because I'm readin', their lives become more meanin'ful. I feel like I'm givin' 'em somethin'."

"Is that what you'd like? For somebody to give you that?" Scarlett whispered in my ear while Tim shouted, "Well, get ready, babe, because you're fixin' to experience an interestin' scheme tonight."

Before I could respond, Tim was out of the car, almost to the sky-blue door of The Blue Flower. Scarlett stared at me from the curb. But I was still inside, embarrassed that I hadn't moved more quickly.

Scarlett stood in front of The Blue Flower, waiting for me.

* * *

I'd never heard of the place, but when I saw the small sign above its plain storefront entrance, I knew I'd seen it before. It blended into the downtown street along with its adjoining buildings, streetlights, and the signs that made the place so ordinary. Dull, chipped paint covered its façade, although fresh sky-blue paint coated the door. Unsymmetrical lines floated in the blue color, the markings of an amateur who hadn't yet learned to hide his brush strokes. Despite that small, loving touch, the painted door wasn't enough to counterbalance the decayed state of the building.

Inside, another world pulsated.

As the heavy door opened, the new-wave music shocked me. It grabbed me by the stomach with hands I wasn't expecting. My arms swung instinctively as I walked through, enticing me to dance despite my usual avoidance of it. A huge, multiroomed escape for Shreveport's gay society enveloped me as the crowd pushed us forward. As a group, we flowed through room after room. We mingled with feminine boys who bounced around us to the tune of whatever song was playing and masculine women who pretended not to notice Scarlett. We passed bars, pool tables, and several small, unofficial dance floors. The handsome men ignored Scarlett, too, but the sexy girls' eyes sparkled when they saw her coming. And maybe even when they saw me.

Bright red and yellow paint covered the walls of each room. On my journey through the odd maze, lights flashed every few moments, illuminating giant blue flowers. Painted over the brilliant, primary walls and even on the ceiling, they ate into the bright color so that most of what I saw was blue. In one shocking flash, I saw a man's light blue face at the center of a navy blue sunflower. Looking closer, I realized that legs, arms, faces, and even breasts were incorporated into each flower. A woman's long thin legs served as a stem for a blue tulip, and on the ceiling, nearly indistinguishable breasts blended into the blue petals of a giant rose.

The amateur had triumphed inside. The flesh looked dead.

Caught at the center of such sexuality and botanical inventiveness, I thought of Darwin, the subject of my term paper, and wondered what, if anything, his survival theory could possibly mean with respect to The Blue Flower. Evolution, I thought. The place shocked me, but I didn't want to leave.

*　*　*

Eventually our group drifted apart, but I continued to follow close behind Scarlett and Tim. Tim introduced me to everyone he knew, announcing each time that I was a Blue Flower virgin.

The response was always the same. "Wait until you see *the* Blue Flower."

It soon became apparent that the Blue Flower was the best representation of their common dream . . . talented, beautiful, unashamed, and, of course, loved by every appetite present. The flower was soon to emerge when George Michael began to sing, "I Want Your Sex."

A charge traveled through the room. It made me tired, and I excused myself to the restroom.

"I gotta go, too," Scarlett said, leading the way.

"Don't take long," Tim called after us, "or she'll miss it."

We waited in line nearly fifteen minutes and then went in together because Scarlett told me there was room for two. She was right, though the shabby bathroom only had one doorless stall and a small sink. "You go first," I said, trying to be nice.

"Oh, I don't really need to go. I just didn't want you to get lost or anythang." She waved her hand toward me, saluting like Tim, and I decided it must be a family thing. "I'll just be right over here." She took a tube of Chapstick from her pocket and stared at herself in the mirror.

I went into the stall and then came out, zipping my jeans.

Scarlett leaned against the door and crossed her arms. "Where are your panties?"

"I'm not wearin' any," I said, like it was nothing, but then I remembered she was lesbian. "I forgot."

She stepped toward me and my knees wobbled. I felt that familiar lethargic dip. "You forgot your panties?" She asked.

Somebody tapped on the door.

"I forgot about you."

"What about me?" she asked, taking a step closer.

"I forgot you like girls."

"We're in a gay bar." She smiled. "You're completely surrounded."

The knocking started again, louder.

I knew I should back away from her but I was too close to the wall.

She took another step forward, bringing her face close to mine. "Do you always go out without your panties on?" Her breath smelled of the Bahama Mamas she'd been drinking all night.

"I don't like panty lines, that's all."

Her hand ran over my arm, soft and buttery. I knew I should push it away but didn't. I thought I might cry. I wanted her arms around me, if only for a moment. It was more a need than a desire. I could smell her perfume and feel the ends of her dark curls on my cheek. Frozen, I monitored my physical reaction the way I'd trained myself. And because I chose not to move away, her face drew even closer, her breasts less than an inch from mine. I looked down at the floor with only my eyes because my face was too close to hers. If I moved, I would touch her.

Staring at a dirty spot on the floor, I finally heard the incessant banging on the door. The gentle tapping so easily ignored had metamorphosed into violent pounding sometime between the moment I remembered she was a lesbian and the realization that I'd been touched by very few women, if any, since the day I was born.

I was afraid to open the door. I was so tired.

"We better go on out now, Angel Duet," Scarlett whispered, her lips nearly touching mine as she emphasized the D in Duet.

* * *

After we made our way through the hostile group of lesbians who had to pee, we joined Tim and stood at the edge of the largest dance floor. Scarlett stood behind me. Tim and Rhett were to my left and right. I held my arms in tight, hoping to avoid contact with any of them. But the crowd drew closer. They squeezed in, as if gathering me up in a communal gay hug. I held my hands together in front of me, pulling my shoulders in. I felt compelled to step onto the dance floor, to break away. But then, out of the darkness, thin green- and blue-tinted spotlights crossed each other over the dance floor, and amidst a pitiful puff of smoke, *the* Blue Flower finally appeared.

She wore her blond hair high on her head. Giant blue petals started at the small of her back, fanning out around her chest and head, making her face the center of a giant flower much like those painted on the walls. Her long legs, covered by light green pantyhose, rose like stems toward a blue petal-shaped skirt barely covering her. Her bright red lips began to sing Gloria Gaynor's song, "I Will Survive," and the crowd cheered. My pale lips were the only closed pair in the place. The Blue Flower circled the dance floor, taking the hands of her fans as she belted out the words that meant so much to them.

Tim yelled, "Isn't she great?" while Scarlett yelled from behind, "Oh my God, he's so talented!"

What a freak, I thought, as the Blue Flower stood before me in all her glory, towering above me, looking into my eyes. Then I recognized him. The freakish Blue Flower wasn't a stranger or weirdo after all. He was someone I knew. Someone I'd stood beside in the high school choir, virtually my neighbor.

In that surreal moment, I realized I was ambushed. My heart stopped. Knees buckled. I felt myself falling, but I didn't. Instead, my body leaned back against Scarlett and she hung on, her arms groping me just below the chest. My head flopped back, and I couldn't breathe. I tried to cry out, but as always, my mouth didn't move. Instead, the muscles remained frozen in some unattractive expression.

I will survive, I thought.

Then someone knocked my head, sending a blazing pain through my skull, forcing it forward, opening my throat. As my lungs filled with air, I tried to calm myself, feeling the drool at the corner of my mouth. I mentally prepared myself to fall at the feet of the Blue Flower, but my new friends continued to hold me up. The Blue Flower moved away to the other side of the dance floor, shuffling his large-heeled feet as he went.

I'd entered The Blue Flower from a world where transvestites weren't real, and gays and lesbians traveled in whispers. Never knowing they were there, I'd passed their homes. They existed in secret cavernous hiding places my southern neighbors created just for them, secret huts they found when there was nowhere else to go. Deep, dark caves in the hearts of normal folks, who did what they were told, had sex with and loved all the appropriate people, and ate balanced meals with their families every night of the week. Their homes smelled of gumbo, Endust, and cornbread, and their grandmothers were all sweet little ladies who never worked a day in their lives. And now, in this inorganic botanical haven, the inhabitants struggled to bring beauty to a place forcing their acceptance. Tim was mistaken. There was no hope for queers in Shreveport, either. Every day I saw the fake and faded smiles of the architects, engineers, and construction workers who'd created the hiding places Tim found.

I'd never met either of my grandmothers, and until Carla moved in, we rarely used Endust in my father's house. But despite all that, cavernous secrets and lies supported its weight. Dilapidating huts had somehow sprouted up around its perimeter—creating my father's hiding place, and mine.

The song ended amidst a passionate cry for more, but the cave dwellers' reigning flower disappeared along with all my thoughts. Then, in a dream, Scarlett carried me all by herself to a red velvet couch. The smell of warm butter swirled around me, as if my father was preparing to sauté dinner. I lay my head in her lap and she bent over me, kissing my forehead, my cheeks, even my lips. Her soft hands moved over me in sync with some sensual tune I couldn't quite make out, warming me, melting me.

Then I began to smell the onions.

"I'm sorry about what I said earlier, about your momma and all," she whispered, and then I knew I was awake. We *were* on a red couch but instead of velvet, it was some type of fake leather, like car upholstery. I wasn't sure if she'd kissed me or not, but I was comfortable and decided not to move, not to care. "Tim told me about your momma." People swirled past, glancing down at us, not caring what we did or said, or who we were. "You can go on back to sleep if you want. I won't let anybody bother you. I'll stay right here all night if I have to."

Her drunken eyes made me nervous, but her lap felt good, like a perfect place to hide. Lights flashed, loud music throbbed, but Scarlett's words, spoken in that singsong manner she'd perfected, rocked me . . . almost dreamlike, and in dreams, the limits were different. Dreams allowed me to love anyone I wanted, to kiss anyone. And they allowed everyone to love me back. Drool didn't exist. "I have a boyfriend," I managed to say.

"But you don't have a momma, now do you?" She wiped away the tear I couldn't suppress. The touch of her hand, smoke, and mascara burned my eyes. "I'll be your momma tonight," she said. I closed my eyes, pretending.

☑ eye

I wiped my face and turned over in bed, hoping to move away from the dark cloud hovering over me. Water ran down my cheeks and onto my neck. My pillow began to feel damp, making me cold. Then the rain poured into my ear, filling it, muting the sound of the thunderous voice calling to me to wakeup.

"Angel, wake up!"

I swung my head around and threw back my aging Holly Hobbie comforter. Water dribbled from my ear into my hair. "What are you doin'?" I moaned. "You got my bed wet."

Carla moved closer, leaning into the space beneath the canopy. Her auburn hair was extra short due to a recent trim, making her face severe. "It was the only way to wake you up, Sleepin' Beauty," she said, and the dark cloud metamorphosed into a gray fog—the kind of fog men like my father get lost in, refusing to ask for help. "Your daddy told me about that little trick."

"If I'm Sleepin' Beauty, who does that make you?" I whispered, wondering how her features remained so chiseled despite the fifteen or so extra pounds she carried around her hips. "You don't look like the prince." Her eyes poked out at me, and I noticed how they matched the color of her hair exactly. I pictured her holding boxes of Clairol up to her eyes, searching for the perfect color. Her eyes were beautiful, but they were rusty. So her hair was rusty, too, as if someone left her out in the rain too long. There was something coarse and brittle about her.

"Do you realize what time it is?" she said, pulling herself back out of the canopy.

Instead of answering, I stared at her, wondering why she'd gone out by herself the night Mac saw her drinking, why she'd gotten drunk all alone. I thought she had friends.

"But no need to get up now," she said, looking at her watch. "I called the hospital about three hours ago, and told 'em you slept through your shift."

"Why did you bother wakin' me up then?"

"I cain't believe how irresponsible you are for a twenty-one-year-old woman. I wish I could sleep my life away." She grabbed the towel hanging over my desk chair and threw it at me. "You're lucky you have a rich daddy, and such a nice one, too."

Sophisticated bitch, I thought, as I blotted up the water on my bed.

"Frank and I have a dinner meetin' with a client. He's in the shower. He asked me to let you know we're leavin'." I tried to ignore her as she walked around, glancing at my things as if I wasn't there. "Said if you woke up later, in the dark, you might get scared, which I thought was strange, considerin' your age."

I wished I *could* close my eyes and sleep for a hundred years like Sleeping Beauty. And it wouldn't just be me. We'd all sleep. The whole city would slither down into that eerie state—the one that keeps the world out, and teases of heaven and hell—that doesn't kill but keeps you from living. Vines, limbs, and dilapidating stuff we accumulated in our waking hours would engulf us. Outsiders would pass, never knowing we lay beneath the rubble. It would be a taste of peace, but only a sad glimpse. I thought about it a lot. Sometimes I even wondered if it was happening. The world was moving on, but my father and I were caught in a lethargic quagmire. That's when it turned nightmarish, with everyone dead and blue. I wanted to slap him and shout, "Wake up! Breathe!" Yet, I couldn't even wake myself.

Tim and his friends from Hope seemed to think they'd found liberation in Shreveport, but they didn't realize their sparkling new playground was my rusty old yard. They didn't see the relativity swirling around us. But I saw it. The same way I saw death around every corner. But when I saw it, I just closed my eyes. A lot of people tried to close out the truth, but I was the one who could do it.

"What's this?" Carla said, picking up a few of the papers strewn across my desk. Without giving me time to answer, her wine-colored lips, trained in debate, began reading. "Intelligent man's trek from the shadowy unknown toward the sun-drenched known began with man himself." I tried to interrupt, but the beauty of her voice silenced mine. "In every cave, in every hut and house, surely there were those who sensed the power of a well-lit place. But among history's faceless crowd, only an enlightened few longed to move toward it, driven to move forward, to the front of the flock, to lead. Theirs are the faces we see when we look back upon that gray crowd. And one face is remarkably clear—the face of Charles Darwin." She smiled. "In every hut?"

"I just started workin' on it, okay?" I said. "And for the record, my dad's not rich."

"Yes, he is, you just never realized it," she said as my father stuck his head in the room.

"Your little angel slept through work again." She tossed the pages of the report toward my desk. "Absolutely incredible," she said, ignoring the two pages drifting to the floor. "I've lived here for almost a month and all she does is sleep." Her hands clenched, almost into fists. She might as well have crumbled my words in her rusty palms.

"Well, I do have a neurological disorder."

"You have a convenient avoidance technique."

I looked at my father. Unable to resist her, he had eased into my room hoping to alleviate the tension. But his strong point had never been speaking up in uncomfortable situations, no doubt why he chose real estate and tax law over the more ball-busting litigious situations in which she participated. He remained silent, and I asked her, "Did it ever occur to you that I might not care what you think?"

"Has it ever occurred to you that you might?" she asked, also glancing at my father, who looked empty, as if he might crumble beneath the pressure. For the first time, I considered that he might understand what being ghostly was all about. "Well," she continued, giving up on him, "I've written quite a few papers, so let me know if you need help." As she turned to walk out, her two-inch heel dug into one of the papers lying on the carpet. "It's not a bad start." She paused at the bedroom door, curious as to what my father would say about my having missed work.

I marched over and shut the door, practically pushing her away.

As the door slammed, my father sank onto my bed in a heap, his tall body squeezing beneath the ruffled canopy. "I don't think that was necessary." Holly Hobbie clones surrounded him, tossing flowers from their baskets, smiling until it made me sick. It was time to redecorate. Carla was right about that.

"Why do you like her, anyway?" I asked.

"I love her, you know that," he said, but didn't sound convincing. "Maybe goin' out last night wasn't such a good idea. Your limitations are different." He rubbed his forehead, perhaps trying to massage a headache away before it took root.

Like Carla.

"Do you really think I have limitations, or do you think I've just perfected a clever avoidance technique?"

Dots of sweat surfaced on his white cotton undershirt. Then the liar said, "We all have those techniques, in some form or another."

"You never thought that before. She told you that, didn't she?" I braced myself, determined to confront him. "How can you love her? She took down our photographs. She won't even tell us where they are. She's rippin' up our home—it's our home."

"She loves me. And she's gonna make this place better."

"You love her because she loves you?"

He didn't answer.

"You didn't love Betty Lou because she loved you. You loved her because she was Betty Lou. She was creative. She had a heart so full it nearly burst. That's what you told me."

He shifted, trying to get comfortable, and the clones of Holly Hobbie stuck out around him, distorted, as if desperate to escape his hot, heavy weight. "I found somethin' unique in Betty Lou," he said.

"But didn't everybody?"

"It's my turn to be loved, to be *found* like that . . . to be worshiped," he said, looking away. "Carla sees thangs. She's harsh sometimes, but she's a brilliant attorney and a very perceptive woman. She's managed to get me plannin' again."

"Well, she doesn't exactly come across as a meek and humble worshiper." I collected the pages of my report, stacked them together, and then sat at my desk, holding them. "She's more like a manipulative fund-raiser, if you ask me."

"Worship comes in as many forms as there are religions."

"But if Carla worships you, where does that leave you?"

"Agnostic, I guess. I've been livin' like an atheist for years. But there may be someone out there. There may be. I don't know. But at least I'm makin' plans now, with Carla. I'm tryin' to love her," he said. "I'm fifty-three years old. I'm almost an old man."

"But aren't love and worship the same, really?"

He shook his head, slow and steady. "You can love but not worship, and I know you can worship without really lovin' at all."

"But all those years, I thought it was love. I never thought you were an atheist. I thought you were a priest. I thought Betty Lou was our religion. Are you sayin' that you worshiped her, but that it wasn't real love? Have you been lyin' all this time? Cain't you love and worship? Wouldn't that be the best thang to have, the best way to feel?"

He reached out for me in his usual way. I left the papers on my desk and went to stand beside him. He put his arm around my waist, hugging me, I think. He may have just been leaning. "You have to find a new religion."

"Well, I can guarantee it's never gonna be Carla."

"It doesn't have to be her," he said. "It shouldn't be her."

"Then who or what should it be? What can I believe in? Do you want me to choose God? Or do I just have to believe in myself, only myself? I need more than that. I don't know why, but it's never gonna be enough." The louder I spoke, the tighter he held me, and the more distorted the Holly Hobbie clones grew. "Everybody else seems to have somethin' I don't. The only thang I've been able to figure out is that it's *mother*. They all have mothers."

"That's a deadend."

"But how can I ignore somethin' so obvious? I keep thinkin' maybe I can find it somewhere."

"It?"

"That *mother* feelin'."

"Maybe what you need can be found, but you've got to start lookin' out, away from this house, away from me. Away from those photographs." He flung his arm out from beneath the canopy as if pushing something away, something invisible. "I tried to give you that feelin'." His arms went limp into his lap and his head fell into his hands. "I made a lot of decisions I'm still not sure about."

"If you mean decisions like not lettin' me paint your nails and all that, that's crazy. And it's not your fault I have narcolepsy. I'm doin' okay. I am, really. Hey, you learned to cook just for me, didn't you?" I rubbed his back, wishing he'd hug me again, even if it was only leaning. "Don't listen to Carla. She doesn't know us like we know each other. She's playin' a game."

"But she's a talented player, and she makes me feel strong. I was hopin' she'd make you feel that way, too."

"I'm always gonna be weak."

He rubbed my arm. "But I want you to feel strong." He kept rubbing. "It feels so good." His voice was sad and tired. "I want you to spread your wings and shoot for the stars and all that corny stuff, you know?"

"I don't have that luxury, but it's okay. I'm strong like . . . like a turtle. I'll just keep pluggin' along and somehow I'll win," I said, but suspected I wasn't getting anywhere. In fact, I decided that as soon as they left I'd crawl beneath my canopy, toss the old Holly Hobbie clones over my head, pull my arms and legs up close to my body, and go back to sleep. "Don't worry so much," I said, grabbing his hand. He'd rubbed continually in one soft spot, and it had begun to sting.

* * *

Before crawling back under my canopy, I decided to wash away the smoky, perfumed smell of the night before. I had the proverbial extra-hot-shower urge. I would stand naked in a human autoclave and hope that the memory I wanted to forget would rise and fade with the steam or go down through the drain, conveniently disappearing by way of a chemical reaction nobody understands, but believes just the same.

Nonetheless, it seemed obvious that once engulfed by a particular smell, or an insidious person or place, one long hot shower lacked the power to clean it away. At its weakest or strongest, science couldn't solve everything. It seemed to me also that, sadly, the urge to cleanse ourselves of what we fear is sin or madness comes from a deeper urge to believe outward appearance has everything to do with what's inside. As if we could scrub the ugly and the poor, the color and the homosexuality off the people we love and off those we hate. We could conveniently slap them into the autoclave and then celebrate as they emerged, germ free.

Spotless.

Sterile.

But nothing ever goes away. Nothing can be washed away. What's not inside already, goes inside, traveling snakelike into secret places, impossible to clean. It hides. My father taught me that.

Standing naked in the shower, I knew this, but stayed, hoping it might work anyway. It was raining on my face again, and this time it felt warm and right. The dark fog had disappeared while encircled by my father's right arm almost an hour earlier. Despite what my father taught me, despite the departed fog and the stubborn stain of reality, I cranked the water hotter. The Blue Flower surrounded me still, blinding me in a new fog as thick as Carla. I smelled of Scarlett, who smelled like Bahama Mamas and Red Hots, or maybe it was cinnamon schnapps. Oh, but I love Red Hots, I thought as I sucked in my stomach and ran soapy hands over my ribs. I liked to pop ten or twenty into my mouth at once, to see if I could endure their engineered heat, to see if I could win. They smelled so good, but this time, the hot was too hot.

I didn't want it.

I spat at the drain.

I turned the water to the scalding point and scrubbed harder, wanting to forget Scarlett and her brother, and the pathetic town they came from. I was just as guilty as the next in putting stock in a hot shower. Tim and his queer cousins held me up in my weakest moment. They shared their strength, and somehow visited an isolated, disordered place inside my head that hadn't encouraged visitors for years. But they'd come bearing gifts I couldn't accept, gifts that kept me scrubbing. Looking straight up into the pelting water, I wished I could take a long hot bath without fear of drowning, but it was out of the question.

See, the last time I'd taken a bath I nearly drowned. I was fourteen and spending the night at a friend's house when it happened. Her entire family ended up in the bathroom, including her burly-eyed father and sixteen-year-old brother. He was the first boy who saw me naked. I may as well have lost my virginity on that ceramic tile floor, surrounded by my friend's family. Before my bath, I'd thought the floor beautiful, friend at my side, showing me where the towels were, handing me her sweet-smelling shampoo.

But as her family stood around my head, shaking me, all I could feel were the dents where the cold tiles connected. I gasped for air but didn't cry. I groped for the elusive towel that was supposed to be mine, but then stopped to put my hands over my breasts. I couldn't cover the rest.

When I finally walked out, their tile became hideous, cold and hard beneath the growing calluses on the soles of my feet. The girl never invited me over again. Either her mother feared another near-death experience or she didn't want me around her son. But that didn't stop the kid from describing my body, down to the freckles on my breasts, to every guy in school. Then they'd all seen me naked, drowning, asleep and vulnerable.

I didn't want to spend the night at her house again anyway.

I forgot her name.

Filled with concern, my father ripped my bathtub from the wall. He replaced it with a large shower stall complete with a seat I'd been more than happy to use. But this time, I sank to the shower floor, bypassing the seat. I hated it. Now the streams of hot water surrounded my head, and this time, as I looked up, droplets shot by me like stars moving past the *Enterprise*, moments after Captain Kirk ordered warp speed. I'd never realized how nice the center of the shower was. It was the eye of the storm, the space behind the waterfall.

To go where no man has gone before, I thought.

* * *

"Things are different now," I said as I stepped out of the shower and wrapped a towel around my head like a turban. "That girl's brother was a jerk." I pulled on my terrycloth bathrobe and decided to eat something before going back to bed.

Halfway down the stairs, I froze.

A sky-blue square, approximately eight by ten feet, was painted over the fresh, champagne-white foyer wall. The hardwood floor gleamed under Carla's care, and looking down upon the earthy brown floor and the floating blue square, I caught a glimpse of Betty Lou's sky again. It was back.

It had to be Carla, I thought.

The giant blue square was light and its edges muted. I could barely distinguish it from the champagne in which it floated, dreamy, sky-like. One photograph hung at the center.

It was the duck.

The new frame hung in the exact spot on which Betty Lou had originally placed it. It was classy and sophisticated. It was glorious. It was a gift.

I sat at the bottom of the stairs for a long time.

☑ flower

"But why did you conk out if you took your medicine?" Tim asked while shoving pizza between his chapped lips. "Why'd you fall like that? You didn't end up crashin' the first time . . . at my apartment."

It was our last day of work in the cotton field. School was starting in four days.

"Well, technically, I'm on medication for bein' tired all the time, not for cataplexy." Our waiter stood next to the table, eager for me to quit talking. "But that was just a really bad night."

"Thank you for eatin' at Pizza Hut," the waiter finally said, placing the bill in front of Tim, who was sitting comfortably between Kimmy and me. Then the guy hesitated, as if wanting to say something to Tim. Instead he walked away, dejected, as if Tim had refused to give his autograph.

"I don't usually have two episodes in one night or even one a day," I said, grabbing the bill so we could divide it. "It's unusual if it happens more than once a week. The sleepiness is the worst." I shook my head. "I don't know. I guess I was just stressed out."

"Yeah, well, The Blue Flower *was* a new experience," Tim said, never taking his eyes off the waiter.

Watching Tim watch the waiter made me feel a little unsettled, although I was trying to be open minded. "Your cousin didn't help."

Kimmy looked at Tim, then at me, and back at Tim. "Why? What happened?" she asked. "What'd she do?"

"You're no longer a 'blue flower' virgin, you know," said Tim. "You've been *deflowered*, so to speak. Now we just have to deal with you," he said, turning to Kimmy. "You're more like the frickin' Shreveport Rose Center."

"What'd she do?" Kimmy leaned toward us, ignoring Tim's comment, displaying a curiosity we rarely saw. "Come on, tell me."

Tim grinned. "Little ole Scarlett took quite a shine to Angel."

"She was just a little bit . . . too friendly." I left out the part about her calling the next day. She gave her telephone number to Carla, but I threw it away.

"She said you claimed to have a boyfriend," Tim said. "Which we know is bullshit."

I tried not to smile, but couldn't hold back. Kimmy chuckled, picking at her pizza. She was torn between her belief in selective listening and her blossoming curiosity. And at that moment, staring at Tim, so crass yet so appealing, and then back at Kimmy, I decided to accept their friendship, to enjoy it. My summer of stumbling through the scorched cotton and burning cow shit had given me something worth holding on to. "Well, I do see someone, but it's not serious."

I wanted to try.

Kimmy looked at Tim as if she'd spent the summer blind. As if she never realized that his let-it-all-hang-out personality had sucked forth bits and pieces of me. Like the tornadoes we southerners feared, he'd swirled into my life, taking me by surprise. The shelter I'd thought sufficient broke down plank by plank until I found myself at the center of an empty flat field with no way out.

"How come you never told us about him?" she asked.

She thought she knew me.

"It's private," I said, not quite comfortable with my decision to confide. "We each owe five fifty plus the tip."

"Considerin' all the crap we've talked about out here ridin' around in the turnip truck, I wouldn't consider that too private. What do you think, Kimmy?"

"He's married," I said, before Kimmy could answer.

"No shit?" Tim grabbed my arm and stood up, holding its dead weight high as if declaring some sort of victory. "You've got more nerve than I thought!"

"Oh, Angel," was all Kimmy said. She looked sad.

The Pizza Hut patrons stared. I tried to pull my arm down, but couldn't. Tim wouldn't let go. "I don't really wanna talk about it, so just fork out the money and let's get outta here."

"Okay for now, but I'll get the info," he said, grinning. "I *will* get it."

"It's my life, and I said I'm not talkin'. I should have just kept my mouth shut."

"Please just sit down and leave her alone."

My arm dropped to the table and Tim sat, looking like a kid in trouble.

"Let's talk about our end-of-the-summer celebration," Kimmy said, attempting to change the subject.

"We gotta go," I said. "It's the last day, but they're still gonna be lookin' for us to get back." I scooted toward the edge of the booth, but Kimmy reached across the table and grabbed my arm.

"Wait," she said, her voice low. "Tim's gonna give me somethin' to try. Somethin' . . . pretty harmless."

"Kimmy's willin' to try it." Tim's eyes looked drunk. "It's part of our celebration . . . party favors, you know?"

"Are we talkin' about drugs?"

"Not so loud," Tim said, leaning toward me, his chest almost in the leftover pizza.

He suddenly looked gay, quite deviant actually, and I wondered how I'd missed it before. I leaned toward him, remembering the huddle he and his friends had formed outside the bathroom door of his apartment. Now I understood the strange grins, the dancing. "I cain't do that. I take prescription medication." I looked around for the waiter, but couldn't find him. "What are you tryin' to do, kill me?" I'd never seen a Pizza Hut so understaffed. People were there, but there was no help available. They were all starving. And looking around the room, at each wasted face, I felt hungry all over again.

"Cain't you just lay off it for a week or so?" Tim asked. "I mean, we don't have to do it tonight. We'll do it next Friday. Just take a nap all afternoon, like last time."

"I don't think I can quit cold turkey like that."

"Look, I figure this stuff's either gonna wake you up or put you to sleep. If it makes you tired, we'll handle it, just like at The Blue Flower. You weren't complainin' that night." He decided to eat another piece of pizza. "I think you enjoyed Scar's TLC." He stuffed it in his mouth while I tried to ignore my lingering appetite.

I shook my head in denial. I'd already eaten enough.

"It's a lot less stressful when you just come on out and admit it."

"I don't need to admit anythang. That's your problem, not mine."

He looked down. "You said your medicine doesn't always help that much anyway."

"Kimmy, I cain't believe you're doin' this," I said. She sat quietly, perhaps praying again. "It doesn't seem like you at all."

Tim threw up his arms. "Hey, just for the Pizza Hut record, she's the one who asked me about it, swear to God."

Seeing Tim's arms in the air, the waiter appeared out of nowhere. "Can I get y'all anythang else?"

"Well," said Tim, staring at the flustered waiter, "maybe some hot breadsticks."

"We don't need anythang, thank you. We're still gettin' our money together."

The waiter left.

"You're disgustin'," I said to Tim.

"I'm sure he's gay."

"That's got nothin' to do with it."

"I just wanna know why I have to do everythang I'm supposed to," Kimmy said without looking up. "I'm twenty-six years old. I'm still in college. I'm fat."

"You're not fat," we both said, forgetting the waiter.

She looked up, but her face was still low to the table. "Well, I've been fat my whole life so I still feel fat. Somethin' like that doesn't leave, you know."

Looking at her tear-filled eyes, I thought of the long hot showers I'd taken lately. Kimmy's showers had filled her to the brink. She was floating, and as her tears began to surface, I knew she'd reached her limit.

"I still live at home with my fat parents. Somethin's gotta give, Angel."

"You could try datin' a married guy like her."

"Will you just shut up?" I said.

"I don't wanna date married men. I wanna fall in love and get married and have babies that I can give names like Christopher and Nicole. I wanna big house and a nice yard with flowers and a bird feeder. All those thangs, you know?" She swept her growing bangs from her narrowing eyes. They were damp. I realized that her tears weren't falling. Instead, her hair was soaking them up. "That's what I want," she said. "Trust me, I worked at the Piggly Wiggly for five years before I started college, and that just ain't gonna cut it."

"But, Kimmy, drugs aren't gonna help with all that," I said. "I mean, the way I see it, you're on your way. You're gettin' an education. You'll meet somebody before too long."

"No, I need a change, some kinda major change." She began ripping her napkin into tiny pieces. She rolled them between her fingers and then dropped them into her empty glass. "I've been in a rut for too long, and I cain't crawl out. I didn't even realize all this until I met y'all."

"What makes you think the two of us aren't stuck in ruts, too?" Tim asked, serious now.

"Well, I don't know. I didn't say that, but if you are, I like your ruts better than mine."

"So you just wanna jump from one rut to another?" I asked. "That's crazy, Kimmy. You're the best outta three here."

"I'm borin'."

"I explained to Kimmy how what I've got will change her," Tim whispered. "It makes people see the world differently . . . most people, anyway. And it's not like you're gonna try it and get addicted, just like that." He snapped his fingers without a sound. "And, Jesus, you could use a little mind alteration," he said to me, sounding like a hippie. "It's twenty dollars a pop and all yah need's one. You don't feel drunk and you won't get a hangover. Who knows, maybe we'll all jump out of our godforsaken ruts."

"Angel, he said it's somethin' everyone should feel at least once in their life. I only wanna feel it once." Her innocent eyes begged, and I knew I might consider it, just for her.

I could tell she needed something.

Tim put his arms around us. "It'll be a religious experience." Then he squeezed my shoulders hard enough to cause a pain in my chest. "You'll think you've died and gone to heaven."

Kimmy stared at her glass. "And then maybe we'll come back to life."

"You'll be frickin' born again."

*　*　*

Mac's door opened, and I fell through it. He caught me like always, but I smelled him first. Before I felt him holding me, I smelled sex, the hospital, and his Polo cologne. Those smells I thought I loved jarred me.

That's when I knew it was happening.

Sometimes, when I fell asleep, I remained in the position I'd been in when awake. Sometimes I froze for several seconds, or even several minutes, but usually, in the end I slumped over, crumpled down, or fell forward. Like ice cracking, there was always an associated sound, a destructive noise that turned ordinary people into gawks and gossips.

But Mac was far from ordinary. "Hey, sleepyhead," he said, smoothing back my hair. It had escaped my ponytail when I rolled down the cab window, trying to stay awake. "You should get rid of that fat ponytail." He held it uncharacteristically, like a beautician, and I wondered who he really was. "Your hair is so coarse and wild."

I pulled myself together, but didn't pull away. He kicked the door shut. "You took long enough," I said. My voice croaked. "What day is it anyway?"

He pretended to laugh. "Ha, ha, you're too funny."

The Mac I knew was back.

He ran his healing hands over my arms as if warming me could wake me. "I was on the phone, but it was only a couple minutes."

"Are you sure? I thought I heard whistlin'." I glanced back at the door, confused. "I rang the doorbell, and then I heard you whistlin'. You whistled a whole song."

"Dreams, Angel, just dreams." He held my face in his hands. A tender gesture that made me feel as if he cared. "Look, you cain't be out runnin' around like this."

"I'm fine. I just . . ." Unable to continue, my mouth fell open as I watched Mac's face change and his hair curl. It grew down over his eyes as his hands fell away. They were suddenly too far away, but he was calling me. I stood, mesmerized, oblivious to everything else because the mind tries to make sense of what the eyes see—and nothing made sense. He stood on the far side of a river, a small one, more like a creek. It was frozen, but not solid enough to hold my weight. He was Darwin. I don't know how I knew but I recognized him. He'd made his way through my mind, out of my dreams, and into reality. I jerked my head from side to side, looking for the place I thought I'd been, but nothing was the same. And then I heard Betty Lou's voice, the voice of *mother*. I couldn't see her, but I heard her singing the song I'd heard Mac whistling. Clouds hovered above me. I concentrated, thinking they were only the white ceiling-fan blades churning above my head. But each one created the shape of something real and true in my life, and Betty Lou was there, looking for them, looking for me, searching like me.

"Angel," Darwin said, "what's wrong? Come on, Angel, come on."

Looking out across the frozen water, hearing the song of *mother*, I felt pulled toward the unbelievable, the impossible. Its painful tug promised ecstasy. Most good things were like that. Everything's a trade-off, a risk, or a scam. I'd drown before reaching my goal. I'd sink beneath the ice like an anchor, the anchor my father cast overboard to hold his lonely ship in place. Unlike sex or the love I'd known, the desire pulling me to the water's edge was sappy. Like a song, ordinary in words, yet so true in its expression, it would stick with me even after I'd come to hate it.

Then the voice of *mother* began to sound like Scarlett's singsong voice, floating toward me from some distant, flowered field. "I cain't," I said. "I cain't do it."

"Angel!"

"I'm scared," I said, knees buckling.

"You'll be okay. You're gonna survive . . . just come on."

As I heard him say, "Wake up," his arms reached across the river. They shook me, but instead of waking me, they rocked me. He rocked my eyes shut. Like a baby's, they closed little by little with each rocking motion.

I fell back asleep.

When my eyes opened again, I knew where I was. I also knew I didn't want to be there. The clock on the wall indicated an hour had passed, and I could hear Mac whistling in the kitchen. His gray townhouse seemed covered in dust, the kind that isn't always visible, but that accumulates when things get old, when they go unattended; the kind that creates drab people and places. I was afraid to be in the house he shared with her. It smelled like them. I stood up and made my way toward the kitchen, groping their furniture as I moved forward. Each possession I touched seemed to bear a story that didn't include me. And the unseen dust swirled up, covering me until I felt sick.

"Why are you so sleepy?" He stood in the small kitchen, looking into the refrigerator. "I've never seen you this bad. You were hallucinatin' back there, weren't you?"

"It happens sometimes," I said, thinking I should keep my mouth shut. "I stopped my meds."

He spun around.

"I missed half my classes this week. And I'm really tired, but I think it'll be okay." I leaned against their kitchen cabinets, yawning.

"What the hell did you do that for?"

"It's just the first week of school," I said, trying to defend myself.

He threw down the dishtowel he'd been holding. "You know that medication is the only reason you're able to get through school." He was bossy sometimes but I liked it. It made me feel safe.

"I slept all afternoon, and . . . I thought I'd be okay."

"Well, you're obviously not."

"The medication doesn't always help, anyway. I'm still tired all the time."

"You just don't realize 'cause you're used to it." He closed the refrigerator. A homemade card on the door said, "Happy Six-Month Anniversary." I wondered how happy it could be.

Mac caught me staring. "It's safer here than at the hospital."

"Are you sure?" Everything was starting to feel different. I didn't like seeing her scarf on the table or her gold earrings on the kitchen countertop. We belonged together at the hospital, but not here.

"Here, drink this," he said, handing me a glass of Mountain Dew. "You could use the caffeine."

"It won't help," I said, staring at the scarf.

"I'll carry you back to the livin' room," he said, lifting me. It was so easy for him, too easy. "Just watch the drink."

We were already to the couch.

"I'd carry you anywhere, you know." He said these things often. Usually, I played along, but as he put me down, I smelled his wife all around me. I didn't want to play along—the perfume was too strong. I decided that he must think me incredibly naive. Or he didn't care that I knew he was a fake.

I didn't care.

Not then.

"I wish you *could* take me somewhere."

Silence.

"How long is she supposed to be gone this time?" I asked, thinking I should just go ahead and unzip his pants.

"Why did you stop your meds, Angel? After all you've been through, I didn't think you'd be so stupid."

I grabbed a throw pillow, but then put it back. "I have good reason."

"Like what?"

"I'd rather not say."

"Does this have somethin' to do with Carla? Did you get your pictures back?"

"She put one back. The duck."

He smiled his perfect smile. "Look, just promise me you'll take somethin' when you get home."

"I promise I'll take somethin'," I said, like a little kid.

"You know," he said, running his finger over my eyebrow in the direction opposite of growth. "You should go out and meet somebody. I've been thinkin' about it. You don't go out enough."

"But what if I do meet somebody? What if I don't wanna see you anymore?"

"I don't know." He lowered me back against the pillow. "I don't know how to answer that."

"Would you get another girlfriend?"

"No." He shook his head, almost sad. "You're perfect," he whispered. "I wouldn't take anybody else."

But I wasn't perfect, that was obvious. I was an anomaly.

I wished Tim could waltz in and rescue me with his ability to prevent people from wasting truthful moments. He would see the truth between Mac and me, and announce it as if we'd been waiting with bated breath to listen. I saw truth, but more times than not, failed to grasp it. I failed to appreciate the unique before it passed away, or beauty in blossom, or gifts that were free. "We haven't even fooled around the last couple of times we were together," I said, trying to be honest.

He smiled again, a not-so-perfect smile, and then undressed me, button-by-button, slow tug by slow tug. But rather than erotic, it was dry and rehearsed. I was not seduced, but I clung to his healing hands and eyes that faked the truth because sometimes he did understand me and sometimes it was erotic.

His wife's scarf lay across the table, choking me.

"I love you, Mac. In a way, I do."

"I know," he said, as if all the women around him do. As if what we had wasn't real and that was okay for him. But I knew it wasn't okay—I could tell by the way he stared at her scarf.

☑ gift

I sat alone in a theater seat, high in the balcony where I could see the bar, the dance floor, almost everything. The smile I wore was different from any smile I'd ever seen or felt.

It was the smile of Ecstasy.

Tim was right. I could feel my resurrection. It started in my fingers and toes. It traveled toward my belly, crashing inward like an orgasm. Then, radiating outward, its warming zoom escaped through the ecstatic smile the drug created. Kimmy was born again, too. She danced below, her body moving as if it wasn't hers, mimicking those around her.

Looking down, I stared at a show rather than a tangled dance floor. Kimmy and the other dancers moved like frenzied angels, dancing and singing in one accord with no need for a rehearsal. They knew the next move, the next word, their minds connected by divine intuition. Their coordination appeared flawless, although some clutched the dance floor railing as if it were their only link to earth, to gravity. The rail grounded them, ensuring they wouldn't fall or rise too high. Big hair canopied the dance floor and a multitude of barren shoulders peeked between the bouncing colors. This was life at its fullest, brilliant with the colors and sounds of the eighties. And the celebration was real yet unrealistic, earthly yet heavenly, purpose in its purest form.

Nothing hurt. Nothing had to affect me personally, neither other people's actions nor my own.

And all the men seemed gay. I knew they weren't, but they had a gay look, as if their minds were enlightened with new possibilities, impossible to ignore. They had new ideas—new lights embedded in their faces, extra eyes opening wide with each beat of the new-wave music. They were beautiful, every last one of them. Unique. Even the ugly grew exquisite.

Kimmy was lovely, too, and I wanted to tell her. I wanted her to feel beautiful. Her bangs, finally long enough to pull back, parted from her eyes like a curtain, and her face, that dark stage, was utterly changed, her eyes open and bright. From my perch, her large body appeared strong but lanky. "More to love," people say. And that was it—more to love. She was larger than the other girls, Amazon-like, a protector. I smiled, knowing she only had to find her place.

That was all any of us had to do, find a place. But I didn't consider mine; mine was in that theater seat. I had no doubt that I belonged, although "Say No to Drugs" floated in my mind . . . a monstrous idea with tendrils embedded deeper than I knew. But I ignored all that and told myself the doctors, engineers, and construction workers had tricked me. I'd fallen prey to their scam at thirteen. They'd tossed all kinds of pretty pills my way while holding back the best they had to offer. It's dangerous, I thought, smiling, and then laughing aloud, louder than I'd laughed in years with not a flutter of an eye or the buckle of a knee.

My eyes were open wide.

And the smile oozed without decision. Its stretch across my face was the spreading-out of everything inside: heart, soul, and spirit; the genetic and the learned; the mind. Released, the fundamental definition of Angel Duet exploded between my lips. I could almost see the smile with my own eyes, beneath my eyes. And nothing else mattered. Bad was bad and good was good. It was life, and it was the path toward heaven. I knew this because I found heaven there, in that theater seat. I learned in those moments what heaven was like. It came to me, a full-bodied wind, rising, blowing my mind with its spiritual glow, bright and blinding.

It healed me.

And I swore never to forget. I thought, smiling, while the others danced below, while some drank and some kissed, while some fed their addictions, and still others wallowed in their confusion, that perhaps I'd felt it before. Perhaps it was the truth I'd failed to recognize, or the free gift I'd turned away. And when this night was over, when my twenty dollars' worth wore off, I'd search it out. I'd dig, no matter what the required depth, no matter how hard or shit-filled the dirt, until I hit upon this lovely emotion. I was sure I didn't need twenty dollars to coax it out. I'd find it again, and life would be different.

"Angel," Tim said, suddenly beside me, smiling the smile. "Is it workin'?"

I smiled the smile.

"It's workin'," he said, and we continued to smile as if that was enough. Looking at those below, we knew that even a friend could die, writhing at our feet, and our joy would not flinch. We would continue to smile the smile, knowing peace lay ahead, and life was but a cocoon holding us tight and keeping us dry until our wings broke free. He sat next to me, put his arm around me, and pressed his lips against my cheek in an almost sensual kiss. "If you wanna sit here all night, that's great, but we were just wonderin' if you wanna dance."

"I don't normally dance," I said, smiling.

"You'll enjoy it now. All that stuff you're feelin', it just comes spewin' out." His words were soft like cotton. "It literally oozes outta the skin when you dance."

"I was never the greatest dancer," I said. "Actually, I was never the best liver. I mean . . . I don't *live* the best, you know." We laughed.

"I know," he said, placing his hand on my knee. "But hey, you're born again, right? And ecstasy breeds creativity."

"I'm creative. I am," I said, as if I'd just found myself. Sometimes it happens that way.

We walked down the stairs of the renovated theater to the bar and dance floor below. Tim told me that seventy percent of those around us were on something. It was that type of place, and they flocked to it like insects to a yellow light. As we moved toward Kimmy, her face glowed and her smile was like ours. She'd never looked happier.

I'd never felt such love for the world, for each person, complete with flaws, armed with pain just waiting to be thrown my way. On that night I could accept their pain, I could actually cherish it for all its worth, for its ability to give me strength. I was strong. Yes, strong. Strong like Jesus, turning my cheek toward them and smiling because no matter what, each was a work of art. No, I would not forget this feeling. Please, God, if you are there, don't let me forget, I thought.

"Angel, Angel, come dance with me," Kimmy invited, smiling. The world was lights and rhythm and motion, and I was part of it.

I came toward her.

We came together.

I kissed her on the chin, the strobe light flashing. My lips easily reached her chin. She took my hand, and we twirled and churned, and clutched the rail side by side. "I love you, Angel," she said, tugging at the leather ponytail clip holding my hair together. "I really do."

Like a flood, my long hair fell over me. It seemed to hug me as if it had taken on a life, the strands resurrected one by one. It didn't matter that I looked sexy. What mattered was the creation of Angel Duet, the individual. I was beautiful. I was a work of art. "I usually try not to love people," I yelled to her, "but you and Tim are different. I didn't wanna love you, but I do," I said honestly, because now, with my soul and spirit stretched across my face, there was no need to pretend. I yelled above the music, "I'm not tired, Kimmy. I'm awake. I'm wide awake!"

And Kimmy yelled, "She's awake! She's awake!" And Tim heard, and whooped and hollered until the entire dance floor churned with the news.

* * *

From the moment I first met Carla at the annual Franklin, Duet &
Mercer Christmas party, I knew she was a success. My father wasn't
romantically interested in her then, but it didn't take long to win him
over, something no one had done in almost twenty years.

So it turned out to be true about her.

One hundred percent went into whatever she took on, whether it
was suing some undeserving soul, redecorating the home of a grieving
man, or waking up his full-grown daughter.

People like her always seemed superior to me. I was sure that God
created our world for them because they fit so perfectly into it. On
my worst days, they were the people I longed to strip down. I wanted
to scrape out their self-love and stuff them with my dull ache and
undercurrent hostility. I wanted to feed them a personality that drives
a timid soul to make all the wrong choices, and to suffer. Their brand
of success bored me to the degree that they discounted mine. But what
set me apart was the resentment.

"Frank," Carla said, "are you just gonna let her lie on the couch
like that, sleeping her life away? You have an obligation."

"She's not a kid. She knows what she's doin'. She's been doin' it
long before you showed up." I could almost hear his smile. "You just
gotta get used to it." I heard a kiss, a faint smack on her face.

"Did you know what you were doin' when you were twenty-one?"
Carla asked.

Silence.

"Well, I didn't," she said. "I was an idiot."

Does she even understand that word? I wondered.

"If she's not up in fifteen minutes, I'm gonna get that medicine
and force-feed it down her throat. She hasn't been takin' it all week.
Frank?" I heard her say. But there was no answer.

His characteristic silence was both weak and strong. It told me he
knew about pain. He'd lost something precious . . . and not in the
regular way. It came at him from all sides. His loss ate him up. And
we ate his grief for dinner. We ate it for breakfast, too. He cooked it
up and served it. And when I tasted it, it was good. Mostly, he fed me
this personality. Like essential nutrients, his loving spoonfuls broke

down, incorporating themselves into my narcoleptic body. My heart grew so swollen and tight that at times I feared it would explode with the sluggish, bitter love he fertilized.

"She just started back to school, for Christ's sake," Carla said, unshaken by his silence. To her, silence was a transaction in which she was the victor. An aloof, puzzling confidence filled her so taut that I couldn't imagine her without it. No matter what her weight, what she had on, who rejected her, or who disagreed with her, her confidence remained, steady and cold. It traveled in her voice like a ball coming at me when I wasn't ready. Forced to throw up my hands, I tried to catch it before I felt the smack. I caught her cold stare as I dragged myself into the dining room, but somehow I still felt it hit. Like a fast, hard ball, it stung, but I remained cool, trying to play on her field. Bippy sat like a sphinx next to her. They both had the same look, Carla's catlike and Bippy's human.

"What are you doin' with that?" I asked, seeing that she had one of Betty Lou's photographs on the table. It lay across a large towel, a precaution against harming the table finish.

"I'm just gettin' it ready." She smiled and reached toward me as if to motion me closer. "How nice of you to get up. It's Sunday, by the way."

"Ready for what?" I stopped. "What are you doin'?"

Bippy meowed as if to scare me away.

"Don't you like what I did with the duck?" She smiled bigger, pretending that I liked her. "I thought you'd like it. I'm not creative, you know." She slid a box cutter over the brown paper back of the frame. "Don't worry, I'm not gonna cut it. I just have to get it outta this old frame before I take it up to the gallery."

"I'm goin' out to do the grass," my father hollered as the door to the garage slammed.

"Which one is it?" I asked, moving a little closer. She didn't answer, but stared down at the back of the exposed photograph, squinting. "What's wrong?"

"Look, real little there. There's somethin' written on the back."
We both bent down close to read the dull, penciled writing. "I think
it says *snake*."

"Yeah, it's the snake cloud," she said. "And it has a date.
Nineteen . . ."

"Sixty-two. It's nineteen sixty-two. She wrote it there when she
took the photograph. She labeled it." We looked at each other. "Did
you see anythang on the back of the duck?" I asked.

"No, I left that one in the frame. But they charged me ten dollars to
take it out so I decided to start takin' 'em out myself."

"It's her handwritin'," I said, running my fingers over the
small word.

"Don't you have anythang with her handwritin' on it?" I could
feel her staring at me, thinking I was pathetic. I'd seen her look at
my father that way, but he never seemed to notice. He never noticed
details so I noticed them for both of us. I noticed when a person had
a tiny hole in their shirt or two dangling earrings in one earlobe that
became accidentally intertwined, detached strands of hair hanging off
people, scuffs on shoes. But Carla was meticulous. She never left those
things around for people like me to find. She made very few mistakes.
She was slow and careful, never allowing others to rush her. I wondered if that was why my father thought she was strong.

"No, everythang's gone," I said. "One day when I was about seven
or eight, he packed it all up and took it away." I stared down at Betty
Lou's handwriting. I didn't want to look up because I felt like crying.
I tried to recall heaven, that feeling I'd found sitting in the theater balcony, but it didn't come rushing back like I'd hoped. I clearly remembered it, but couldn't feel it. I also remembered my promise to find it.

"Well, I cain't even believe that." Carla put her hand on my back
and oddly, I wanted to lean into it, to feel it harder against me. I
wanted to lean into her, tight and warm. Thinking of it turned my
body heavy and sad. I wanted her to grab me, to force me into that
leaning hug, taking my imperfection into her. By some miracle, she
might sift it through her impregnable spirit, and then return to me the
best parts, the parts that were interesting and loveable. All the other

parts would fall away like the dead strands of hair that never stuck to her, but landed, clinging, across the backs of people like me.

"She had her own darkroom, but he gutted it and made it his office. And I think there were more photographs. We have a couple of photo albums, but those are different. These are all he left me," I said, turning the snake photograph over to look at it. "He told me this was really a huge cloud that stretched for miles across the sky. She used some kind of special lens to get it all in the photograph. It's funny how, when you look at it, you cain't even tell how much sky it took up. There's no perspective."

Carla said, "Well, he told me that for each of these photographs there were probably fifty more. So maybe these are just the best ones. For all we know, she only wanted you to see the best stuff. Maybe he knew she'd want all the crappy ones thrown out."

The crap I would never see made me sad. "Do you think this handwritin' could be evaluated?" I asked, but she didn't seem to hear.

"It does surprise me that he actually got rid of her stuff . . . and just think, that was only eight years after her death."

I didn't like her tone. "What's that supposed to mean?" I asked, swinging around to face her.

"Well, he still isn't over it. I never knew anyone who could hang on to the past like your father. I mean, I feel really, really bad for the woman. It's tragic, actually, but there comes a time when you just gotta look in the mirror and get over it. You all have been cryin' over spilled milk so long it's all dried out and crusty. It stinks."

"I don't smell anythang."

"That's 'cause you're used to it. Trust me, it stinks to high heaven around here."

"He's just . . . a sensitive person. And if you think he's so pathetic and . . . smelly, why do you keep hangin' around? You could leave, you know."

She began gathering up the things she planned to throw away. "I have my reasons."

"Dad says you're perceptive. He says you see somethin' special in him, but it sounds to me like the stuff you're perceivin' isn't all that great."

"Sometimes people just wanna be seen for exactly who they are, even if it's not pleasant. It's liberating. I think your dad's startin' to feel liberated." She smiled.

"From what? From her?"

"You haven't reached the point in your life where you can truly appreciate what I'm talkin' about. Just trust me, he's stronger than he thinks. He just needs someone to show him, and he knows I'm capable."

I felt smacked again. "He's a lot better than he used to be."

"Yeah, and I bet he didn't really get rid of all her stuff, either."

"I don't know. That day, I asked him not to take it away. He was cryin' a little, takin' boxes out to the car. He said it was time to get rid of it. And once, when I was about fourteen, I asked if he had anythang of hers left, and he said no."

"That's weird, don't you think?" She sat down at the table.

I shrugged a shoulder like I didn't care. "He said he didn't wanna talk about it, like he always does." I stared at the table while she stared at me.

We didn't speak for a few minutes. Then she said, "Who's the guy who calls you all the time? The one who always gives a different name? Don't you think that's a little odd?"

"He's a friend of mine." It was Mac. "He's just different, that's all."

"I know you're doin' somethin' that's gonna get you in trouble. I can see it comin'."

"Just don't worry about it, okay? You need to stop worryin' about me in general. Isn't that what Dad just told you?"

"That's not what he meant."

Silence.

Finally, she said, "Did you do any more work on your Darwin paper?"

"A little," I said, finally sitting down, wondering why I was still there.

"So what about Darwin? What was the evolution of his theory?"

"Well, he made all those discoveries supportin' an idea that had been around for centuries, but his religious beliefs, Victorian society, and his family's beliefs kept him from comin' forward with his data." That was all I had to say.

"And?"

"Why do you care?"

"I happen to be interested. I told you I'd help, didn't I?"

"Well, he struggled with the implications that resulted from the theories he set out to prove. Actually, he didn't really set out to prove anythang. He just saw the implications, the answers, starin' him in the face. I don't think he wanted it to be true." I kept going, realizing it felt good to show her I was actually smart. "He wanted to believe God created the earth just the way it says in the Bible . . . that the answers are all simple . . . that they just require faith."

"He was certainly intelligent enough to believe in the complicated."

"Well, he didn't wanna hurt his family by supportin' somethin' that would threaten their beliefs. He couldn't deny what he'd found, but at the same time, he hated it. In the end, it wasn't even his own beliefs he struggled with, it was the family thang . . . and society."

"But does a man owe his family so much? He was an educated man who forged a path few men even tiptoe across. Just think what his life could have been like if he'd been able to get over all that goofy guilt. He very well may have been nothin' but a big coward."

"Well, I guess *he* believed he owed 'em. Isn't that all that matters? He loved 'em, I guess. That was the kinda man he was . . . so he suffered. And besides that, he wanted to publish his data when it had a chance to be accepted."

Later, I realized my father was like Darwin, suffering for the sake of those he loved—not brave enough yet for anything more. I still have the paper I wrote that year. Every now and then, I take it out and read it again, and like a song, it takes me back to the world I once lived in.

"I can understand, but I cain't sympathize," she said, shifting her weight. "It sounds to me like he denied his greatness for too long. He was pretty cowardly when you consider what he had to offer." She stood up and stretched, slow and ritualistic.

I watched her body, noting its imperfections one by one, and fought my urge to consider Darwin a coward.

In my opinion, Carla was just a great bullshitter, one of those people who insist the sky is green and you believe it. Even as you stand looking up into the clear blue, you shake your head, yes, yes, the sky does look a little green today. I never considered she honestly believed it was green, that her eyes were liars, and that I was also right when I thought, no, I think it's only blue.

As I watched her place the snake photograph between two pieces of cardboard, I decided I didn't hate her because my father loved her. I despised her because I could never be like her. I could never walk around as if I deserved not only the space I took up, but a little extra, too. She was a bitch. And I was a bitch for hating her.

Surely, I thought, that's all we have in common, besides our love for him.

☑ horse

Lying by the pool later that day, I thought about the tiny date on the back of Betty Lou's snake photograph. Knowing she was exactly my age when she penciled it in caused me to wonder if I should be doing something more creative with my time. I was staring into the water when Kimmy came around the side of the house in her typical lethargic style, but from the looks of her, the Ecstasy *had* caused a change. Tim was right. Kimmy and I had both changed in ways that were clear and simple at the time, but in the dull aftermath they emerged insidiously false. He was right about a lot of things. I didn't wake up a drug addict. I didn't have a hangover either, but I'd been sleeping since that giddy smile wore off. I'd been dreaming and my memories of the night were questionable. I was counting on Kimmy to help me sort things out. I usually didn't have a friend handy to identify the fictitious and the real. By now, my whole history needed sorting, but I'd come to the realization that it wasn't going to happen and that my history wasn't necessarily factual. Every time I fell asleep, history changed. Looking back, I couldn't identify the pattern of my life.

"Angel," was all Kimmy said as she sat down at the end of my lounge chair. I pulled my legs up to accommodate her.

"Are you okay?" I asked, realizing it was an insensitive question. She'd lost her virginity to a stranger—of course she wasn't "okay." Though, I still couldn't understand why she should be sorry. Actually, I couldn't remember the details, the exact situation. I'd slept with a couple of guys I barely knew, never caring or wondering if I'd made the right decision. I almost preferred it that way, reveling in the seductive moments and then gladly walking away. Knowing they couldn't handle my screwed-up body, I released them before they had to face the responsibility of narcolepsy. I thought I was doing them a favor, but sometimes it hurt.

She finally spoke. "I wanted to do it, but it happened so fast." She started to cry a little, and I put my hand over hers. Her swollen face allowed me to see how she must have looked for most of her life, bloated and desolate.

"Kimmy, you're twenty-six years old. I think the whole thang was really slow. Fast is fifteen. The night of your fifteenth birthday. That's fast. Not this. I'm not sayin' this to make you feel worse. I hope it makes you feel better."

"But do you understand? Do you know how I feel?"

I let go of her hand at just the moment I should have held it tighter. "Maybe it's too fast no matter when it happens."

She put her hand on her stomach. "Once my mom told me that love should be like two big polar bears tumblin' around in the snow, or pigs rollin' through the mud." I thought she might throw up. "Or like a litter of puppies packed together so tight you cain't tell 'em apart."

"I don't understand that at all," I said, shaking my head. "That sounds like brothers and sisters."

She touched my leg. "Neither of us have any, you know." It was an unaddressed lonely fact we shared.

At least she has a mother, I thought. "But, still," I said. It was all I could say.

"I guess my mom thinks a person ought to feel free and comfortable. I guess you're supposed to be havin' fun."

"But what about passion?" I asked.

"I doubt my mom's ever felt passionate in her life. She's a really large woman. I guess it was good they adopted me. I fit right in with the two of 'em."

"Passion makes the world go round," I said blandly. "I guess it's what made Tim jump out of the truck that day. It made us all better friends." I shrugged a shoulder. "I cain't believe I'm sayin' this, and it's really corny, but passion's what keeps us alive." I didn't tell her I was guilty of stifling my own, that I constantly tried to keep it in check. "It's there somewhere in everybody, even your mom."

"I thought it was money that kept the world turnin'."

"I don't think the source of passion has to be another person. I don't think it's the money. It's the emotion behind it."

"I felt passionate with that guy."

"Are you sure it wasn't the drug? I felt it, too. Just not over a guy."

"Can you believe what we did?" She stared down at her large, sandaled feet, and I realized I'd never seen her toes before. They were painted the color of boiled shrimp. I wondered if she'd kept them painted all summer or if it was something new. "I know I'm gonna be thinkin' about it for a long time. Do you ever have experiences like that? Ones you know mean somethin' important, but you don't really know what yet?"

Of course I did.

"After we left the old theater and went to that guy's house . . . I never even got his name . . ." She paused, and I thought, here comes the truth. Then she continued, "I still cain't believe those people were just layin' there naked." She bent down, picked up a loose pebble, and threw it into our pool as if it was something she'd always wanted to do. But as it skipped across the water, she flinched, knowing we wouldn't want rocks in our pool.

"Don't worry about it," I said.

"They didn't even care. Did you think that was weird? 'Cause you didn't act like it."

We'd walked in to find the guy and his girlfriend lying naked on his sofa bed. They snatched the covers up around them as Tim, Kimmy, and I filed into the room along with all the other people. Tim seemed to know everyone.

"I thought I dreamed that part," I said. "And the circle . . . did that happen?"

"Don't you remember? I remember everythang."

"I remember. It's just that sometimes I have trouble tellin' what's a dream and what's real."

"You mean it doesn't have anythang to do with takin' drugs?"

"No, it's the narcolepsy."

* * *

No one told me the names of the couple who lay naked under the thin white sheet. After yanking it over them, they both tucked it neatly around their bodies like a shroud made for two. Their private parts bulged, and I fought the desire to strip the cotton sheet away and gawk at their nakedness. Kimmy, Tim, and I hung at the end of the bed. We were still smiling the smile, but a low glow had settled over us, which I attributed to the fact that five hours had passed. It was three-thirty in the morning, a time I never expected to see.

Kimmy wandered away, and I let her go much too easily.

The sofa bed situation fascinated me. I couldn't believe that two naked people who'd obviously just had sex would welcome an entire crowd of people into their presence. Some they didn't know, for that matter. But they were smiling the smile, so I figured it was okay. I smiled back, although it was beginning to take a bit more energy. I had the dreadful feeling that I'd soon be sprawled across the floor.

More people filed in, around the sofa bed, into the kitchen and back out, while mosquitoes flew in through the perpetually open door. It was practically a party. Tim and I eventually left the naked couple's bedside to join the circle forming in the center of the room.

They called it the truth circle. Most of us sat cross-legged. Two joints and a few cigarettes appeared among the participants. As the lights went down, Tim began to explain the game to those of us who were new. Everyone was to take a turn. Tim was first, and I would be last. "When your turn comes," Tim said, "you're obligated to speak the truth about somethin', anythang you want to talk about. The person facin' you must then ask a relevant question that you *must* answer." He patted my leg. "It's easy."

We sat quietly for a moment. Then Tim said, "I'm gonna have sex dreams tonight." It wasn't funny. His voice was true and deep, as if telling a secret he trusted each one of us to keep.

"Well, don't dream about me, okay," I heard someone say, someone who couldn't grasp the seriousness and tragedy of truth the way I was trying to.

"Why not?" Tim asked. "I don't care if you dream about me. It doesn't mean anythang."

The guy directly across from Tim finally spoke. "Have you ever dreamed about having sex with somebody in your family?"

I squirmed, feeling my smile fizzle. Heaven descended upon me, heavy like cream, thick like crap. And despite the dim light, the room seemed much too bright. Heaven still blinded me, but now in a way that hurt my eyes.

I looked for Kimmy and saw the bedroom door close behind her. I'd smiled as if she were entering a unique place and not the dark cavern of wrong. The guy she followed had smiled the smile at her, and at me, and at Tim. He'd smiled it too well. As my own faded, I knew that the smile was corrupt and that Kimmy was making a mistake. It might have been okay for me, but for her it was wrong. There were no white fences, no children named Nicole, and no big houses inside that guy, behind his sickening smile. He was empty except for that joy the drug fed him.

Tim smiled, answering, "Yeah, of course, everybody has those dreams," his voice turning oppressive.

I thought about Betty Lou and then Scarlett and Kimmy, and in that moment, with that truth floating through the drugged-up circle, heaven's last glow drained from the room. All heads turned toward the door Kimmy lay behind, screaming from pleasure, or from pain. It was hard to tell which. And as I froze in cataplectic shock, eyes bulging, mouth wide open, I thought I'd rather be screaming behind that door than forced to speak the truth out here. Kimmy's breathy scream was the last sound I heard before I hit the floor, happy to be out of the game.

☑ ice

"What *is* your type?" Tim asked as the bartender slapped three napkins onto the splintered wooden bar. We were jammed against it—a
lady's hard purse dug into my back. Before I could answer, a drunken
guy bumped into her, shoving the purse into my arm. My elbow slid
across the bar toward Kimmy. It collided with her napkin, which she
grabbed as if it was precious.

Tim didn't notice the scuffle. He was too busy checking out the
place, gawking at straight men. Without looking at me, he hollered,
"You wanted to come to a normal place, but you're still not satisfied.
That's a pretty shitty attitude."

"So what will it be?" the bartender asked, staring at us.

The place was normal all right. It was ordinary, dark and crowded
like bars should be, but a creative wasteland compared to The Blue
Flower or the old theater. All three were old, but this place was somehow dying. Still, it was obviously a hot spot. The crowd proved it,
though something was missing. I guessed it was where I belonged, but
I didn't like it much. Of course, I wasn't going to tell Tim that. So, seeing his point, I ordered a Diet Coke and took a moment to consider a

description of my type, to find someone to show him, but apparently, my time was up.

"Face it, you're just the kind who's never content," he said. "It's a personality thang. You really shouldn't feel bad about it. You cain't help it."

Ignoring him, I continued to survey the bar, homing in on the men who appeared available. They were typical. A few wore suits. There were also preppies and of course rednecks; however, I'd learned that attire alone could not identify a redneck. Clothes gave away the preppies but never the rednecks.

Redneck trickled through us all. It diluted our blood. It's what softened our hearts, I think. Some tried to escape it, pretending to have unbreakable hearts, while others cherished it. They were the ones who thought it made them strong. I thought being a redneck involved a special brand of escape—escape from all the other types of people one could choose to become.

Continuing my search, I came across the crossbreeds, the guys who were preppie from the waist up and redneck from the waist down. They tucked their white, starched button-downs or their short-sleeve Polo shirts into dark blue Wranglers, tight and big-stitched. Semi-large belt buckles, like funky tools, held their garb together, but the boots gave them away. They never left their boots behind.

I didn't care for the muscled preppie guy Tim and Kimmy were admiring. He was too sweet and pretty, like pink cotton candy I didn't have to taste to know it would eventually melt into nothing but sugar. "There," I finally said, "see the guy in that reddish sweater, sittin' over there . . . with the glasses. He's my type."

"No way," Tim said, shaking his head. "He looks a little too geeky."

He didn't look anything like Mac.

"Well, maybe I like geeks. You like queers."

Tim smiled and shrugged his shoulders.

"He's lookin'," Kimmy said, poking me in the arm. "I think he saw you lookin' at him."

"He's *definitely* eyeballin' you," Tim said. "Come on, let's go talk to him." Before I could stop him, Tim headed toward the guy and his three friends. Kimmy, who was a little drunk after one drink, followed close behind.

"But you don't even know him," I said, too late. Tim's motor mouth was already moving. His slender hand was pointing me out. I had to go. Fate called as clear as I'd heard Mac whistling and Betty Lou singing. The band played a new song, and its eerie melody fed the situation. The full-bodied music meandered past Tim's pointing finger, through the crowd, around the suits, the rednecks, and the crossbreeds. It made its way toward me as I stood transfixed, an offering rather than a person. It swirled around my head. I could almost feel it seeping through my ears, filling my head with lies.

Christian saw me that night as enticing, something shining and new, maybe even valuable. In reality, I was cotton candy to him. But the way he seemed to savor the idea of eating me was deceptive. I thought I could stay that way I was forever.

I glanced back at the muscled preppie but he was already gone, melted.

When I looked at Christian again, the people between us parted, providing a better view of his wavy auburn hair and the dark holes in his head. His eyes were liars, not windows like they say. The view looking in wasn't the same as being inside. It was abbreviated, lacking perspective, and there was a trick to getting in that I didn't know.

I couldn't find the door.

To me, men were like skyscrapers, teeming with cavernous windows and short on doors. Their windows kept me hungry, showing me what I wanted, deceiving me, but their doors starved me. So, feeling famished, I moved forward, toward the promise of fulfillment. On my way, a moment like one of those Kimmy and I had discussed by the swimming pool struck me, a moment of unclear significance. I still remember what I wore that night, and I remember Christian's reddish sweater, his khaki pants. His Bass shoe tapping on the floor. Sometimes, I try to remember more but can't. Only that walk toward him—that ringing moment is clear. It was so clear, in fact, that it's become transparent and empty after all these years. But on that night, the clarity of the moment wrapped me up, making me strong and safe in my conviction that it was indeed critical. It was a drug moment—running loose, artificial yet real, majestic with promise, yet sure to wear off.

*   *   *

"Do you actually think I'd drive a vehicle like that?" Christian asked as he opened the car door for me. "I hope you have more confidence in me than that." He snickered, quite sure that he was far above even his dark gray Audi. The holes in his head flashed, and that's when I knew he lived in a perfect world, a world with no room for undesirable cars or clothes or even people. I was suddenly sure that even his around-the-house clothes displayed designer labels and his bathroom always smelled fresh.

He'd be driving a BMW in no time.

"I didn't know which car was yours," I said. It was our first date.

Unlike those perfect people like Carla whom I sometimes wished to disembowel, Christian had no bowels. While the others stored reality, proof of their imperfection, deep within carefully constructed façades, he sported an empty compartment, clean and hollowed out. At least that's what I thought I saw in his eyes. Each time they flashed, I saw a bright, blinding place just large enough to contain me.

I felt sorry for the owner of the old Monte Carlo parked next to Christian's Audi. *His* reality was a shell he rode around in all day. Its paint peeling, its tan exoskeleton rusted. It had numerous dents and a broken headlight, besides. But then Christian, walking around his car, caught my attention, and I had to admit that regardless of how sorry I felt for the driver, I wouldn't be crazy about riding in it, either. The back of Christian's shirt puffed out, hard with starch, between his leather suspenders—the kind of outfits I'd seen in men's magazines at the beauty shop. Watching him, I knew I didn't want a man forced to wear his reality, or one who felt compelled to hide it. I wanted a man who had no reality. For that man, it could be anything, really. *I could* be his reality. I could cower inside his shell, enjoying the beauty and emptiness of my haven. I could sleep.

I'd told my father I was strong like a turtle. I wished I hadn't said it.

"I didn't want to insult you if it was yours. Not that I really thought it was."

"I wouldn't even sit in it, much less own it." He laughed. "Give me a break," he said, but not in a mean way.

Christian wasn't handsome like Mac. He wasn't James Bond, but he had kooky good looks, the kind photographers recognize as star quality. He was as tall as Mac, but lankier, more agile, wiry, even. Mac was built like a football player, whereas Christian seemed more suited for baseball. Mac could play the warrior, Christian royalty. Mac's weight landed on his heels whereas Christian's stayed on his toes. I wondered why he couldn't seem to touch ground.

I was still a little tired. I'd taken a half-pill of Ecstasy thirty minutes earlier. I was waiting, but then—somewhere between my house and the restaurant—I felt that surge, waking me, allowing me to dismiss the Monte Carlo and its owner. Whatever I felt or thought became acceptable, an integral part of who I was, narcolepsy and all. I sat back, relaxed, and glowed from loving myself so completely that I didn't need anyone else. And once I was rid of the need, anyone would do. Christian was drawn to that pure love of myself, thinking it was for him. I could lie and not feel like a liar. The lies were justified simply because they came from me, proof of my humanity.

I could stay awake.

Many of my dates ended before they began, me asleep by the time we reached our destination. But this time was going to be different. Tim promised. I wanted to see how long I could date Christian without him knowing about my narcolepsy. It was immature, I knew, but my desire to be rid of my disorder surpassed maturity. Narcolepsy was my growing tumor, and I'd reached the point at which no risk was too great. I was determined to create a new perception of Angel Duet; I wanted to see what she would look like, just for a little while.

"Aren't you sweet," was all he finally said.

I didn't know what to say.

"So," he said, "Do you go to CPL a lot?"

"CPL?"

"Oh, I forgot, you're so young," he said, turning on the radio. He was twenty-eight. "It stands for Centenary Packaged Liquor. That's what they used to call the Centenary Oyster Bar before it was a bar." That was where we met, that normal place I hated. "They changed the name a couple years ago. New owners, I think." I couldn't hear him very well, but I didn't want him to turn down the radio. It was a love song. "Maybe we can swing by later," he said.

"I don't go there too often. I don't go out much, actually."

"Well, I guess I'm lucky you were out last night."

Again, I didn't know what to say.

He smiled and turned the radio up a little more. I was sure we made a perfect couple. I could tell that he didn't care if I said anything or not. At the time, I thought that was a good sign.

*   *   *

I moved through Christian at an incredible rate. Instead of resting inside him like I'd hoped, I slithered like licorice through his hollowed-out system.

☑ jar

Patty, the ER nurse, said, "Head injury comin'," the way you might expect her to announce an abrasion or a stuck fishhook early on Saturday morning. But it wasn't early. It was nearly six-thirty in the evening.

In the twelve years Patty had been an ER nurse at the hospital, she'd seen very few life-threatening head injuries, but we still trusted her tone as a gauge for the event's seriousness. "Girl got hit in the head with a bottle," she said, folding up the newspaper she'd been reading in her downtime. Her chunky Avon rings scraped the countertop, but she didn't seem too concerned. "And not a little girl, either. ETA—five minutes." Mac headed for the bathroom, probably in case he couldn't go once the ambulance showed up. I watched Patty watch his ass.

There were four of us: Patty, one LPN, Mac, and myself. I took out the necessary insurance forms and attached them to a clipboard in case I had to go into the treatment room to get information directly from the patient. The LPN continued to stock the supply carts. Other than that, we more or less just sat, waiting for the ambulance. I watched the clock, considering what I'd do when I got home . . . before falling beneath my canopy. I only had to survive twenty more minutes and the short walk home.

We heard the ambulance's wail, and within seconds the fall pine air burst through the wide ER doors. Mac and Patty rushed forward to meet the paramedics as they spouted out information I didn't understand. All I heard was "twenty-six-year-old female," and all I saw was Tim's white face as he came rushing in behind the gurney.

I looked for Kimmy but only found knotty gray blankets, medical equipment, and plastic tubes. Tim grabbed my shoulder, but I didn't turn away. I knew she was there somewhere, at the center of those trying to save her, her face hidden beneath the seeping blood.

Patty's tone sharpened. "You'll have to go sit yourself down over there," she said to Tim, pointing toward the small waiting area.

"But is she gonna be all right?" Tim asked, his voice screeching.

"You'll have to sit yourself down over there," Patty repeated, implementing her broken-record technique. Tim watched as they rolled the gurney into the trauma room and its doors shut us out. His pale face began to splotch. I took deep breaths and pinched my forearm three times.

Tim didn't try to stop me, even when I drew blood.

I wiped my arm with a tissue. I said, "What happened?"

"We went to happy hour at The Blue Flower, and we were leavin' and this car drove by. They just yelled. First they yelled."

"Did anybody call her parents?"

"They came back. They threw a goddamn bottle out the window and hit her. Shit, Angel, the bottle hit Kimmy right between the eyes." He turned a few tight circles as if chasing his tail, mad at his tail. Then he stared at me. He looked dizzy, and I watched the blotches on his face and neck turn dark red. His eyes pooled. "I hate you sometimes." He turned another circle. "How can you be so calm? She's your friend, for Christ's sake."

"It wouldn't matter if she was my mother."

"Bullshit!"

I threw the bloodstained tissue away. "I'll freak out later," I said, heading for my desk, "in my own time, okay?" I felt myself being sucked into one of my recurring dreams, the one where I'm driving down the interstate that passes through the middle of Shreveport like a zipper. Inevitably, the moment comes when I lose control. Either I forget how to drive or my foot presses the pedal involuntarily or the road suddenly dips or narrows or splits. The zipper begins to open. I pinched my arm hard again. "I have to fight gettin' upset so I can do my job, so I can live my life." I took a deep breath. "Is that so hard to comprehend?" I felt like a bitch.

He stared at me as if it were a stupid excuse.

"And I have ways . . . to try . . . to stay normal."

He continued to stare.

"I already explained all this to you."

Once, two years earlier, the paramedics had brought in a nine-month-old baby who had been pinned beneath a tumbling cord of wood. The baby died, and as the mother screamed, I collapsed at her feet. I looked up from the floor and saw tears dripping off her face. I tried to move, to get up, and when I felt a tear hit my face, I tried to grab her ankle but couldn't. Just as Patty led her away, the lady looked down at me as if I'd killed the baby myself. It's hard to believe, but they just left me lying on the floor. I figured they thought it was clean, and besides, they knew my problem wasn't something they could solve. I remained frozen there for ten or fifteen minutes, learning that, when you look close, clean-looking floors are still filthy. That upset me more than being ignored. It was depressing, staring at all the filth people can't see.

"She's not even queer," Tim said. "They called her a queer. They called us queers and threw the goddamn bottle."

"Angel, take him to waitin'," Patty hollered as she ran out of the trauma room. "You know the drill." Her scrubs were a mess, spotted with Kimmy's blood. She grabbed something from the backup cart and then disappeared again through the doors separating those who could save Kimmy from those who could not.

"Okay," I said, nudging Tim in the right direction. "We gotta try and fill out some of this paperwork."

"She was just tellin' me how she always wanted a horse, how her parents laughed about it, like she was crazy or somethin'. She was sayin' how they didn't have the land or near enough money."

"Somebody will bring her driver's license out in a minute, and I'm sure she'll be okay. That lady, the nurse," I said, referring to Patty, "she didn't seem too concerned and she always knows."

"Kimmy was sayin' how she's still gonna get a horse one day when the yellin' started. I just ignored it. I looked right at her and said she would. I said she'd get a frickin' horse." He sat on the blue plaid couch taking up most of the waiting area and picked up a magazine. "I was wrong to ignore the yellin'."

The hospital didn't have a separate waiting room, only a small, open area that forced family and friends to sit on the sidelines as if expected to cheer the ER staff on. I always thought it strange, but Mac liked being watched.

As I sat down next to Tim, I thought about his cousin Scarlett for some reason.

We sat staring into the ER as if waiting for a game to start, as if the hospital provided our seats not for waiting but for witnessing, for watching from behind the bright-taped line marking off the perimeter. I was often surprised how many people struggled to keep from stepping over that line, as if invisible walls shielded them from the players, and often, from the reality they faced. At times, the waiting area filled and the witnesses overflowed like people crashing through a barricade. They practically fell across the line, propelled in my direction. I was forced to overhear their conversations, their tearful concerns, and sometimes even their cruelty. My desk wasn't far.

I wondered what Scarlett was up to, up in Hope.

"Most people who come here walk out by the end of the night," I said. It was true. "Mac's a good doctor," I assured Tim as he flipped through *US News & World Report*.

"What's this crap got to do with us?" he said, tossing the magazine onto the floor. We watched as it slid across the line.

"I know the doctor," I said. "I *know* him." We exchanged a blotched look.

I pinched myself again as I watched a huge man and woman waddle through the double ER doors. Their rotund figures filled the emergency entrance, blocking what was left of the summer sunlight. Only a slit of it peeked in above their heads. They didn't hurry because they couldn't. I got the feeling they were moving as fast as they could.

Kimmy's parents, I thought as I grabbed the clipboard from the blue couch. They were larger than I'd imagined. As I walked toward them, Kimmy's life became clear. And it wasn't simply their size that clarified her. It was their four small eyes, the heavy lines framing their mouths, their tiny hands, and their feet squeezed into flip-flops. It was their unkempt hair. Her life stared at me, exposed, sad and noble. I couldn't help gawking back. I listened to my businesslike voice inquiring about insurance and tried to focus on getting the information. I was still awake and that was a triumph.

* * *

"Well, at least the scar's on her fore 'ed," Kimmy's father said. "She can just keep her bangs over it and nobody will be able to tell the difference, no-how." Mac said her parents were in denial, but I wondered if the unattractive faith filling them merely kept their lives simple and their eyes small. I pictured them shopping at Piggly Wiggly in flip-flops.

Even after two weeks, Kimmy's hospital room was bare. No flowers. No cards. When I mentioned that flowers would be nice, her mother said I shouldn't bother. She said she'd never had one speck of green on her thumbs and didn't want to be responsible for keeping anything alive. "Don't waste your money," she said. "Kimmy won't know about 'em, no-how."

I should have gotten the flowers anyway, but instead, I wrote a poem and tucked it beneath Kimmy's pillow. I figured it was for her alone. The fat, flip-flopped couple could go to hell. But, still, I found myself staring at Kimmy's head lying across the words I'd found for her, trying to imagine her mother as the owner of a good heart. After all, she did adopt Kimmy. I tried to believe that someone worse had abandoned her.

I tried to believe flip-flops were okay.

"There's nothin' really wrong with flip-flops," I told myself out loud. I imagined that, upon seeing Kimmy's big, sweet face, the woman had rescued her from a motherless life like mine. "There's nothin' wrong with flip-flops," I told Kimmy.

There was a solitary chair in the room, and I'd spent every afternoon sleeping in it. But Kimmy hadn't moved. I stared at her a lot, trying to imagine her straddling a horse, trying to see her mother's good heart. I wondered what it would be like for her when she woke up, when she saw her bald head and the stitches running down her forehead in a rough line.

I peered down the hall. The two nurses on duty were busy at their station. One was writing in a patient chart while the other read the newspaper. After closing the door, I stood next to Kimmy's bed, staring at the zipper sewn into her head.

I touched it, but only for a second.

I knew it was odd, but I lay down next to her. There wasn't much room. I knew not to move her, so I shifted onto my side, draping my leg over her. She was under the blanket, and I was on top, but I could still feel her warmth between my legs. My head fit into the space between her jaw and shoulder, connecting us like a socket. I fell asleep next to her mother-soft skin, rubbing against it, dreaming she was Betty Lou, wishing my name was Nicole.

Then, in a dream, Betty Lou and I were on the floor. She was dead. I groped her, hoping to pull her back into the world that made sense, the one I understood. I wiped at the blood smeared across her face, trying to find her mouth and nose and eyes, but they weren't there. My hands were too small and the blood too thick, too coagulated; like a web, it kept me from her. Then we were on opposite sides of a river. We bordered it like sister cities. It flowed between us, connecting us while keeping us distanced until a time when the earth moves. But the earth rarely moves. And when it does, it's slow, its changes undetectable to those waiting. It doesn't lurch.

Only my heart lurches.

When my eyes opened, Tim was sitting in the chair. He smiled that devious Dennis the Menace smile I didn't like. I started to move, but he said, "It's okay, I'm watchin' the door. I locked it." His understanding justified my need to feel someone soft in my arms. He knew Kimmy was my chance.

I closed my eyes again and drifted back to sleep. Just before I fell into that familiar place—my haven—my odd need to lie next to Kimmy moved over me like an unexpected growth spurt. Even if I hated it, even if it turned me ugly and awkward, I knew the desire wouldn't go away. I also knew that it might not ever be satisfied. No matter how many times I climbed into her bed, I would never really be there.

There was a knock. "What's goin' on in there?"

It was Mac.

When we didn't answer, he started banging.

I managed to move to the chair before Tim finally opened the door. I slumped into it, still half asleep. "You two cannot lock this door," Mac said as he marched into the room. "There is absolutely no reason to lock the door." He looked at Tim and then glared at me. "Do you realize that if your friend here needed immediate medical attention, several minutes would be knocked off the response time? Do you wanna be responsible for your friend not gettin' the attention she needs?" he asked Tim. "And what happened to your hair?" he said to me, sounding too familiar.

I smoothed down my rumpled hair with my hands. "Tim, this is Dr. Boyd, the ER doctor who worked on Kimmy," I said, ignoring Mac's outburst.

Mac lowered his head to acknowledge Tim. "Angel, you should know better," he said.

I could feel Tim's perceptive eyes staring at me, staring at us. "You're the one, aren't you?" he asked Mac. "You're the married guy she's been screwin' around with."

"What the hell are you talkin' about?" Mac said to Tim while staring at me. He wasn't convincing.

"I told him about it," I said as my energy reserve swirled toward the drains I seemed to have on the soles of my feet. "I didn't mean to. It just . . . came out."

Tim smiled for the first time in two weeks.

"He doesn't really care," I said. "He just likes to get people worked up." I didn't know what else to say. I didn't know how to fix it. "He doesn't judge, I swear. He's gay."

"Oh, well, I guess that makes it okay then. Is that what you're tellin' me?" He reached back and pulled the door closed without looking.

Tim said, "Do you wanna lock it now?"

Disgusted, Mac turned to open the door again, to leave, but then Tim said, "What's wrong with Kimmy? Her parents said there's nothin' really wrong with her brain, so why doesn't she wake up?"

Mac stopped and turned around. "Her brain reacted to the bottle's impact by swellin', just like any other part of your body would, but it's trapped in her skull," he said, shifting into doctor mode.

"And her head bounced off the brick wall when the bottle hit her."

"Right, and her brain's cuttin' off its own blood supply, which is coma inducin'. I advised her parents to move her to a hospital that's better equipped for this sorta thing, or at the very least, to get a neuro consult. Her intracranial pressure needs to be measured." He shook his head. "Their first mistake is stickin' with that family doctor of theirs." I watched him watch Kimmy and saw for the first time that his reasons for becoming a doctor surpassed his need to be watched. People would always watch him. It didn't matter if he saved lives or dug ditches. They'd stare just the same.

"He's an internist, I think," Tim said.

"Pretty much functionin' as a family doc. The guy's ancient, for Christ's sake. That's one of the shitty thangs about bein' an ER doctor. Once they're outta the ER, you've got no control. She's not my patient anymore."

Tim said, "Her parents are just selfish, that's the problem. There's nothin' I hate more than people who can't break outta their frickin' mold when necessary."

"You don't know that. Maybe they can't afford to do anythang else," I said, struggling to stay awake.

"Well, they have insurance, don't they?" Tim said.

"Yeah, but . . ."

"Well then, don't waste your bad breath tryin' to make up for those people . . . like they're Kimmy or somethin'. They're nothin' like her. I bet they drained the life outta her before she hit kinder-garbage." He paced back and forth across the room. Each time he approached Kimmy, he hesitated, searching her face for clues. "It doesn't surprise me at all that she's sufferin' from *unexplained unconsciousness*."

Mac's eyes fixed on Tim, causing him to stop as if trapped. "Everythang can be explained," Mac said. "It just may be above your level of understandin'."

"Are you callin' me stupid?"

"Well, it's just the swellin'," I said. "Right, Mac?"

"You are—you're callin' me stupid, aren't you?"

Mac rolled his eyes in my direction, and I laughed inside, the way he always managed to get me laughing. "I think you're overreactin'," he said. "You just need to relax."

"Okay, how about you *explain* to us why you've only been married a couple of months and you're already screwin' around? Can you explain that?"

"Who *is* this guy?" Mac looked more irritated than angry . . . as if dealing with a kid.

"I, for one, would be very interested in hearin' your explanation," Tim said, not backing down as usual. "How about you, Angel?"

"Tim's my friend, you know, from my cotton field job."

"Yeah, I remember. I also remember tellin' you not to take that job."

Tim sank down the wall, landing cross-legged on the floor next to Kimmy's bed. "I'm the one who probably got her wonderin' what the hell she's doin' hangin' out with you." He whispered just loud enough for us to hear.

I wanted to remind him how he'd cheered me on at the Pizza Hut. How he'd held my arm up until it hurt.

He wasn't always honest either.

Mac stared at me with wide eyes, and I focused hard, hoping this time I might see the real him and not the distortion to which I'd grown accustomed. The room holding his lying windows was dim. But in the shadows, I saw a good heart that made mistakes, a heart like mine. "What the hell is wrong with you people?" he asked.

"Nothin's wrong with *me*," I said. "Why do you think somethin's wrong with me all the sudden? I finally made some friends, that's all."

"And I'm just speakin' the truth . . . at least as far as I'm able to understand it," Tim added.

"You're the one who told me I should go out more," I said to Mac. "You just didn't think I'd get out with a couple of queers, did you?"

"Hey, I'm the only queer here . . . as far as I know."

"For Christ's sake, the truth is a delicate subject," Mac said. "You cain't just dish it out indiscriminately."

"Bullshit. People either don't really wanna hear the truth or don't wanna speak it," Tim said.

"The truth didn't get you too far the other night, did it?"

We all looked at Kimmy.

Tim shut his mouth.

"What were you doin' lockin' the door, Angel?"

"I was lyin' on the bed with her." My knees were jelly. "She's my friend, and I don't know what's wrong with her, and I don't know what's wrong with me. Everythang's changin' . . . and I didn't wanna get in trouble with the nurses. They already think I'm weird."

Mac looked sad. "You shouldn't compare yourself to her. You should be thankful for what you have instead of focusin' on what you're missin' all the time." His face changed. "Jesus Christ, Angel."

I slid back into the chair, mentally fighting to stay alert. When I didn't respond, Mac came and knelt between my knees. He looked at me with those eyes I thought I loved sometimes. He kissed my jelly knee. "Kimmy's a good friend for you. It's okay to have friends, and to be a good friend. But she's not your mother."

I couldn't speak. A sound like whistling rushed through my head as if it was empty. As if no one had bothered to fill it, to clog it tight with hugs and kisses, with good and bad advice, with soft skin that glues on with its crazy love—the kind that can't be washed away.

"Just leave her alone," Tim said. "She's gonna have an attack. You're doin' it to her." He seemed to have forgotten how many times he'd done it to me.

"Angel, I'm your friend, too," Mac said.

"No," I said. "You don't understand. You never did."

"Of course I did. I do."

"No," I shook my heavy head. "If you really understood, you wouldn't care if I wanted to pretend she was my mother, just for a minute." Mac's head shook as if he was my father, telling me I was wrong. His face swung back and forth, swinging all doors shut. I was shut out. "You don't understand. And you know what? I don't even wanna see you anymore. I met somebody else, anyway. Just like you told me I should."

His large hands dropped from my knees. "Does he know about your narcolepsy?"

I looked at Tim. "I'm takin' care of that for her," he said, smiling. He'd been feeding me small doses of Ecstasy for weeks, giving me just enough to keep me normal for Christian. For the first time in my life, I had a relationship without sleeping through it.

Mac sat silently, looking dumped. But when he realized what Tim meant, his face caught fire. His head swung to look at Tim and then back at me. "Shit, Angel. Shit!"

Mac was smart.

"There she goes," I heard Tim say. Mac held me for a moment and then leaned me back against the chair. "Kimmy's her friend, not her goddamn mother. She's not your mother, Angel. Shit."

"She cain't hear you."

"Yes, she can."

I could see Mac's boots. I stared at his boots.

"She's lucky she can just fall outta conflicts like that," Tim said, as if nothing much had happened. "I wish I could do that."

"No, you don't," Mac said. His tone was somehow different, the words filled with compassion, and I realized he did understand. Then he asked Tim, "Are you gonna be here awhile?"

"Yeah, I'll hang around." As Mac left the room, Tim added, "Hey, maybe sometime we can pick up our conversation."

"Yeah, sure. Look, just stay here. And don't give her anythang. Don't give her so much as a goddamn piece of candy, and don't lock the door again unless you feel like gettin' thrown through it."

Then Tim said, "He's gone, Angel. If you can hear me, he's gone now."

All I could think of was the pressure in Kimmy's zippered head. I knew Mac was right, but no one was listening, no one was measuring.

☑ kettle

"Why do you think this one's so special?" Carla asked as she handed her VISA card to Nina, the gallery owner's daughter. "It looks odd—compared to the others."

Nina threw me a jolting glance, and I decided I was getting paranoid. It was Tim's fault. Tim and Scarlett's.

Carla said, "I mean, am I missin' somethin' here?"

I gazed at the photograph, trying to remember if my father had specifically mentioned it. It was the largest, and the only one without a recognizable shape. Betty Lou had positioned it at the bottom left corner of her arrangement, placing it out of the way, I thought.

"Maybe it's an aberration," said Nina.

"What's that?" I asked.

"In layman's terms, somethin' wrong in the picture caused by a defect in the camera. A distortion."

I looked at Carla and shook my head. "No, I cain't figure it out, but it's somethin'. It's gotta be somethin'." I turned to Carla. "Didn't you look at the back when you brought it in?"

"I forgot," she said as if she couldn't care less.

"You know that's important to me. I wanna know what it says. I wanna know what all of 'em say. I'm sure it would explain, because this has gotta be somethin' we just cain't see."

Nina said, "Probably an aberration."

Carla rolled her eyes, irritated. "Well, it's too late now. And that frame cost more than all the others put together, so you can forget about takin' it apart."

"How could you just forget?"

She waved her hand through the air. "It probably just says *cloud*."

"Still," I said. "Now I'm gonna have to look at it every day wonderin' what it says . . . wonderin' what she was thinkin'."

"These were probably pretty expensive to develop at the time they were taken," Nina said. "Back then, most people around here were still usin' black-and-white film for these types of photos."

"Did you happen to see the year written on the back?" I asked.

"It was nineteen sixty-somethin'. I'm not sure—maybe '65 or '67. I cain't remember."

"Musta been '65," Carla said.

"Well," said Nina, "I'm really not sure. It *might* have been '67."

"No, the woman who took these died in 1966."

"Oh . . . well, I guess it was '65 then." She smiled and swiped Carla's credit card, making a loud noise that echoed through the gallery.

* * *

During the ride home, Carla asked, "How's Kimmy doin'?"

"She's still in a coma, but they're sayin' she'll come out of it." My eyelids were closing. Every man in every car on every street looked like Darwin. "I don't know how they can tell." I knew he wasn't real, but I watched him each time I caught a glimpse, each time I imagined him there. Then I decided it was Mac. Mac was everywhere. "They finally moved her to a better hospital," I managed to garble out.

"What was wrong with the first one?"

"She needed a special neurology unit for her brain."

"Have they made any arrests?"

"Tim was the only witness. Carla, I have to sleep now."

"You don't *have* to do anythang," I heard her say above the rush of the car and the river now surrounding it, the red river that seemed to be in all my dreams and visions. "You wanna sleep, but you don't *have* to. When are you gonna realize that? You don't give yourself enough credit."

"Tim couldn't even remember what kinda car it was. And you're wrong. I do wanna stay awake. It's my eyes. They won't stay open. It's like sinkin'."

"You want to sleep, don't you?"

"He cain't remember," I said, trying to decide how I could get away from her, how I could swim through a river that wasn't really there.

"That happens."

"I wish he could remember," I said. Then I wished I could remember. I wanted to remember every detail of my life before narcolepsy, but the memories only surfaced in short, unconnected shocks. Vivid dreams had filled in the blanks until I wasn't sure which moments were real, which were lies, and which were mere fantasies. Betty Lou's presence permeated my dreams of childhood. That's why I missed her. I knew her in those dreams as sure as if she were Kimmy or Carla. She handed me things, and I felt her touch. She spoke to me. She fed me. I smelled her. If soft could smell, it would be Betty Lou Duet. It would be the smell of mother.

"He's probably scared," Carla said, determined to torture me.

"He's not like that. If he could remember, he'd speak up."

"People will surprise you. Trust me. Remember that I've had a lotta experience with this sort of thang. Most people remember what they wanna remember." She paused long enough for me to thank God, but then she spoke again. "Go ahead, sleep your life away. It's no reflection on me."

* * *

Carla left me sleeping in the car. When I finally woke and stumbled into the house, she was hanging the large frame in the exact place it had hung for over twenty years. She knew the spot without measuring

because she had already nailed the wall. In fact, she had already nailed
the entire wall.

She ignored me at first, but then said, "Well, you've been sleepin'
an awful lot, but when you're awake, at least you seem a little more
'with it.' I can say that for you."

"Carla, why don't you just tell me where all the photographs are?"

"Because I like the element of surprise."

What a jerk, I thought. "They're just photographs."

She picked up Bippy and stroked him from head to tail, slow and
steady. "So when do I get to meet Christian?"

"You don't." I went to the kitchen to get a drink and she followed.
Bippy, having had his fill of petting, followed Carla but kept against
the wall.

"Well, why not?"

"Why do you need to meet him?"

"Because I'm interested in your life."

"Sounds like you're nosy," I said, between gulps of Mountain Dew.
I had to wake up. I had plans.

"I'm tryin' to have a relationship with you, Angel. Why are you so
nasty all the time? Cain't you be a little more mature than that?"

"No."

"Just tell me what you like about him."

"Why do I feel like I'm on the witness stand?"

"Look, I know for a fact that you're not used to havin'
someone around to talk to, except your dad, of course. Just play
along, okay?"

"Well," I said as I sat down at the kitchen table. Bippy peeled
himself away from the wall and jumped onto my lap, a first. "He's
the best-lookin' guy I've ever met." She smiled, and I didn't like it.
"You know, not necessarily good-lookin' to everybody else, but he's
my type. I literally picked him out of a crowd. He drives an Audi.
He has very good taste in clothes. He won a marathon last year.
Did I tell you that?"

"No, you didn't," she said, staring at Bippy in my lap.

I wondered if watching the cat sleep made her sleepy. If it made her want to curl up tighter and tighter until she was a ball on a bed, covered up, dead to the world.

"Well, he did," I said. "And he's very polite and funny and interestin'. I don't know, all that regular stuff." I swung my head, catching my ponytail in my hand. I started braiding.

"Sounds like you're pretty crazy about him." She stared as if expecting me to tell her something else, as if she wasn't convinced. It was her courtroom face, carefully practiced to cause uncomfortable feelings, to make people feel like they were lying even when they weren't.

She made me doubt myself.

I didn't tell her, but I'd never met anyone who seemed so perfect for me. He laughed at my nervous jokes and didn't care when I didn't say anything. He made me feel good. He didn't care about my freckled chest because he was freckled, too. Tim thought I only loved the Ecstasy; he thought Christian sounded boring. But I reminded him that Ecstasy doesn't have freckles. It was Christian's freckles I loved.

Mac was married and Christian wasn't.

I rinsed my glass and turned to leave, but then she asked, "Have you gone to visit Kimmy lately?" I was trapped.

"I was there the other day. She has somethin' stickin' in her head now. It's kinda gross, but it's what she needed. Like I said, they're still sayin' she's gonna wake up soon."

"I'm takin' the horse photograph in next," she suddenly said, and I wondered if it was to keep me trapped, to keep me talking. I couldn't imagine her feeling lonely. Not because she had so many friends, but because she didn't seem to need them. She began to load the dishwater, and I realized she looked matronly standing there with a spatula in one hand and a pot in the other. "Why don't you just take all the pictures at the same time?" I asked.

"I told you, that's not my style."

"That's weird."

"Oh, well. I guess you'll just have to deal with it."

"Can I see it? Do you have it here?"

"It's in my car. Go get it if you want, I don't care."

When I brought the horse photograph into the house, my father and Carla were standing at the center of Betty Lou's wall like a wedding cake couple. He kissed her forehead, and I looked away. She had already taken the photograph out of its old frame. I pulled it out from between two pieces of cardboard. Then I turned it over, searching for Betty Lou's scrawl.

"Oh my God, it's 1966," I said. "She took this photograph the year I was born." It seemed as if I was getting closer to her. Holding her photographs and touching her writing were involving me in her life, albeit after her disappearance from mine. Touching what she touched made her death less severe, her life less erased. I stared at the numbers, thinking how I was inside her when she wrote them; thinking I could have heard her muffled voice and somehow looked through her eyes as she'd captured the horse forever. She'd found something fleeting, mathematically temporary, and impossible. "These photographs should be published in a book, a coffee-table book," I said, turning to Carla. The crow's feet around her eyes deepened. She liked my idea.

But my father yanked the horse away. "Let me see that," he said, nearly ripping the photograph.

"Dad, what are you doin'? You're gonna ruin it." I stayed calm, checks in balance, knowing that something new was happening. I didn't want to miss it.

"Carla, just get the pictures framed." His face was angry but his voice was soft like the cat lying in a ball. "I don't want you two handlin' 'em."

"Frank, what's the big deal? Angel likes to see Betty Lou's handwritin', that's all."

"Look," he said, nearly yelling now. "I don't want these handled! If you wanna get 'em framed, you frame 'em." He shoved the photograph into Carla's chest. "And you just let her do it," he said to me while Carla quickly tried to smooth out the bent photograph.

Carla and I stared at each other.

"I want 'em back on that wall. Period." He marched out, leaving us staring. We looked at each other longer and harder than we ever had.

"You're makin' me crazy," Carla hollered. "You are, Frank."

Within moments he was back, holding Carla's face in his hands, bending over her and saying, "If you wanna stay here, in this house with me, don't ever say that to me again." His hands shook, making Carla's face shake. "Don't ever say that again," he repeated. Then his hands dropped to his sides, heavy like balls attached to chains, and he walked out.

Carla was speechless.

Finally, to break the tension, I said, "Why did you put all the nails in ahead of time like that? If you're not gettin' the photographs framed all at once, don't you think it would look better, and make more sense, if you left the nails out until you're ready to hang each photograph?"

I didn't want to talk about my father.

"But then I wouldn't have as much incentive to get it done, now would I? This is the way I do thangs, Angel." She stared at the wall, and I stared at her narrow back and wide hips. "Throughout my life," she said, spreading her arms out as if to say that the wall was her life, "I've set goals, mapped out a course of action, a measurable plan, and then step-by-step, I've accomplished those goals. I accomplish the goal in question and don't concern myself with what thangs *look like* or how my plan is perceived along the way. Only the end result matters, the culmination of multiple parts, tiny steps I recognized early on as critical."

"Carla, we're talkin' about hangin' photographs here, not changin' the world." I didn't know why I was still there, talking to her.

"Well, you don't know that. The smallest little thang can change the world, don't you think? It could change *somebody's* world. We all live in different worlds. You didn't think we all lived in the same one, did you?"

"Oh, please . . . I don't think these clouds are gonna change anythang."

"You know, you really are extremely negative," she said.

"I just think you're makin' a big deal outta nothin' . . . hangin' photographs . . . my photographs, I might add. Photographs nobody gave you permission to take down in the first place."

"Well, my methods have always led to success, so I'll just continue on if you don't mind."

"I really don't care what you do."

"There you go again, thinkin' you don't care when you do. If you're so uninvolved, why did you even bring it up?"

"I was just wonderin'."

"Maybe you should consider developin' a few more methods yourself."

"Are you sayin' I'm not successful?" I sat at the foot of the stairs. Rather than jumping up in arms like most folks would, I shrank down, down into my own arms; they wound all around me, thin and weak, until I grabbed my braid. Pulling it was another strategy I'd developed to keep alert. Pulling my hair as hard as I could without being noticed usually did the trick when I didn't feel comfortable pinchin' myself. "With what I've had to deal with, I think I've been pretty successful." I pulled my braid hard again in my sneaky way so that she couldn't see. I didn't want her to know she was puttin' me back to sleep instead of waking me up.

"I'm simply sayin' that, from what I see, your methods are conceptual rather than methodical. While they're based on spiritual or intellectual awareness, they revolve around your *perceived* physical limitations."

"You're wrong," I said, yanking my hair even harder.

"See, I charted a course with these nails, a course I now have no choice but to follow. If I pull out the nails without filling the holes, I'll just have a bunch of holes, and that would look horrible. It would look even worse. At least now, my plan is apparent to anyone who comes in here."

"You still have a choice, Carla. You can change your plan."

"No, you have to decide what you want and chart a course. If you keep yankin' nails you're just gonna end up starin' at a bunch of holes on down the line. You're not gonna get anywhere, Angel."

I shook my head. "Carla, I have the same plan I've had since I started college. I'm goin' to grad school."

"Are you? I haven't seen a whole heck of a lotta studyin' goin' on lately, and every time you skip class, you're addin' to your collection of holes. Do you realize what happens when you get too many holes?"

I didn't answer.

"Eventually they merge and your wall crumbles." She spread her arms out again as if to embrace the blue square she'd painted.

"I should have known what this was about," I said. "Why don't you just quit worryin' about what I do and what classes I skip? This is my last year of college, and I've just skipped a few classes lately . . . more than I usually do. But I have it under control."

She finally turned to look at me. "If your wall falls, Angel, you've got nothin'—no place to hang your creation." Her eyes were wet. I'd never seen her cry, and it made me nervous.

I tried to resist the urge to pinch myself, to bleed. I dared not stand up, so I focused on one nail near the edge of the blue square.

"You've got nowhere left to even chart your course, and then your whole house can fall. You've lost support. Your security is gone."

She seemed so sad, and I didn't know why. "I have to get ready," I said, standing up because that falling feeling had passed. I reminded myself that I couldn't stand her.

"Are you goin' out with Christian again tonight?" She called after me as I headed upstairs.

I didn't answer and didn't look back. It was none of her business. As I reached the top of the stairs, I envisioned my home crumbling behind me, but then remembered Carla's nails. She'd generously refilled the holes Betty Lou created. My father was right. She was a brilliant woman. She'd known not to leave a single void unfilled.

☑ ladder

Christian took me to the Lobster Fest at the Kon Tiki that night. I lied when he asked if I liked lobster. I told him I did although I'd never tasted it. We'd been dating for nearly a month. I hadn't told him about Kimmy or Betty Lou. I wasn't sure why.

He hadn't asked.

When the waiter handed me a lobster bib, I almost laughed. Everything was fine, even comical. It didn't matter if I'd lied about the lobster; I knew I could pull it off. I ate slow and steady, watching Christian's every move, but it was messy. We sat, a perfect couple, eating a perfect meal in a perfect place, not really saying a lot. We were too busy cracking our tails. But I was happy. I knew I would make love to him later, and I would remain awake for the entire experience, alert and attentive.

Tim told me sex was great on Ecstasy.

I couldn't wait.

My tail cracked, and I smiled the smile.

Then I laughed.

Tim was right about the sex. Christian soon insisted that I get on the pill. He said it was crazy that I wasn't.

As the weeks went by, I slept, woke, went to class, worked at the hospital, and saw Christian two nights a week. He wanted to see me more often, but I didn't have the waking hours to spare. My grades slipped. I was a little sick of school—my father called it senioritis. Tim began charging me for the Ecstasy, and I canceled my sleep clinic appointment three times in a row. Mac hadn't called. Kimmy hadn't woken up. Scarlett called twice. My Darwin paper was nearly due.

Things were rolling out of control, like a turtle careening down the mountainside unable to get its arms and legs out long enough to grip the ground, to stop. I knew because I heard Carla say to my father several times, "Something's wrong with Angel, Frank." Each time, I waited to hear my father's response, but all I heard was that loud, lonely silence—the one he'd mastered long before Carla considered us part of her plan. Then she would say his name like a hammer falling on my head. "Frank?" she asked. "Frank? Frank?"

In those moments, I realized she was nailing me to the wall, and that my father was relearning the alphabet faster than I could read it.

"Dad, what's wrong with you?" I asked one night when Carla wasn't home. "Why'd you get so upset about the photographs? I think they look better now, don't you?"

He stared at the fireplace.

"What's wrong?" I asked again, wondering how many holes he'd filled in his life, if he'd charted his course like Carla, or if he'd just been lucky. I put my hand on his shoulder.

*   *   *

"What's that noise?" Christian asked as we approached the down-town building that housed my father's law firm.

"It's just the mailboxes." Thirty or so little metal mailbox doors clattered in the wind; the building had apartments on the top floors. Although I had the key, Christian seemed nervous about going in after business hours. We'd gone to the Kon Tiki Lobster Fest again. We'd become regulars. When my father heard I'd be home early to work on my Darwin paper, he asked if Christian would stop by his office so I could get some files for him.

"My father always talks about those mailboxes. He likes that noise."

"It sounds like machine-gun fire."

"Have you ever heard machine-gun fire?" I asked as we walked in. I was sure that I'd find Betty Lou's photographs in Carla's office.

"No, but I bet that's what it sounds like."

I rolled my eyes.

We made our way to the twenty-sixth floor. Christian kissed me on the elevator. Franklin, Duet & Mercer took up half the floor. I hadn't been to my father's firm in a while. It was the first time he'd given me the key. I was to go straight to his office, pick up the stack of legal-sized manila folders marked with the name Porter, and bring them home. It was an easy enough assignment, but I had my own agenda.

"Where are you goin'? Your dad said office fifteen. I think it's this way," Christian said, pointing to the right. "This place is really classy. They probably have surveillance. I don't think you should poke around."

"Just relax. My father works here, remember? His name's part of the company name, you know. I just need to look for somethin'. You can just wait here if you want," I said, patting the big leather chair in front of the reception desk. "We have *clearance*."

"All right, but you're makin' me nervous."

As much as I was crazy about Christian, I thought Tim wasn't too far out of line in calling him Mr. Boring. As I headed down the left hallway, I glanced back at him. His face looked boring, as if there was no beat to his heart or race to his blood. For me, being in a place I wouldn't normally go, alone at night, woke me like nothing else could. I couldn't believe my luck. I'd been trying to figure out how to get into the building after-hours for weeks. I wasn't about to waste the opportunity to look in Carla's office and see if that's where she'd put the photographs. I knew that finding them wouldn't change anything, but I needed that connection, the link they provided.

Her office wasn't hard to find. Photographs of Bippy were everywhere. She had a cat calendar. It was immaculate. Unfortunately, there were no piles of cloud photographs leaning against the wall. Nor were they stashed in the one small closet.

"Angel, are you comin'?" Christian called. "Let's get outta here."

"Just give me a minute," I yelled back. I sat in Carla's desk chair looking around the room, disappointed that I couldn't find anything. Finally, I decided I should just get the stupid folders.

I began falling the moment I opened my father's office door. Despite the half-pill of Ecstasy I'd taken, despite the thrill of finally getting in there at night, I couldn't hold up. I crumpled. It was an old story that played out over and over again. I was the star, but to me, it was boring; there'd been too many takes. To those who'd never experienced it, however, it was a major motion picture come to town.

Christian must have heard the thump of my fall because he came down the hall looking for me. He didn't run to rescue me, instead walking hesitantly down the long, door-lined hallway, even after he spotted me lying half-in, half-out of my father's office door. His footsteps were quiet because he stayed on his toes—his heels just wouldn't go down.

From where I'd landed on the floor, I could see the clouds.

The liar had allowed Carla to hang the photographs we both loved on his wall. He knew exactly where they were. He looked at them every day—that was the deal he'd made. He'd let her take Betty Lou from me. He had allowed her to feed my mother back to me in slow spoonfuls, while he gulped her down as always.

I felt that sort of backwards crying that happens to those who know the regular kind isn't always enough, shallow by comparison, washable. Those backwards tears filled me, making my body more rigid. I couldn't look away even if I had wanted to. Ironically, I was forced to stare at Betty Lou's photographs hanging on my father's wall for twenty minutes. It was, quite possibly, one of the longest cataplectic attacks I'd ever had. I stared at the wall, at my father's lie, while Christian became more and more agitated.

"Holy shit," he said, nearly whispering. "Holy shit." He leaned down to look at my face, but didn't touch me. He blew on my eyes. He walked back down the hall, his footsteps a little faster now. I heard him make the emergency call. There was no way I could stop him.

While he waited for the paramedics, he walked down the hall toward me, stopped for maybe ten to fifteen seconds to look at me, and then walked away. He repeated this procession until they came, but each time he walked away he stayed in the reception area a little longer. He never touched me. Too afraid, I guessed. He didn't say anything, but I did hear him pass gas. He didn't know I could hear. It baffled me how people could clearly see my open eyes and still assume I couldn't hear. As soon as I heard the gas, I knew he'd hate me when he found out.

Lying there on the floor, listening to his heel-avoiding steps, I realized that Christian wanted me to believe he was perfect more than he wanted to be perfect. He wasn't even close to being perfect. I stared at Betty Lou's photographs, wondering how to love a man after seeing his guts. Whether cleaned out or filled with shit, it was not a pretty sight. How could I believe in love when that light shines suddenly in, illuminating what I thought was beautiful, turning it grotesque? I couldn't love the ugly. After all, no one seemed to love me when the room lit up. Very few people are gorgeous from all angles, and I doubted I could ever catch sight of the ugly and still love the lovely. It made me sad to know I was guilty of the same selfish thing I saw in Christian—the need for someone else to make me perfect simply by thinking it was true.

I didn't like him so much anymore, and I could feel him not liking me. I could feel him looking down at me as if he hated me, as if he hated to admit I was only human, that I had saliva. Screw him, I thought.

By the time the paramedics arrived, I was loosening up. The larger of the two men was there in time to help me up from the floor. His partner pulled my father's chair into the middle of the office, and I eased into it, feeling exhausted. My muscles ached. I didn't tell them about the photographs. I wiped my mouth and asked for a glass of water.

"I have narcolepsy," I explained after drinking two glasses. "It's a sleepin' disorder." Both paramedics shook their heads as if trying to tell me I was right. "I take medication that keeps me under control." I didn't mention my new illegal dosing regimen. "And I also have cataplexy, a condition that pushes a person into REM sleep within seconds, causing a type of paralysis. My medication is just runnin' out, that's all. I'll be fine."

"I'm a little familiar with that," the larger paramedic said. "You're sort of catatonic but you can still see and hear. Cain't communicate, though, right?"

His partner's head continued to shake. He said, "Never got called for this one." Both of their bellies were big. They reminded me of good ole Southern boys, the ones who thought their soft hearts made them strong. I knew I wasn't looking at the real story, though. Their bellies were probably rock-hard.

It was a southern thing, to *seem* soft, so destroyed into being tender-hearted and kind to the point of stupid. Most people, who aren't southern, don't understand that the softness isn't real. They don't realize that destruction carries us forward, that we can rebuild and relearn a million times over. We don't make the same mistakes twice. Each time we make them, they're different. We're different. Many of us, people like me, can't be jarred up, stereotyped, forever. The jar we grew up in was so hot and stifled we eventually had to bust out the only way we knew how. Those who get out, seep out by way of their melted hearts. The paramedics' soft-looking bellies didn't fool me.

"I'm sorry you had to come. He didn't know about my problem," I said, finally looking at Christian. He sat in one of the chairs my father sat his clients in—one of the chairs for people needing help. His head was in his hands.

"I cain't *believe* you wouldn't tell me somethin' like that." His voice was ugly. "What kinda person are you?" He looked up at me. "Your whole life's a buncha bullshit."

"That's not true. You know me, Christian. You just didn't know about this one small thang. It doesn't change who I am."

"You know how much I really know you?" He looked at me as if I was a stranger he'd passed on the street.

I didn't answer.

He held up his hand in the shape of a zero. Apparently, I hadn't known him either.

The paramedic took my pulse and blood pressure. He turned to Christian. "Maybe you better take her on home, okay? I think y'all are gonna be able to work this out."

"I don't really wanna take her anywhere," he said to the guy, but looked at me. "How long were you plannin' on keepin' this from me, anyway?"

"Look, there's no need to be gettin' so upset. She's got a legitimate medical problem. Maybe she just didn't wanna share it with you just yet," one paramedic said. "I think you need to try and be a little more understandin'. Just take a deep breath and count to ten." He chuckled a little. "Look, my brother was married to his wife ten years before he realized she had epilepsy, and they're *still* married. I think you're overreactin'."

Christian didn't feel like counting. "It's just too weird. If I'm supposed to be lookin' after an invalid, don't you think I should be informed? What if that had happened to her in public?"

"Well, heaven forbid!" hollered the paramedic. "You would've had to do exactly what you did here." He was ready to leave.

"Well, I wouldn't want the whole world watchin' her drool all over herself, and I don't think she would either."

I felt nauseated.

"Gee, wouldn't that be embarrassin' for you?" the partner said.

Son-of-a-bitch, I thought. I looked at the big-bellied paramedics and was sure we were all thinking the same thing. Except for Christian, who was too busy thinking of himself.

After the paramedics left, Christian and I went outside to his car. He didn't hold the door open for me like he usually did. That's when I set the folders on the ground next to his Audi and ran. I ran even as he yelled, "What about the folders?" I looked back only once. I kept running until I couldn't. Then I walked until I fell.

☑ mother

The sidewalk in front of The Blue Flower was so hard that when my head hit it, I was sure it was my last fall. I lay rigid, eyes fixed on the tire of the car parked at the curb. It was tan, and I wondered if it was a Monte Carlo. I thought I was bleeding. My head felt heavy, as if my brain was swelling like Kimmy's. I thought I was dead until I heard the voice of the stranger who'd been touching me ever so slightly, lifting my arms, my head, and my legs. The voice said, "She's not bleedin' anywhere. She's just sorta passed out or somethin'." Another voice said, "Is she drunk?" but I didn't quite catch the answer because more voices interrupted. A crowd gathered quickly, increasing with each blast of music that came through the opening door of The Blue Flower. Then I heard the word *ambulance*.

"What's the problem here?" It was the same paramedic. "What the hell? Not you again," he said. "Okay, everybody, break it up!" he shouted and the crowd began to disperse. Music blasted nonstop as the gawkers went back in. The paramedic leaned down. "Look," he said. "You're not makin' my night any easier here. Believe me, I understand your problem. And I honestly feel for yah, but if you're in this bad of shape, you need to be at home, not out walkin' the street. At least until you can get a handle on this."

I suddenly hated his long face staring down at me as if I needed pity. "Don't be alarmed, but I'm just gonna look in your purse here and get some identification. We'll call home for you." He patted my leg. "You're gonna be just fine."

I wanted to scream at him to stop, to get away from me, but all I could manage to do was part my lips wide enough for an embarrassing groan.

His partner stood near the car tire, keeping the new gawkers away. Just as the paramedic said, "I got a number," I felt soft, familiar hands lifting my head. Then my head was in her lap again, and I heard the voice that sang when it spoke. It sang a song I didn't want to hear, a song so sweet it made me sad. It practically sang, "Oh, hey y'all, it's just not necessary to call anybody. This is Angel Duet, my best girl-friend. I know her."

"Is that so?" the paramedic said. "Well, ain't I lucky. I just had the pleasure of meetin' her best boyfriend, too. He didn't know crap about her."

"Well, I know all about her. I'm her best friend. I've been waitin' here all night for this girl to show up."

"Oh yeah?" the paramedic asked, "Twenty minutes ago I didn't get the feelin' she was plannin' on meetin' up with you." He turned to glare at the door of The Blue Flower. He knew what kind of place it was.

"Well, I'm sorry if you don't believe me, but she most certainly was. She was supposed to meet me at," Scarlett looked at her watch, "ten-thirty. She's late. That's why I had to come on out here lookin' for her," she lied, the tension in her voice mounting. "Look, I know how to handle her, so if you don't mind, I'll just stay right here until she recovers. See, she's limberin' up already, probably 'cause she knows I finally came on out to get her." Her voice crossed slow and steady from the realm of song into a dark, angry place. For the first time, she sounded tough, the way I thought a lesbian should sound.

"And whatdayaknow, here I fuckin' am, so I'll take her home if you don't mind!"

I was just loose enough to look up and see the paramedic's face. He recognized Scarlett's beauty but stared down at her as if trying to figure out what language she was speaking, and exactly *what* she was. He was a gawker, too. A voice crackled over the ambulance radio. The paramedic was forming a conclusion about us when his partner called, "Hey, sounds like a real one," and leaned into the front seat, saying they were on it. They left to attend to their next emergency, but the paramedic griped all the way to the ambulance, saying that he hadn't even had time to eat tonight. He hated nights like these. At least if he was gonna get paid to save lives, he didn't want to waste his time on people who were just tired as shit. "White college trash," I heard him say.

I wanted to yell, "My father's a lawyer!" but couldn't. Then I remembered that he already knew; he'd just been in my father's office. I couldn't understand why he would mistake me for white trash.

My head stayed in Scarlett's lap for a few more minutes, long enough for me to wonder how my head kept ending up there, and long enough to realize how much I enjoyed it. Finally, she helped me to my feet. As we approached the blue door of The Blue Flower, I couldn't help but feel as if someone was throwing bottles at me. I couldn't help but think I was like Kimmy, and that there might be real solutions to the problem in my head. I just had to sleep a little longer. I wiped my mouth and focused on the blue door. Scarlett was oddly quiet.

Once inside, I began searching for Tim. I walked slowly through the dark maze, trying to spot his pale, boyish face. Boyish faces were everywhere.

The half-pill of Ecstasy I'd taken four hours earlier was wearing off, and I was getting tired. I didn't want to lose myself again, not at the feet of the gawkers surrounding me. I pictured myself sinking into the strange crowd, unnoticed. As they trampled over me like a dent or a strange gouge in the painted blue floor, no one would realize I was there.

The music seemed too loud. My head pounded. And for some reason the smoke stank more than usual. Everywhere I looked there were
women. "Where are all the men?" I asked. "Where's Tim?" He went
to The Blue Flower every Thursday night. I knew because he relayed
his social activities to me in excruciating detail. Ironically, I think I
was the only one who listened without falling asleep.

I walked and Scarlett danced along beside me through the botanical
strangeness engulfing us. She slid her arm through mine. She bounced
up and down, and I felt like Eeyore, dull by comparison. My long
ponytail was Eeyore's tail. I was swollen and blue.

She didn't seem fazed by the fact that she'd found me lying outside
on the ground. "Angel, what brings you back here?" she asked, her
voice singing again. Although she crawled like Tigger beneath the skin
of those unlike her, she was fresh and honest. I could easily believe
she belonged in the same family as Tim. Somehow, they both had a
knack for endearing themselves to people who couldn't stand them.
"You never called me back. I was worried I'd never see you again. Of
course, Tim always keeps me posted on how you're doin'." I swung
my head around, searching for him. "How come you never did call
me back?" she asked. "You're not afraid of me, are you, baby?"

"I'm not your baby," I said.

"Maybe just a teeny, tiny bit, I bet . . . *afraid*, I mean." She smiled,
and seeing the droop of my eyes, quickly added, "You're so tired,
aren't you? Come on, we can fix that."

She practically dragged me to the back corner of the room. Still
dancing and hanging on to me, she said, "So I heard Tim put you
on a new prescription. Is it runnin' out on you now? Because if it is,
I can help." She smiled again. "I can help you with a lotta thangs,
actually, if you just give me a chance. You know, Angel, all I need is
a chance—to be your friend." She smiled her Scarlett O'Hara smile,
and I wondered if her voice was somehow related to the shape of her
mouth. I had a small mouth, surrounded by freckles, like little nails
hammered flush, locking it in place.

"Yeah," I told her. To hell with it, I thought. "I took half a pill four
hours ago. I only take half. A half keeps me normal."

Without speaking, she turned her back to the crowd. And when she turned back toward me, she held her fingers close to my lips. "Here," she said, "another half. I want you to be awake so we can dance. This is The Blue Flower's new Ladies' Night. Does that make you a little bit nervous?"

"Just give it to me," I said, suddenly aware of the dark and small corner she'd backed me into.

"I promise it'll taste better this way, trust me. Didn't anybody ever tell you that?" She leaned even closer and said into my ear, "A pill, bitter or honeyed, large like a horse or small like my tits, tastes sweet and slides down easy when slowly licked from scarlet fingertips."

I rolled my eyes and took a breath. Her breasts weren't that small. "Where did *that* come from?"

She giggled. "I just made it up, but I know it's true. Here," she said, offering her fingertips. "Go ahead and take it." She smiled again, and I couldn't tell if it was the Ecstasy smile or a real one. I took the pill with my mouth as she instructed. I felt the tips of her fingers and her long painted fingernails on my lips and for a moment in my mouth, too.

"Where's Tim?" I asked, looking past her. "I thought he always comes on Thursdays. I need to find him—I gotta talk to him."

I wondered what Christian was doing. He'd stood in front of my father's building, watching me run away. Within minutes, his gray Audi was slowly following me. He'd followed me until he saw The Blue Flower and realized where I was headed. I suppose that's when he knew for sure that all the things he'd said about me were true. He didn't really know me at all.

"Well, as of last week, Thursdays are Ladies' Night. Tim's not here, at least not right now. But I'm here. I'm his cousin, so don't you think I'll do for now?"

I didn't answer but let her lead me to the dance floor. At first, I just stood there, surrounded by lesbians. They were both sexy and sexless. Scarlett was sexy. She bounced like Tigger on his tail, happy to have a tail. Then suddenly I felt like bouncing, too. The blue of my bruises faded. My head began to tingle. My ponytail felt erotic as it swung from side to side.

She moved closer to me. "I've always fantasized about cuttin' off a ponytail like yours," she yelled in my ear. "It would feel so great to just chop that baby off." She moved even closer and reached around to grab my ponytail.

I didn't stop her.

She pulled it around until it hung between us as we bounced. "I love this tail of yours. I wanna hold it for a while and then I wanna cut it off, right here. I wanna take these long thick horse hairs and toss 'em all over the frickin' place." I smiled because I couldn't help myself. "Will you let me do it?" she begged. "Aren't you tired of havin' this heavy thang hangin' off your head all these years? Don't you wanna have a lighter head, Angel?" She ran her hands, alternating strokes, down the length of my ponytail.

I stared at her hands, squeezing and stroking the long tube of hair, thinking that although it was part of me, and had been for so long, I would never feel anything with it. I couldn't feel her hands in my hair. It was dead weight. I was going to answer. I was going to say yes, yes, cut it off, please lighten my load, when Tim crashed into us.

"She's awake! Kimmy's awake!" he hollered above the music and the bouncing crowd of lesbians. And then Scarlett was close behind me, cutting my hair. Where she got the scissors, I'll never know, but she had them and she cut my ponytail off. My head flew up, propelled by the knowledge of Kimmy's awakening.

She was alive.

Scarlett flung the hair she'd cut high into the air. The three of us looked up in disbelief as the long hairs separated. Caught in a strange breeze created by the incessantly bouncing lesbians, they surfed over our heads, reflecting the flashing light like gold. The Blue Flower suddenly looked a hundred times bluer. There was an explosion of blue: flowers, faces, and breasts on the ceiling. My head felt light, like a sore muscle finally released from its burden.

Christian deserted me at the first sign of trouble. He was like all the others, but I didn't care. Not when my head felt so goddamn light.

I was floating. My hair fell all around me, but few people noticed. It fell everywhere. It landed on everyone, on their heads and arms and backs. Bunched together, it was heavy. Separated, its weight became undetectable.

"Where's Christian?" Tim yelled. "You didn't bring Mr. Borin' here, did you?"

I shook my head and smiled the smile at Tim, and then at Scarlett. It was half the smile, half mine.

"What happened?"

"I found my mother's photographs tonight," I hollered. "I found 'em!"

Scarlett looked confused. She'd never thought to ask me what happened; I wondered if she even cared.

Tim yelled, "And Kimmy woke up. She woke up tonight!"

☑ nail

After Scarlett cut my hair and my braided rope was gone, I began to grasp the dichotomy of loving the departure of what I thought I loved more than I actually loved the departed thing. I thought I loved that rope. It's funny how thoughts of love can sometimes be stronger than love itself. Now I know thoughts of love are weak. They tie the knots that real love loosens.

I thought I needed that long, burdensome rope, at least for tugging on when I couldn't pinch myself. Nobody liked the pinching. Pulling a rope, hanging on, was somehow easier for them to see. Perhaps it was the rope's utility. Perhaps it was the destruction, the sores, and the bruises pinching inflicted that turned heads and opened mouths in shock. Now my rope was gone. Those wide eyes and gaping mouths could no longer lead me to it.

I began to let go because I had to.

After Scarlett cut my hair, I let her touch me. When I looked up and saw my long hairs flying through The Blue Flower, when I saw them landing, one by one, twisted and shimmering on the lesbians' backs, I knew I'd let her.

When we were finally alone in Tim's small bedroom, I clung to her. I closed my eyes and smiled the smile. I groped and fondled her in places I knew she wanted to be touched. I touched her where I wanted to be touched. My energy stunned her. It was as if I knew those free moments were all I'd ever have, all I'd ever taste.

But as she stroked my shocked hair, as she finally ran her hands over me, the Ecstasy smile slid away, and I told her I couldn't imagine a world without men.

"Oh, I don't wanna world without men," she said, her eyes shining through the dark. "I just cain't ever see myself bein' intimate with any of 'em, that's all."

"I can see it, but I cain't feel it," I said, turning away. "I cain't seem to feel it."

"Maybe just not yet, you cain't," she said, stroking my back. "Maybe you need somethin' else now." Her hands were warm. They were small and narrow, but seemed to cover more territory than any I could remember. "Maybe you don't really know what you need. And it doesn't mean there's anythang wrong with you. A lotta people go through it. They go through it all the time. I promise." There was a scar in her voice, a glitch of uneven terrain in what was normally smooth despite the ups and downs of her melodic speech.

"How do you know?" I asked, but she didn't answer.

The night seemed to grow darker as her hands stroked more than just my back. They moved down the sides of me, moving toward the inside. They stroked my loneliness. Her narrow fingers seemed to soothe each lonely memory as if they were stored throughout my skin. And those memories built upon the dark, solitary times before I slept, before I dreamed of Betty Lou, cried for her caress although she couldn't possibly hear. I closed my eyes and wished my mother had lived.

I cried backwards tears again, but I didn't wish or cry long before I saw Betty Lou. She stood before me like a real angel, separate from me and everything else, but real in my narcoleptic dream. And then Scarlett's hands weren't the hands of a lover. They were the hands of *mother*.

Mother at last.

Mother cutting my rope.

Mother lying next to me in the dark, flesh against flesh, almost one again.

"You know," Scarlett's scarred voice whispered, "men never really seem to do what they should anyway when a girl's fallin'. And you, you *really* fall, and I can perfectly understand why they don't hang around to catch you."

The dream was over.

"Once they see a girl fallin', especially fallin' hard, they don't like it, and I think it's partly because they're immature that way. They're great big meatheads who always think they're God's gift to women, so when one really does like 'em, when a girl really spreads her heart wide open, they consider her ordinary. And they never want ordinary." She laughed low, almost cruelly, and I could feel the spurt of her breath against my neck. "But women are the real gift," she whispered, "all wrapped up nice and pretty, ready and wantin', hopin' really, to be unwrapped, to be explored and discovered like a treasure." Then she turned me over, unwrapped, explored, and discovered me.

I took long, deep breaths and let her do as she pleased. But although I was her treasure, she wasn't mine. She was less and she was more. Scarlett was rare and she was *mother*, but she wasn't Betty Lou.

I tried to calm myself, to catch my breath without having to pinch myself. "I think it's human nature," I finally said. "Men are just different."

I didn't look at her.

"Well, why shouldn't women be loved the way they wanna be?" Her hands were on me again, her whole body against me.

"Mothers love that way, don't they? I think that's how it is," I said.

"Mothers cain't do this," she said. I gasped again at how nice her touch felt. It was warm and dangerous, like a bath in which I might drown. But the heat was numbing. I was falling asleep, and I knew that when I awoke, I'd want to leave. As my eyes fluttered, I thought of Christian, regardless of his meathead status. There's something lovable about meatheads, I thought. There's something more to it that Scarlett doesn't see—something she can't see. I was afraid then of losing sight of it myself. I feared I'd be blind before I ever really saw, before I ever really woke up next to a meathead I could love. I fell asleep wondering how I could ever shake my crippling need for *mother*. It was a rope I couldn't cut, one that dangled through my life, knocking me down, lowering me. I knew then that it wasn't the kind of rope that pulled up or liberated or rescued. There was no cloud-filled sky in which it hung, only darkness, only loneliness. I hated it, and I hated Scarlett for making it so clear.

Tim drove me home before she woke. At first, he was quiet—upset, I think, that I'd left Scarlett asleep in his bed. But halfway to my house, he woke me up. "When are you gonna go see Kimmy? Do you wanna go tonight? I can pick you up."

"No, I gotta finish my Darwin paper soon or I'll be screwed."

"I know she wants to see you. She's been awake for almost twenty-four hours. You'd think Ma Piggly and Pa Wiggly would have called us right away. We were both up there all the time, probably more than them."

"I don't know if I'll have time to go until after finals. Finals are always bad for me."

Suddenly he grinned. "So how was it?" he asked.

I looked out the window. "I don't wanna talk about it."

"Okay, I'll just ask Scar."

"She's not gonna tell you anythang."

"She tells me everythang."

"Isn't anythang private to you people?"

"If you wanted privacy, you should have slept in someone else's bed."

* * *

A week after Scarlett cut my hair, I found myself examining the plastic window I'd peed on, trying to convince myself that the line was too dark, too purplish to be considered blue. A blue line meant pregnant. I called Christian and he agreed that I should come over.

He didn't agree that I should give birth.

He sat in the corner of his living room, hiding in its shadows. He was the first guy I'd dated who owned his own home. And it was perfect, so organized. Mature. His furniture wasn't new, but rather had that quality of old money and an antique flare that someone truly tasteful can create. He created it by simply choosing it.

His mouth was a straight, organized line and his flared eyes were blank.

"It's just not fair," he said. "I don't wanna be nor did I choose to be a parent yet, and besides, you're not exactly the picture of health." His auburn hair curled over his forehead. "You're crazy, if you ask me." His house sat immaculate around him while he struggled for control. I wondered how he managed to keep the white doilies so perfectly positioned atop the furniture. Not one was askew. I wondered how he kept them so white.

His legs were spread, his hands clenched.

In many ways, he seemed more ready to be a parent than I was. He had a life of his own while I barely lived enough to call mine a life. That's the unfair part, I thought. It was unfair that I should sacrifice so much while he hid in the shadows clenching his hands, trying to wring me away. It was unfair that I *wanted* to accept the sacrifice, that his curse was my gift.

I stared at him, as silent as I'd always been.

"What are you lookin' at?" he asked.

I wished I could make him see what I saw. I wished I could make him feel it. But he was slippery and hollow inside. He was too perfect to ever view an imperfection as a gift. He was doomed to live his life looking impeccable while the aberrations, the imperfections, and the oddities of nature grew up around him. In the end, I thought, he'll feel weird. He'll be lonely.

I felt sorry for him because he couldn't love his child. Then I cursed myself for feeling sorry. If he's happy with himself, I thought, it shouldn't matter. Then I decided he was like a man blind from birth, content with his life, with what he knows, but tragic in the loss of his sight, of his inability to comprehend something so inspirational, so glorious. Instead, he seeks glory elsewhere. He is forced to find alternatives for the thing he can't possibly understand.

Does that make him innocent? I wondered.

Determined to remain calm, I gripped the edge of his sofa. "Look, I'm basically healthy. Narcolepsy's a condition that affects sleepin'—nothin' else. And I've had this for a long time. I'm used to it. And I'm off my meds now. And I even did some research. I found a couple of articles suggestin' that narcolepsy actually gets better durin' pregnancy."

"But what about after? How are you gonna take care of a baby? You cain't even take care of yourself."

"I don't know," I said.

I didn't know.

"But if I just have the right support," I said, "I can get along."

"Well, I don't think you should count on me for it, if that's what you're gettin' at."

I pictured him murdering runts and yanking wildflowers out by the roots.

He still looked good to me. I'd never forget how I'd picked him out of the crowd, how that hadn't worked. "I wasn't really countin' on you," I said, wishing I could.

He squeezed his head as if it hurt. "I mean, what the hell do you think you're gonna do?" He stood up and paced across the living room. "How are you gonna take care of a baby?" He made a sarcastic chuckle, and I wondered if he realized he'd already asked that question. I'd already answered. I *had* answered. "You really are crazy." He stared up at the ceiling.

"I'll graduate by the time it's born. I can get a job, or if my father agrees, I can still go to grad school." I shook my head too much, the way I had all summer. "It's not impossible." My head wouldn't stop shaking. It was shaking, yes, yes, as if to convince me that what was coming out of it was true.

"You're livin' in a dream world." He looked at me as if I *was* white college trash, something I never thought existed until I met him. I thought college, an education, lifted you from the trash heap. I thought my educated father had lifted me out of the heap long ago. "Look, I'll give you the money to do what you gotta do." He looked down.

Yanking up the wildflower, roots and all, didn't bother him. But I wasn't fazed. I'd already guessed he'd want to kill the runt. "Save your money."

"You don't know what the hell you're doin'."

"I know you think I'm gonna end up like some big fat lady livin' in a trailer, wearin' stretch pants, and hangin' laundry out to dry, but you're wrong." I stood up, hoping that I wouldn't conk out. "People like you always think I'm weak, but I'm not weak. I can do anythang I want. I just have to get a plan. I'll get a plan goin'. I'll nail the wall, and I'll see it through."

His eyes narrowed and his head shook. "What are you talkin' about? I cain't even communicate with you. I cain't believe I got myself into this circus."

I sat down again, tired. I wanted to tell him how I'd felt when the doctor confirmed my pregnancy.

I was asleep when he called. The doctor's words filtered through my brain like a dream in which my mother was closer than she'd ever been. "No matter what you decide to do about this pregnancy, you have to call your neurologist immediately," he said. "You gotta promise."

I didn't know what to say.

"It's critical. Angel, are you there? Hello?"

"I'm here."

"Call him right away. I don't know how this will affect your narcolepsy. You just call right away, you hear me?" His doctor face flashed through my mind. His smooth skin combined with his white hair made his head look like a giant pearl.

I wondered if he'd ever felt like dirt.

After I hung up, I continued to lie across my bed. I pulled my shoulder-length hair out from under my head, positioning it around my face in what had once been a gigantic circle, a web. I could feel my heart growing. A smile emerged from that deep place I'd only found through Ecstasy. I smiled the smile. It burst into my face like a flood. I rushed to my large bedroom window and opened the blinds in a loud, quick clatter. The sun shone across the room, scorching every last Holly Hobbie. I hadn't felt so awake in weeks; my heart hadn't beat so hard. I looked at myself in the mirror. The Holly Hobbies would be gone soon.

Everything would change.

I would never be as lonely as I'd been. I would know that mother feeling now in this way. I would possess it and give it to someone who loved me despite my disability, my imperfections, and my mistakes. It was a gift I could give my child and myself. I would not look it in the mouth. I would not question whether it was meant to be, and I would not count the class rules that would be broken. If it made me white college trash, so be it.

I would only count the blessings. I would make it work.

The baby wasn't a mistake. It was right in a way Christian would never understand because he didn't understand who I was at all.

The clouds shifted and a new light flooded the room. Its warmth embraced me, as if I'd emerged from beneath a muted ocean, pearl-like again. Then I fell among my burning Holly Hobbie girlfriends and cried. I cried until I couldn't move, and I saw Darwin again, beckoning me, while in the background Betty Lou's voice called, "Don't be afraid. Just take a step. The water's not nearly as cold as it looks." Then I conked out again, and this time there were no dreams.

"Wake up!" Christian hollered. "See, you cain't even sit here for thirty minutes without dozin' off. What's gonna happen when you're holdin' a baby and you fall asleep? What if you fall down like you did at your dad's office? You're gonna end up killin' your own kid."

I wiped my eyes. I was past the point of letting him startle me. I'd made my decision. I'd spent my life searching photographs and walls and my father's eyes for that elusive feeling, for Betty Lou, for *mother*. All I'd wanted was to find my mother, so if I couldn't find her, I'd become her. I said, "You can participate or you can fall by the wayside." But I knew he was already falling into the past, away from me and my baby and the life I would make for us. I wished he would look up and suddenly see. I wanted to cure his blindness, but I knew it was impossible. Looking back, I saw that I hadn't given him much to love. I'd willingly played the part of the cotton candy, holding my real self back, and that was my fault.

He'd once shared a theory with me. He said nobody was actually bad in bed, that it just took the right combination. At the time, I thought it made a lot of sense, and now I wondered if it was also true that no one was truly coarse and unfeeling. Perhaps it was just the situation that made them behave badly. In a way, I didn't blame him. Maybe he wasn't really a jerk.

"It was just a fling, you know," he said, looking older than twenty-eight. I pictured him at forty, wondering if he'd have kids by then. I wondered what kind of father he'd be.

"It was a lot more to me."

"Well, maybe you just don't know the difference."

I felt older, too.

☑ oyster

"Exactly how did she die?" I asked my dad the next day.

Blank face.

"What was the *exact* complication?" I stood in our large hallway, studying the few photographs Carla had returned. "Don't you think I should know? You never give me any details."

"I didn't understand all that grandiose medical talk," he said. "She bled. That's all I remember." The words came easily, but like always, they relayed nothing. "There was a lot of blood."

"Come on, Dad. You're a smart man. You're a lawyer."

Suddenly, he stood close beside me, and without looking, I reached for his warm, sweaty hand. We'd stood there a thousand times, gazing at her priceless clouds. "I'm a real estate attorney, Angel. Not a genius."

We both studied the wall with narrowed eyes.

"You could understand if you wanted to." It was the farthest I'd ever pushed. "You just don't want to, do you?"

I never dreamed he was lying.

His shoulders slumped then, and he rocked as if about to fall. "She looked so peaceful with you lyin' next to her." He paused. "She did love you."

"But how could she *really* love me. She didn't even see me, did she?"

His head shook. "She saw you."

He dropped my hand and wiped both of his on his starched white apron, one of the gifts Carla had given him for his fifty-third birthday. As his hands fell away, I saw steak juice smeared across his chest. The taste of acid flooded my throat and reality hit. I was pregnant. No amount of creative pretending or willful denial would alter the truth.

My father must have seen the sick look on my face because his look finally changed. "She saw you and she loved you. She would have loved you more every day if she'd been around," he said. As always, his emotion breathed life into the woman whose dead body had lain between us for so long, cementing us together, making him inflexible and me hard. He looked down at his manicured nails, and I knew I was torturing him. He still couldn't bear acknowledging her death.

Now I know why.

"I just cain't understand," I said. "I wanna know exactly what killed her, that's all." I took my favorite photograph off the wall and glanced at the back of it. "Is that really too much to ask?"

"Do you love her, Angel?"

"Of course," I said. The cloud in the photograph formed a perfect horse galloping across the sky. "I see her in my dreams."

"You saw her with half-open, baby eyes and you love her. So just imagine how much she loved you with grown eyes that knew they were dyin'. She knew she was dyin'." He had muddy brown eyes that had never cleared, instead growing thicker and thicker each time I looked. If I focused hard enough, I could almost see the words *Betty Lou, Betty Lou* layered within them, making my father blind.

* * *

"Mac, it's me," I said. "I need a favor."

"You shouldn't call me here. Who answered the phone?" His voice was heavy like the rock that seemed to hold his feet to the ground.

"I don't think she recognized my voice."

"Okay, so what's the favor?" He didn't sound angry. He always seemed to forgive people so quickly. I used to think he forgave too fast, but this time I was glad.

"Well, you know how you always talk about bein' like James Bond and all?"

"Yeah, I was born for that part, but . . ."

"Hollywood just doesn't know it yet," I finished his sentence.

"That's right. You're a smart girl. I always said that about you."

And sleepy, I thought. "Well, I need you to investigate somethin'. You're the only one I know who can pull it off." I lay across my bed, staring up at the canopy.

"Well, what is it?"

"I need you to look at my mother's medical records."

"Christ, Angel, you've gotta get past all that."

"I gotta find out how she died. I *have* to know, now."

"Why the sudden urgency?"

I grabbed a pillow and squeezed. "Well, because . . . I'm pregnant."

Silence. Then, "Are you sure?"

I wondered if he thought it might be his. "I've been to the doctor," I said.

"It was that new guy, wasn't it? What a dick." He still didn't sound angry. "It should have been me, you know."

"But you're married."

"I know, but we would've had a kick-ass kid. We're both good lookin' and intelligent and decent. People like us should populate the world—we should be havin' six or eight kids—not all those welfare mothers. They're increasin' exponentially." He sounded like a preacher coming to the main point of his sermon. "People like us have an obligation. We're decent. Before long the decent are gonna be scarce, you know. They'll just be a few of us, workin' our asses off to support all those welfare kids."

"Do you really think we're decent?" I asked, solidifying my opinion that his egotism was a cover. There had to be more.

"Sure we are. We're as decent as the next guy," he said. "But, hey, why don't you just ask your dad again. Surely under the circumstances, he'll be willin' to talk about it."

"I've tried that, and I don't wanna tell him I'm pregnant yet. I cain't until I get some kind of plan together. I've got to think, and I just cain't think right now." It was true. I felt right about what I was doing, but I still didn't know how I was going to do it. I didn't know how I'd manage to keep from falling and crushing my own child. "You're the only one I've told . . . besides Christian. He wasn't exactly thrilled."

"Of course—he's a dick. Look, this isn't a normal situation. Your dad's gonna have to be a major part of your plan . . . and Carla, too. You better start bein' really nice to her. I don't think this is somethin' you should be keepin' to yourself." He stopped and didn't say anything for almost a whole minute. Then he said, "If you need anythang, you call me. I'll do whatever I can . . . under the circumstances." I heard the same blip in his voice that I'd heard in Scarlett's. A scar. And then I realized they had somethin' in common. I just wasn't sure what it was.

"I didn't expect you to be so willin' to help."

"Well, I am. I don't know, somehow I feel responsible. Believe it or not, I miss you. I still wanna be your friend."

"Can you please just try to find out about Betty Lou? It would mean a lot to me if you could just do that one little thang." I paused. "Her maiden name was Brown. I don't know if you'll need it. And I was born at LSU."

"Why were you born at the Med Center? You know, they'd probably release her records to you."

"All I know is she was there because of some other medical problem and she went into labor early. I called and asked about it and they said there's some kinda legal letter on file sayin' the records cain't be released to anyone except my father."

"Your dad's tryin' to hide somethin'," Mac said. "So you basically want me to steal 'em?"

"I just want you to look at 'em and tell me what they say."

"LSU's pretty lax compared to other hospitals. But I don't know. It's really against my professional judgment . . . my oath, you know."

"You've broken oaths before," I said.

"That's true."

"And you still consider yourself a decent person. You just got through sayin' that."

"You got me there." I could tell he was smiling.

"So cain't you just try? Please. I know you have a lot of friends there."

"I'll try."

* * *

"What do you think you're doin'?" my father said, startling me. He was coming up the attic stairs.

I froze, not because of my disability, but because I'd been caught.

"What are you doin'?" he said again, louder this time. "You know you're not allowed up here."

"Don't you think that's ridiculous at this point? I'm almost twenty-two years old." I tried to hide what I'd gotten into. I tried to change the look on my face.

He grabbed the box in front of me as if he knew exactly what was in it. I couldn't decide if his twisted face meant anger or grief. It usually meant grief, meant the lack of something that had once been present. It was that void, that missing element, which made me see the ghost in him. I'd always thought the entity was Betty Lou, but now that Carla had him planning, I realized it was something else. "I didn't want you in this attic," he said, "not when you were a kid and not now. There's nothin' up here that belongs to you."

"Well, I think there are thangs up here that *should* belong to me," I said, looking at the box. "What are those photographs all about? Why don't you want me to see 'em?"

He grabbed the box and held it tight. "I've raised you, and I love you, but you're gonna have to accept that some thangs are better left as they are. There's nothin' for you in this box or any others in this attic."

"I don't believe you." I stood up and began rummaging through the junk filling the attic as if it had grown there. It grew wild from the cardboard boxes that served as fertile ground. I imagined his junk had started small, tiny buds tossed across the worn hardwood floor. But now the junk was alive like long spiraling weeds whose roots connected. Drawing upon all the types of tears that filled our home, they'd grown longer and stronger than my father ever expected. "You haven't been up here in years, have you?"

He looked around as if he hated the place. "No, it's all junk."

Before the buds, there was death. It all started in death.

"I saw the pictures," I said. His twisted stare made me sick with anger. "What is wrong with you? They're only photographs, photographs she took, and I want 'em. I wanna see all of 'em." His immobility made me nauseated. "Don't you get it? I wanna understand who she was. You got to know all about her, but for me, everythang's a mystery. There's a big blank space in my heart. All I've ever seen of her, all I've ever really understood is those photographs in our hallway and your cryin'. And I'm sick of your cryin'."

"I haven't cried over your mother in quite a while, Angel." He was trying to appear calm, but I could see he was uncomfortable. His head nearly touched the ceiling, causing him to slouch. His free arm swung every couple of seconds. He wanted to sit but there was nowhere to go except down on the floor or down out of the attic. He wanted out.

"You cry every day. You cry when you don't tell me the truth. When you refuse to let me in on Betty Lou. You just wanna keep her all to yourself. You don't wanna share any of your memories. Maybe you think they'll be diffused or somethin', but I deserve 'em. You didn't even tell me you let Carla hang my clouds in your office, and then you didn't even care enough to realize I'd see 'em when I went to get those damn folders."

"You're lucky your boyfriend had the sense to bring 'em here," he said. "You don't *deserve* anythang, Angel. You've had a better life than most, and I don't wanna hear you talkin' that way. I've told you quite a bit through the years. And I'm sorry, but you're never gonna have memories."

My dreams, my dreams, I thought. What about my dreams?

"The memories are mine and the stories are yours," he said, "and you're just gonna have to accept it. Now get on outta here."

"You know, I used to think you told me everythang . . . *all* the stories, but now I realize you just told me the same stupid thangs over and over . . . stuff about fields and clouds and cameras. And it's all shit!"

He wilted further, if that was possible. "Look, the truth is, I only knew her for three or four years." The box was slipping, but he held it tight with one hand. His other hand went deep into his pocket. "She was only nineteen when I met her." His face went gray, his eyes blending into the dusty attic. He was part of the weed—he was the rotting vine. "So there are no more stories. I've told you all the stories I have." He pulled his hand out of his pocket to prevent the box from falling.

"Well, I don't believe you." I wanted to water him, to splash him with the nutrients, the health he needed, but I didn't know how. "And I'm sorry, but you're not gonna stop me from findin' out about her."

"You're talkin' crazy. I mean ridiculous," he said. "I told you I don't know exactly why she died." With his free arm, he pulled one of my old dolls out of a nearby box by its head. "It used to be so easy," he said, staring at the ragged doll. "You used to be so . . ."

"I used to be a kid but I'm not anymore. I don't wanna be a kid my whole life. It's bad enough havin' to live here, havin' to be looked after. I want my own life. I need to know who I am and who you are and who Betty Lou . . . who my mother was. I'm twenty-one years old."

He dropped the doll and put the box on the floor. Then he pulled his arms toward his body as if wrapping himself up the way I used to, when that rope still dangled from the back of my head. Before he could unwrap, I went for the box. I managed to grab a handful of the five-by-seven photographs before he could stop me.

"What is this?" I shook the prints in his face. "What does this mean?"

"They're just pictures," he said sadly. "You said that yourself."

"But they're not. These aren't *regular* clouds—they're not normal. They're so . . . disturbing." Each one was dark, with distorted shapes and odd angles. Many contained streaks of lightening. In one photograph, a woman's spread legs, my mother's legs, pointed into the clouds, bare and white.

"Clouds were her creative interest. Period."

Looking at them, I could clearly see her creative vision, but I could also see her outside the photograph, behind the camera, standing alone in those lightning-filled fields, those beautiful fields turned ugly and gray like my father. She stood vulnerable, wrapped in her passion, a human lightning rod. Asking for it. Her vision was doom, and she seemed to be begging for some cloudy manifestation of her emotion, hoping to be stricken. I imagined her finger pressing the button. Perhaps her final goal was to obliterate clouds and shapes of clouds.

I held in my hands pictures of her obliteration.

"Those are just another example of what made her unique," he said, finally. "She wasn't afraid. She was driven to capture somethin'."

"What was she tryin' to capture?"

"I don't know."

"But this looks dangerous. Why didn't you stop her?"

"I couldn't," he said, as if he had wanted to. "There was no stoppin' her."

"Well, you must not like these photographs, either, or you would have framed them like the others. If these are so creative, why'd you hide 'em in the attic?" I held out two of them, trying to force him to look, but he turned away. "You cain't even look at 'em. You always said she was Miss happy-go-lucky, but this is somethin' different," I said, shaking the photographs. "This is a different person."

"They're just photographs that I didn't consider to be her best work. I don't understand why you're makin' such a goddamn mountain out of a molehill."

"You did this to me. You made the mountain and now you're forcin' me to climb it. I didn't ask for this."

"People are adopted every day, and they don't have a clue to who their real parents are."

"But at least they have a mother . . . like Kimmy. She was adopted."

"You had me," he said. "You still have me. I've tried to be a good father."

"It's not enough, and I'm not gonna pretend anymore that it is." My face was hot and there didn't seem enough air in the attic. As I looked around, I had the sensation of being inside a bubble. I was floating inside, wondering how much oxygen was left, while my father stood out of reach.

"There are no answers to your questions, Angel," he reminded me.

My head hurt. "How did she die, Dad?"

"There are no answers to your questions."

"Are you gonna marry Carla?" I asked, surprising myself.

"I don't know. Not now." His voice came at me from the opposite end of a tunnel where every fact and lie bounced back toward him, echoing until he'd lost his mental balance. He was far away. Even he knew he was far away.

I continued to stand in front of him with outstretched arms. The backs of the photographs in my hands had no dates—nothing—written on them. My father looked at me like a narcoleptic stone, and I knew he would soon fall. I thought I was going to fall over, too, but I didn't. I didn't move until he was gone.

Once recovered from the shock of standing still, I went to my bedroom and ripped the Holly Hobbie comforter and sheets from my bed. Stuffing them into the silver trash can on the side of our house in a tight, hard ball felt good.

I had no regrets.

☑ pot

For those who believed in divine creation, few problems existed. For them, each species had been created in its still-existing form, and it was not necessary to know on which of the six days of creation each had come into existence. Six days might seem a short time for the work, but this difficulty was already being removed by the more daring, who tentatively suggested that "day" might be a purely figurative word, and that the period involved might be as long as the latest geological argument demanded. Darwin most likely fit into this staunch group of believers, and it would be over the course of his lifetime that he would slowly lose his faith. His reluctance to publish his realizations and therefore tackle man's history was due not only to his wish to avoid stirring up opposition, but to the outcome of his innate desire for a quiet life and his hope for success. He himself had only begun giving up his faith under the pressure of accumulating evidence. In public, he dodged the issue of his findings as long as he could and felt it possible to claim of his work, with almost Jesuitical casuistry, that it need not offend the emotions. If politics is the art of the possible, Darwin knew that the art of survival consisted of not offending.

In 1858, Darwin was backed into a corner . . .

* * *

Mac backed my father into a corner the day I turned in my paper.

"Hey, you! Need a ride?" Mac's grin was as bright as his white Corvette, his hair black as its top. Seeing him on campus was strange. He didn't belong—his car was too nice. "Is class dismissed?" he asked as he drove beside me through the parking lot.

Finally he stopped, and I leaned over the passenger door. "What are you doin' here?" I asked, although I knew—he'd discovered something.

"I thought we could have a picnic. I brought all the stuff."

The car behind him honked. "Shouldn't you be at work?" I asked.

"Day off, my dear. Come on." His smile was enchanting, his knowledge irresistible.

We drove out of town, further south, past planted fields and empty pastures. Tracy Chapman sang about fast cars, being someone, and things getting better. I turned up the music but Mac turned it back down. "It's too loud," he said, "I won't be able to hear you."

"But I wasn't even talkin'."

"Well, in case you do," he said, and I remembered how Christian hadn't cared if I opened my mouth or not.

So we rode in silence, straining to hear the radio until I finally asked, "What did you find out?"

"I'll tell you when we get there."

"Where are we goin'?" I asked.

"I'll know it when I see it. Rest for now, and I'll wake you up when I figure it out."

I laid my head back, almost glad he hadn't told me yet. I wished I could sleep in his car, traveling to a place he'd know was right for me. I wished he *could* wake me when we got there. I closed my eyes and listened to his familiar whistling, in sync with the beat of his thumb on the steering wheel. I wondered where his wife was. She didn't seem to exist, but yet she sat between us. I could feel her breath on my face. I could hear her voice in his whistle.

I felt like a welfare mother.

Mac took me to a field, one that was still somewhat green despite it being mid-December. It was one I knew well. "Why'd you bring me here?" I asked.

"Well, I thought you'd wanna talk."

"No, I mean here, to this place."

"It looks good," he said, looking around. "Why, what's wrong with it?"

I lay down on the blanket he shared with his wife and stared up at the clouds. He unpacked the red cooler that was hers, too. "I've been here before, with my dad."

The day my father brought me to the field had been beautiful. He laid out a blanket similar to Mac's, and we lay side by side looking straight up. I was five or six. My father started to cry, and turning to him, I watched the tears fall from the sides of his weathered face. I didn't know it was unusual for a grown man to cry so often. I thought I'd like to place a bowl beside his head and see how high his tears could fill it. "Why are you cryin'?" I'd asked, but he didn't answer. Instead, he pointed to the sky. Straight above, there hung a gigantic cloud, shapeless at first, but it soon began to change. It took the loose shape of a tree, the kind children draw. Its trunk fat and straight and its top comprised of five connected circles. "You cryin' about the clouds?"

"Betty Lou should see this," he said.

"But she ain't here, Daddy."

He didn't correct my grammar as usual. Instead, he said, "She should be."

I wondered if he meant instead of me, but I didn't ask. I didn't cry, either. If I cried, my father would cry more, and I wanted him to stop. To me, the clouds looked like giant sponges that could dry all tears. But no matter how hard or long he looked, my father never saw the sponges. He only saw her. I don't think he even saw me until the narcolepsy. Narcolepsy gave me an identity in my father's eyes while erasing it for everyone else.

"I made ham and cheese sandwiches," Mac said. "Do you like Doritos?"

I nodded. "Yesterday I found more of Betty Lou's photographs in our attic."

He continued taking food out of the cooler. "I brought a lot since I thought you might be extra hungry lately." He grinned as if my pregnancy was an everyday affair, as if I was planning to go to Wal-Mart and buy a doll that could eat and pee—as if I was married.

"They're so different . . . the photographs I found. They're clouds like the others, but they're storm clouds." I propped my head on my hand, my elbow sinking into the grass cushion. "And you'd think even those kind would be beautiful, but they weren't. They were scary. I don't know if it was the angles or what."

"She must have been very creative," he said. "Maybe she was a creative genius."

He held a ham sandwich to my mouth, and I took a big bite. I *had* been hungry lately. And it wasn't a normal hunger. Every cell, organ, and thought needed refreshing. My heart and head were starving. I couldn't get enough, but I hadn't gained weight. The baby was feeding off me. It needed me.

I wished I had more to give.

I stared at the sandwich. "So I guess you found somethin' out," I said.

Mac rubbed my back. "It's pretty strange but not totally unexpected—at least on my part. Are you sure you really wanna know?"

"Just tell me, okay?" I said, taking another bite from his outstretched hand. He was eating from it, too. His bites were much larger than mine, and not much was left.

"I only had a few minutes, but from what I read, you had a normal birth." He closed his wife's cooler.

I sat up. I tried to swallow the ham, which seemed like a large, shitty bolus, down my throat. I choked until my eyes began to tear. I looked over what lay before me . . . his spread . . . and I knew it wasn't enough.

"It's good news, I guess. As far as your worryin' about yourself and all."

An incredible thirst came over me. "Did you bring any drinks?" I managed to say, wondering why he hadn't offered me something already.

After I drank enough to send the ham where it was supposed to go, I said, "I always felt as if I could literally see those clouds she found. I could almost feel her *wonder*, I guess, when I looked at them. Do you think that's the sign of a good photographer, of an artist, or do you think I was just desperate? Because when I saw the photographs in the attic, I felt the same way." The ham was gone but the shitty bolus was still lodged in my throat. "I know she felt horrible when she took 'em."

"I don't know, could be a little of both. I do think it's possible that she had a gift. But I'm not too creative myself, so I don't know."

"I'm creative."

Mac was silent, and I wondered if he believed me. Then he said, "Your mother didn't die durin' childbirth, Angel." It was as if he thought I hadn't heard him the first time.

I tried not to cry. "I know I'm creative," I said. Mac held my hand. "Have you ever wanted somethin' so bad, not even wanted it, really, but needed it for some reason, so much that you started to hate it? Did you ever hate the way that thang you needed controlled you in the end, but you still couldn't stop wantin' it? It takes you prisoner. I'm a prisoner, Mac." He wanted to kiss me. I knew he wanted more, but I was empty except for the life inside me, the one that had no memory, no idea of the pain of my father's lie. "Why do people lie?" I asked him.

"I don't know," he said. "I don't know why we do."

"Why do you lie to your wife?"

"I don't know." He shook his head. "I think maybe it's a weakness, a sign of a need for somethin'. Maybe attention. I don't know. Somethin' more than what I've got. Maybe I'm a prisoner, too."

I touched his face. "Is it so bad to want more than what you have?"

"It is if it breaks the rules, if it hurts people. Maybe if it imprisons you."

"I don't think my father would lie because he wanted somethin' more. What more could he want? What more could I give him?" The tears came then. They were big, and they rolled down slowly until they spilled over the curves in my face. Then they dropped, heavy and final, like the beliefs I'd held, like my father falling out and away. "What more could he take from me?"

Mac's large arms surrounded me then, and he told me everything would be all right. He would help. He said he didn't know why he lied or why my father lied, but that we'd find out. We'd find the answer to both questions. It was only a matter of time. He said, "Your father's a prisoner, too."

"He always says there aren't any answers to my questions."

"I found an address in her chart, a Florida address. The last name was Brown. I wrote it down." He held my shoulders, forcing me away from him so that he could see my face. "I called the number, and I talked to an old guy who's related to the Browns. He lives there with his sister." I shook my head, afraid to listen. "I'll take you there," he said, shaking me, forcing me to look at him. "We'll go and find out what happened."

"You cain't just go out of town like that. Maybe Tim will take me," I said, afraid to go, afraid of what I might find.

"That little dipshit is not takin' you anywhere. Besides, you'll be better off with a doctor lookin' out for you, not a drug dealer."

"He's not a drug dealer."

"Like hell he's not."

"He's upset with me right now, anyway, because I haven't been to see Kimmy. Not since she woke up."

"Forget about them. I'll take you. And don't worry about me. I can manage."

I believed him.

As we rode back toward town, I told him that being pregnant was somehow making me healthier. I tried not to think about my father's prison and how he'd taken great care to trap me in it, too. He'd invited me through its heavy doors and then slammed them tight. Then, from its windows, he'd shown me the sky and all her clouds. He'd shown me a place I could never go.

"Maybe it's hormonal," Mac said. "I can check into it, if you want."

"It's just funny how somethin' that's supposed to be so wrong is makin' my life better. And it's not just the narcolepsy." I stared out the window. "I mean, that's a big part of it. I've been sleepin' better at night, and I haven't been as tired durin' the day. And I haven't conked out in a couple of weeks. But anyway, it's *me*, too. It's changin' me. I haven't seen Darwin."

He touched my knee. "Maybe you don't need Darwin anymore. Maybe you've found out how to survive," he said, smiling. "Survival of the fit, you know?"

"So you're sayin' I should stay barefoot and pregnant?"

"No, I'm talkin' about the other changes. Those thangs won't go away when you have the baby. They won't ever go away."

"How do you know?"

"Because I'm a little older than you. I know that death and life are two of the few thangs that change us permanently. I've seen it."

"At the hospital?" I asked.

"Well, that . . . and four years ago . . . my youngest brother committed suicide, and then less than a year later, my other brother turned into a frickin' vegetable."

"Oh my God," I said.

"He was in a car accident," Mac said, staring straight ahead. "He's a vegetable." His voice was filled with scars, blips in the mask he'd so beautifully created. "There's nobody left but me and my mom." Sunglasses hid his eyes despite the sun's descent. "My brother, the vegetable, helped me carry all those tools, my dad's tools, up to my room, and that son-of-a-bitch who shot himself just watched. He was always like that . . . standin' by, never gutsy enough to join in, to start findin' his own frickin' life."

I didn't know what to say.

"Life is a gift," he said blandly.

I touched my belly.

"I'm really happy for you, Angel. You're lucky. You just don't realize it yet. Me, I'm waitin' to find enough life to balance all that death and shit. But I know I will."

"I wish you weren't married," I said and turned away.

I wasn't sure if he'd heard me at first, but then he said, "Sometimes I wish I wasn't either." Then he began to whistle, and again I heard the shrill cry of his wife.

☑ queen

When I first got into Tim's car, I didn't see Scarlett. It was dark, and she was lying down in the backseat. It was one o'clock in the morning. I'd woken up an hour earlier and couldn't go back to sleep. I kept thinking about Mac and Betty Lou and those people in Florida, and besides, I'd slept the entire day. Sometimes that happened. I'd sleep so many hours during the day that I'd toss and turn at night. Usually, I'd continue to toss, but this time I had something else in mind.

"What's she doin' here?" I whispered to Tim after he shut the door.

"Is she asleep?" he whispered back, twisting around to look at her.

I looked, too.

"I'm awake," Scarlett announced, her rhythmic voice penetrating the still night with absurd volume. She sat up, smiling. "Hey, Angel, how's it goin', girl? I've been thinkin' about you a lot lately, you know." Her dark curls pointed toward me in messy clumps. I turned back around and stared at my father's house as Tim backed away. "Been to any good sleepovers lately?" she whispered into the back of my head. "Or have you just been hangin' out at home? 'Cause we haven't seen much of you."

I wanted to turn around and smooth her hair. "Yours was the last sleepover I attended, if that's what you're gettin' at."

"Hey, girls, chill out. We're on a mission here."

Our goal was to sneak into my father's office so I could take a closer look at Betty Lou's clouds. I'd decided that the middle of the night was the only time I could take my father's key without him knowing.

Tim said, "You're lucky I was up when you called."

"You're lucky we were home at all because you know how we get around, right, Tim?"

Ignoring her, he said, "Well, I'm still pissed at you for not goin' to see Kimmy, but I'm not gonna ask you about it. I'm just gonna sit here and drive you to the scene of the crime."

"It's not a crime. I have the key."

"Kimmy's goin' home next week," he said. "Did I tell you that?"

"No."

"Well, she is."

"And he really wants you to go see her either before that or after," Scarlett added. "She misses you and is wonderin' why you haven't been to see her. Why you've deserted her, pretty much. Kinda like you deserted me." Her melodic quality continued despite her obvious resentment. A dark lullaby.

"Shut up, Scar," said Tim.

"Yeah, I guess it's a little different situation with us, right, Angel?"

"It's a *lot* different," I said, twisting to face her again. "Why'd you come if you're just gonna pick on me?"

"Because I like you."

As we approached my father's office building, the mailboxes began to cry. Tim scooted past as if under attack. Christian's voice echoed through my head, saying, "Christ! It sounds like gunfire," and I wondered if all men felt as if they were under attack. "Can you tell me again what exactly we're doin' here?" Tim asked.

"I just wanna take a look at some photographs in my father's office."

"But why's it such a big secret?" Scarlett asked. "I like doin' thangs like this. It's excitin' and all, but why all the secrecy?"

"It's a long story. Right now I just wanna get in and get out."

"Are you back on that medicine that screws you up?" Tim asked.

"You guessed it," I lied, shaking my head as fast as I could so he'd believe me. He'd already been questioning why I hadn't required a refill.

Once in my father's office, Tim plopped into the big leather chair. "Your father must be loaded," he said, squinting to assess the plush office. We'd decided to keep it dark, for security purposes, which Scarlett found exciting. We turned on two small lamps.

Scarlett stood close beside me, insistent on helping take down the photographs. Unlike in our hallway at home, they were hung in two tight, straight lines, each photograph only an inch or so from the next. I chose the last three: the nail, what looked like a giant piece of hard candy, and the angel. It was obvious that Carla was framing and replacing them in order because the first several photographs had been replaced by duck prints. She'd hung the nails in here, too, I guessed, so she wasn't about to pull them out.

Scarlett and I placed the frames facedown on the small conference table in the corner of the room.

Tim spun in the chair until he became a blur.

"So, what now?" Scarlett asked.

"Now," I said, pulling out the box cutter I'd brought in my purse, "I'm gonna cut 'em open." She stared at the instrument, her eyes glistening. I hesitated, and looking down, noticed the points on her breasts. Her face was shadowed except for her bright eyes, but her body was brilliant in the lamplight.

"You know, Angel, your hair really looks good," she said, brushing it behind my ear. "I'm glad I cut it. I really hope you don't regret it, 'cause I'd just hate that, you know?"

"Are you gonna cut the picture or not?" Tim asked. I'd stared at Scarlett for too long. "Why are you doin' this, anyway? Are you gonna let us in on what's goin' on here or not? I'm gettin' the creeps."

Scarlett smiled. "I'm not," she said. I wondered how she could understand, be so vulnerable, when I'd treated her so badly. Perhaps she was a girl falling hard. If so, she'd been right. To a lot of men, she might have appeared desperate. To me, she appeared kind, unselfish, and loving. She was still beautiful.

I cut into the paper backing of the first frame, careful to keep my line straight. "Can you please bring that lamp over here," I asked, and Scarlett ran for my father's desk lamp. I held the photograph up to the lamplight and pried the paper as far open as I could without ripping it. The date, "1964," along with the word, "candy," were clearly written on the back of the photograph.

"Isn't there usually cardboard or somethin' between the photograph and the brown paper?" Scarlett asked.

"These were done cheap. They're old," I said. "Carla's havin' 'em reframed. I just wanna look at the dates on the back. My mother took these photographs."

"They're incredible," Tim said.

"Yeah," I said, disappointed that the second photograph was dated 1965. "One left to go," I said. It was the angel, and I knew if there was an answer, I would find it there. I sliced the paper backing while Scarlett rehung the other two photographs.

"A little to the left . . . no, that's too much," Tim said. His voice droned on and on, left, right, left, right, and then disappeared. Everything disappeared as I stared at the date beneath the tiny word "angel." It was 1968.

"I was born in 1966," I said, but Scarlett and Tim didn't hear. They were too busy aligning Betty Lou's photographs across my father's wall. But I knew then that they could never be realigned. They would remain forever crooked, bent, and twisted like the attic weeds tangled around my father's neck, the chains he'd created for himself.

☑ racket

Florida is full of pork rinds. Most people associate the state with Mickey Mouse and oranges, but I always think of those translucent animal skins and their smell of meat and grease. I think of thin-skinned people, cooked by the sun, people who care more about what other people think than anything else. Of course, I didn't fully grasp the concept of *people rinds* until after my trip to Florida and the long journey back. Only then did I realize how thin my own skin had become due to my father's incessant whittling.

In Florida, I tasted pork rinds for the first time and discovered how incompatible they were with my system. That was my choice, but I was forced to taste and swallow the human kind against my will. Digesting those took much longer and made me sicker than I realized. Only when the remains were cleared away, out of my system, could I begin to see the havoc and appreciate the miraculous recovery.

Five days after my last final exam, I stood on the Browns' doorstep. Mac and Tim stood to my left and right, ready to throw me into the past, yet at the same time hoping to guard me from it.

I told my father I was going to Disney World with Tim and some other friends. Carla protested, worried that something would happen to me. My father just sat, holding on to her. He had a pained look on his face, and I realized later that he must have been feeling the gut-grinding anguish of human rind digestion. They break down the slowest in men like my father. When Carla got to Z, he'd pass the last of them. He'd be free.

I didn't know what Mac told his wife. I didn't ask. I should have known that Tim would.

Four days after my last final exam, I bought the pork rinds at an old Mobil station in northern Florida. A black man who read the gas tank meters through a set of rusty binoculars managed the station. He was too lazy to walk out and take a look. That's what eating too many rinds will do. Either they make you too complacent to take an up-close look at life, or they freeze you in your tracks, so burdened you can't look even when you want to. Either way, you're stuck. You're doomed to view the world through your own, rusty set of binoculars. Like tiny windows, they alter reality.

Afterward, none of us spoke for nearly two hours. I sat in the back-seat eating my rinds while Tim sucked on his boiled peanuts in the front.

Mac wasn't hungry. He drove pokerfaced.

"I still don't see why Scarlett couldn't come," Tim finally said. "It would have made the trip a little more excitin', don't you think, Angel?" He turned to face me. "You two are about as excitin' as a church on Monday. Scarlett always revs thangs up."

I didn't answer, but he was right. Scarlett wasn't a normal person, really. Like Tim, she overstepped bounds, doing it in a way that suggested the boundaries shouldn't have been there in the first place, that such things were silly. She showed me a world to explore rather than conquer. Each time Tim stepped over a line, he only made me realize that it was there for self-inflicted reasons. He called for conquest. Mac overstepped bounds, too. But, unlike Tim and Scarlett, he never even saw them. For Mac, there was no exploration, no conquest—only situations he created for himself. I feared he was blind to all consequences.

Tim's life would be triumphant and Scarlett's a celebration, but Mac's future was unsure. Surprisingly, his was the one life I wanted most to follow. When his nails were finally all hammered in the wall, I wanted to see the photograph he'd hang.

"Look, this is not a frickin' field trip or joy ride," Mac said. "You're lucky I agreed to let you come along. And I'd better not be transportin' anythang illegal across state lines."

"I'm not *that* stupid."

"You're stupid enough to have the shit."

"Can we please just all get along?" I said from the backseat. "This situation is stressful enough."

They didn't talk for another hour, or at least I don't think they did. I fell asleep.

Then I awoke with my head in a toilet. I looked up and saw boards all around me, wood paneling on every wall, even on the high ceiling. It stank. Tim stood beside me. "Where am I?" I asked before vomiting again.

"We're at a rest stop. You were talkin' in your sleep, sayin' you had to throw up, and Mac thought we should stop . . . just in case."

"Is this the women's bathroom?"

He shook his head. "We couldn't wake you up all the way, so we thought one of us should come in here with you. We agreed that I'd be a little more inconspicuous than Mac." He snickered, and I threw up again.

I spit into the toilet. "This is so embarrassin'."

"Don't worry about that. It's not like I haven't thrown up before. Are you gonna be okay? Are you carsick?"

"No, I think it was the pork rinds."

"I told you not to eat that crap. I think it's like poison. I mean, what is it, anyway? It cain't *really* be the skin of a pig, and if it is, that's disgustin'."

* * *

Mrs. Brown took a long time to answer the doorbell, and when she finally did, she stared at us as if we were door-to-door church people out to convert her. Her small, suspicious eyes combed over us. I wondered if she was related to Betty Lou and if she thought I looked like her. I wondered if she was my grandmother, but she gave no signs of recognition.

I hoped she wasn't so old that she'd forgotten the details of her life.

Mac finally spoke. "Hello," he said. "I'm Dr. Mac Boyd. These are my friends Tim Logan and Angel Duet." Mrs. Brown's squinty eyes narrowed even further. "We would like to know if you're related to a Mrs. Betty Lou Duet, formerly Betty Lou Brown."

"Betty Lou's my niece." Her leathery, tanned skin reminded me of pork rinds. I thought I might throw up. "Her mother was my sister, but they're all gone now. They're all *lates* . . . my husband, my sister."

I waited for her to say, "my niece," but she didn't.

"So . . . are you Mrs. Brown?"

"Heavens, no, I'm Mrs. Bernard."

Mac smiled, his white teeth flashing. "Your brother told me on the telephone that his sister was Mrs. Brown and that he lived here with her," Mac said.

Mrs. Bernard flashed her best false-teeth smile in return and waved her hand over her head as if swatting at insects. "Oh, he's always gettin' all kinda thangs mixed up. *Baby* was Mrs. Brown, our baby sister. She was married to Robert Brown, but all's left now is Brother and me," she said, "and we just do the best we can, helpin' each other along. We take care of this whole yard ourselves." Her face brightened around her blinding teeth. "We have oranges, bananas, and avocados." We all looked around. "This house belonged to Baby—that was my sister. I think I told you that. But when Baby passed, Brother and I took over. There's a lot to keep up." She sighed. "It's a lot for us."

"It's beautiful," Mac said. "Mrs. Bernard, would you mind if we came in and asked you a few questions?"

"We wanna know how Betty Lou died," Tim blurted, and then turned to Mac and me. "I think we should just get to the point."

"Well, somehow, this young man's got thangs confused," Mrs. Bernard said to Mac. Tim and I stared at each other. Mac returned Mrs. Bernard's romantic gaze. He knew she liked him. After all, she was female, even if she was close to eighty. We all knew he was the one who would be able to get the information we wanted. "You can come in, but only because Brother's here. He's my protector now," she said, motioning us into the house. "Are you really a doctor?" she asked Mac.

We all shook our heads in amazement as we walked into her home. I'd never seen so much green and pink in my life. Almost every picture frame, vase, and knickknack was a shade of either pink or green. It was everywhere. The carpet was bright green, the walls pale pink. Her house was like a piece of candy and we walked in, our heads turning from left to right like kids in a candy store, feeling as if nothing there could possibly hurt us.

Mac and I sat on the edge of a green bamboo love seat with pink rose-printed cushions, and Tim sat in the green vinyl recliner. "So what happened to ole Betty Lou?" Tim asked. We all stared at Mrs. Bernard, whose own health appeared questionable. I was glad there was a doctor in the house.

"When Baby, that's Betty Lou's mother, *my sister*, died, she asked me to look after Betty Lou. And I do." Her leathered chin rose with pride. "I march down there and see her every couple of weeks or so." As she spoke, I fell backwards, my head hitting the top of the rough bamboo frame. Mac jerked my arm, pulling me forward, making me dizzy. Mrs. Bernard stared at her feet as she spoke. "It's gettin' harder and harder, mind you. I'm gettin' too old for that sorta stuff."

"So she's alive, then?" Mac asked, squeezing my hand tighter than he ever had. I'm sure his grip was the only reason I didn't conk out from the shock. My eyes rolled twice, but his squeeze steadied them.

"Of course she is. She's only forty-somethin' years old. Of course she looks a lot older. Before Baby passed, she used to go on and on about how lovely Betty Lou used to be." Mrs. Bernard stared out the back window of her living room. "Betty Lou was Baby's only baby. I always said it wasn't good to have just one. I used to tell her she should have more. Me, I couldn't have any."

I sat speechless, listening to her knotty voice drone on. She looked at me and smiled. "You're her daughter, aren't you? That's the only reason I let you in here, of course. Well, that and because Brother's here."

My lips parted, but no sound came out. All I could think of was my father. Rather than focusing on the long-awaited facts Mrs. Bernard could provide, my mind was stuck back in Shreveport, back in my father's attic, back at the side of the swimming pool he'd built for me. Through Florida, Alabama, and across the Mississippi River, I could hear his cries. I could see his eyes searching for the clouds Betty Lou found, trying to make sense of his life. I could hear him saying, "Angel, I don't really know how she died."

"She's her daughter, isn't she?" Mrs. Bernard asked Tim and Mac when I didn't respond.

Mac squeezed my hand again. "Her father told her that her mother had passed."

"It might have been best that way, dear. Baby and her husband blamed your father for what happened, for her illness. They didn't want anythang to do with your father or you. Of course, you're innocent, but it was all just too painful. People can only handle so much. At least that's what we all thought back then. And of course, there was such talk. Baby just couldn't bear it."

"But why?" I asked. "Why did they blame him? What's wrong with her?"

"She's not right." Mrs. Bernard tapped her head. "She's not right at all."

"But why would that be my father's fault?"

"You'll have to ask him that. I don't know the whole story."

Tim leaned forward in the green recliner. "I think you're lyin'."

"How dare you call me a liar in my own home."

"Hey, I just tell it like it is, lady."

"What's goin' on in here?" an elderly man demanded from the front door. He stood blocking the sun for a full minute before moving into the house. Everyone had stood up by then. I realized I'd fallen. I couldn't seem to separate myself from the love seat. "Why'd you let these people in the house?" he asked Mrs. Bernard.

"They're relatives. Well, she is, Brother," she said, pointing at me. "She's Betty Lou's daughter, Angel."

"Betty Lou hasn't had any angels since 1965," he said, staring at me. "I'm gonna have to ask you all to leave."

"But, Brother, she's our relative."

"I don't care. She's somebody else's relative, too. The son-of-a-bitch who drove Betty Lou away."

She waved her hand over her head again. "Oh, don't listen to him," she told us. "He's always getting thangs mixed up."

"Are you blind, Sister? Look at all those freckles! You get them outta here or I'll throw 'em out. You know that's what Bob and Baby would have wanted."

"But she's innocent. None of it was her fault."

"What wasn't my fault?" I demanded. "I wanna know the truth." Brother stormed out of the room, hollering, "You better get 'em on outta here before I get back."

"We're a very close family," Mrs. Bernard said. "Well, we were when we were all here. When you get old, all your friends and loved ones start passin' on. After a while, you don't know what's worse: bein' the one who passes or the one left behind." She held out a white bowl filled with pink and green mints. "Would you like a mint, dear? It'll make you feel better." Tim reached for the bowl, but she suddenly pulled it back. "Wait!" she said, and then plucked out the only two yellow ones. She popped them into her mouth and Tim's hand was back, scooping up half the bowl. "I only like the pink and green." She smiled.

I didn't take a mint. "Please tell me where she is."

"I'll tell you how to get there, but I'm not tellin' you anythang else. You've gotta ask your father. He's the only one who can tell you. It's his responsibility. It always was. We all agreed on that, even Baby."

"He always says there's no answers to my questions."

"But she's tellin' you there are," Tim said. "You know that now. You've just gotta be brave enough to hear 'em, and he's gotta be brave enough to tell you."

"My father isn't very brave."

Mrs. Bernard said, "I think he is."

☑ snake

The next morning, Mac, Tim, and I drove toward the address provided by Mrs. Bernard. It was only the three of us, but I was beginning to fear that as long as Tim was around, Scarlett would be there, too. I thought that perhaps I should break my ties with Tim, but then realized it wasn't that easy. He was one of those people who stayed with you despite annoying behaviors or odd mannerisms. They slither beneath your skin, and however irritating the process may be, you end up feeling as if they'll always be there, as if they're part of you in a comforting way, like family.

But I wanted to forget Scarlett. I wanted to forget how she'd cut my hair, tossing it with complete abandon, and how she'd shown me that Christian was second best. She'd shown me a world that's hard to discount once you've walked its streets, tasted its wine, and reveled in its warm waters.

I looked at the back of Mac's head, hoping there were other streets to walk and wines to taste. I knew there had to be something more. Perhaps Scarlett had only shown me I was farther behind in finding it than I'd realized. Mac held his head steady when he drove, rarely taking his eyes off the road. I suddenly realized I hadn't heard him whistle at all. Not once had he whistled in Florida.

Mrs. Bernard hadn't bothered to tell us where we were headed, but we knew. It was an unspoken fact none of us brought up during the thirty-minute drive from Siesta Key. The closer we got, the further from Scarlett I felt. Betty Lou was just around the corner, and when I saw her, I was sure Scarlett would fade into the past, into a memory that would serve only as proof of my love for Betty Lou. But when we arrived at the Florida Sunshine Mental Health Care Facility, I began to have second thoughts. I smashed my shaking hands between my thighs. As Mac parked the car, I said, "I don't think I can go in." I pushed myself into the corner of the backseat and grabbed the door as if to keep it from opening. "If I go in there, I'll be sick. I know I will."

"What the hell are you talkin' about?" Mac asked without turning around. Instead, he stared into the rearview mirror. "You're goin' in there even if I have to carry you in."

"You've been pukin' your guts out since we got to Florida," Tim said. "Why are you so sick all the time, anyway?"

"I just need a little longer to get used to the idea of her bein' alive. Then maybe I can come back. I'll come back, and I'll get to know her then."

"I don't know if I'll ever be able to bring you back," Mac said. "Look, if I found out my dad was out there somewhere, I wouldn't hesitate to see him, even if it turned out he was a frickin' vegetable like my brother . . . so you're goin' in."

"But you *knew* your dad. He loved you, and he'd know you if he saw you again," I said, staring into the rear-view mirror. "I just don't feel so well."

"My dad was no bargain, believe me. He was a carpenter, basically a laborer, and that's what he did. He labored. He wasn't much for relationships." Mac's eyes dropped out of sight for a moment. "That's probably what fucked up my brother."

"So what about you?" Tim asked. "What happened to you?"

"I don't know. All I know is I swore that when I grew up I was gonna make a livin' with my mind, not my hands. Nobody's parents are perfect, no matter how much you want 'em to be."

"You didn't answer the part about relationships," Tim said. "How are you with that?"

Ignoring Tim, Mac spoke to me. "You can spend your whole life imaginin' how she would have been perfect, but she would have failed, somehow, at somethin'." He stared at me again in the rear-view mirror. "So you're goin' in there and facin' what you've got. Besides, you're gonna feel sick regardless."

"Will somebody please tell me what's goin' on here? Why are you so sick?"

"I'm pregnant," I said.

Tim's face exploded with the light his wide eyes provided. "No shit?"

"No shit," said Mac.

"Well, at least we know it's not Scarlett's," he said, snickering. "Is it yours?" he asked Mac.

I said, "It's Christian's."

"Mr. Boring's responsible?"

"What do you mean, it's not Scarlett's?" Mac asked. "Why would you say that?"

Tim looked at me with raised eyebrows. I wanted to give him an I'll-kill-you-if-you-tell look, but I didn't have the energy. "Let's just say Angel and Scarlett had a pretty good time together. If Scarlett was a guy, the possibility would definitely exist."

I got out of the car as fast as I could, but Mac followed. "You fooled around with Scarlett?" Tim stayed in the car. However, he rolled down the window enough to eavesdrop.

"I don't wanna talk about it, okay? It's nobody's business." I put my hand on my chest. "It's my business."

"When you climbed into Kimmy's hospital bed, I thought it was just a one-time thang. Trust me, I was only concerned about her health. I didn't care that you did it. I didn't think it meant you were gay." He leaned against the hood of his car, watching me pace. "I just tried to tell you that nobody's gonna replace your mother. I never realized you'd go as far as to sleep with somebody like Scarlett. What the hell were you thinkin'? You're not like that."

"I was thinkin' that I wanted to, that's all. Is that so hard to understand? She touched me, and it felt good, if you really wanna know." I stopped pacing and stood close to him, shoving my face up to his. "Do you wanna know more? Do you want the details?"

"Jesus Christ! What the hell's wrong with you? I care about you, and I'm afraid you're makin' mistakes you're gonna regret. Look, now you're pregnant with that borin' idiot's baby. At the very least, it ought to be mine. I told you that."

"Yeah, and now I'm in Florida with a married guy. Do you really think stayin' involved with you is the best thang for me?"

"This is a friendly arrangement. I'm helpin' you out as a friend."

"Is that really what you want it to be?" I asked. "You didn't want Tim to come. You know you didn't. Right?"

He refused to answer. Instead, he said, "You need to go in there and face your mother because despite her medical problems, she's still your mother. She's the one who took those photographs and the one you've been cryin' over since the day I met you. I'm not lettin' you come all this way just to walk away."

"Fine! Just get away from me, okay?"

"Fine," he said. Then he got back in the car and slammed the door.

"She's tough," I heard Tim say.

I leaned against Mac's car, staring at the place that had housed my mother while all the time I'd thought she'd been in heaven.

"You love her, don't you? You're in love with her," Tim said, laughing. He always laughed when he was sure he'd uncovered some buried truth.

"I love my wife," Mac said. "And stop laughin' or you might not have a mouth to laugh with."

"Oh, I'm *so* afraid," Tim said, still laughing. "You are so cool, you know? You think you have your whole life figured out. You think you can have it any way you want. I just think it's funny, that's all."

"Well, I don't. And you're wrong. I don't have shit figured out."

Tim had forgotten that the window was down, and Mac didn't know. I strained to listen.

"So where is that wife of yours? How do you get away with the shit you pull, anyway?"

"I love my wife," was all Mac said. He started to get back out of the car when Tim said, "Hey, Dr. Mac! You know why the truth is so delicate and valuable? It's because everybody hoards it." Mac slammed the door.

He put his solid arms around me, hugging me for a long time. Then he put his hands on my shoulders and turned me toward the clinic. "Just walk toward that door. When you reach it, it's gonna open and you're gonna find somethin' you've been lookin' for a long time. I don't think many people get that chance."

"Don't be afraid!" Tim hollered from the car. "Seek the truth!"

"Yeah, seek the truth," Mac said. His eyes moved in his head as if he was trying to understand something himself. And for the first time, I considered that maybe there were no doors after all. Maybe when you look for a man's door, you create it. You create the door that shuts you out. I looked past him and focused on the door I could see. "I might be awhile," I said.

"Don't worry, maybe I can finally talk him out of his recreational activities," he said, motioning toward his Corvette.

Maybe he can do the same for you, I thought, as I walked toward the door to *mother*.

* * *

"Excuse me," I said to the receptionist. "I was told that my mother, Betty Lou Duet, lives here."

The lady studied me, considering what to say next.

"I'm here to see her."

"Please have a seat, and I'll get her doctor. You'll need to talk to him first."

The receptionist returned with a tall, thin doctor. His face was handsome but a bit pinched. "Hello, I'm Dr. Angus," he said, extending his hand. "I hear you've come to see Betty Lou."

☑ turtle

Dr. Angus stood just outside the door to Betty Lou's room. His eyes gave the final push I needed. They fixated on me as if waiting to see the number on which the dice would land. He'd shaken me up with an hourlong speech about expectations and love and mental illness. Then he walked me down the long hospital corridor toward her room and tossed me in. I knew he was waiting to see what would happen, probably holding his breath. He'd waited for years, knowing that eventually I would surface.

What happened in the months leading to that moment and in the weeks following was not a coming of age. It was an awakening. The life my father had built was a circus shrouded in fog. And as the fog began to lift, what was once a hazy joy town quickly filled with trash and liars. I stood very still in front of the door, there in the Florida sunshine, preparing to see my mother and face that tragic circus. The air had begun to clear months earlier in the Ag Center fields, in Mac's apartment, and in my father's secret attic. But when I actually saw her face, I would look upon the liars and the trash, the contrived thrills. No one wants to see it that way. We want to keep our foundation intact. Our anchors. The stories.

"Who's there?" she said without moving from the corner in which she cowered, face to the wall. The bleak room seemed to envelop her slight figure. Varicose veins created a map down each thin, bleached leg. Her short, white robe merged with the white walls around her. Dull blond hair hung over her shoulders, hiding the sides of her face and her neck. The back of her hair was matted, but the curls were there, struggling to rise.

"It's me," I said, barely able to speak. "Angel."

She turned to face me and a broad smile grew, as if painful, across her haggard face. Instead of the smile I knew from photographs, it was but an afterthought. I was staring at leftovers, but my belly-swelling hunger gave me the strength to remain standing, hoping she could satisfy me. I needed more.

"Betty Lou Brown," she finally said, looking at the ceiling. She sighed. "You have found me."

My heart hurt.

Glancing back at Dr. Angus, I read his lips. "Don't be scared," he said, motioning me forward.

"No, it's Angel," I said, stepping closer. "I found you. You're Betty Lou Duet. Brown was your maiden name."

She smoothed her hair as if embarrassed, and then said, "Yes, Betty Lou Brown is gone. I almost forgot," while shuffling over to look in the flimsy fake mirror bolted to the wall. She touched her sharp cheek, unhappy with her distorted reflection. The beauty she had once possessed had left her hollow-eyed, thin, and saggy. "If I hadn't been born so beautiful, I wouldn't have been so tempted," she said, speaking like a sane person. "I wouldn't have wanted so much." Then her voice changed and she spun to face me. "But Angel's gone, too. She's dead. Cain't you see her on the floor there? I cain't look." She stared at the ceiling, avoiding me. "I cut her arms and she's just lyin' there. Look!" she yelled.

I stepped back. The odd, barely there scars on my arms began to ache.

"Blood keeps flowin' down that there creek," she said, her southern accent suddenly more pronounced. "There's a sign by the bridge—1968, it says." She looked at me then, her eyes staring without recognition. "It's nothin' but a bloody creek. It's gonna pull you in." She smiled weakly. "I know what I'm talkin' about."

I tried to see. I tried to understand, but the only creek I found was formed from the tears running between her premature wrinkles. The tiny streams spilled over the sharp edges of her cheeks. And there wasn't just one or two. There were enough to fill an ocean.

An ocean called Frank.

And one called Angel.

My father's lies had been for her. She was all around us like a choking sea. "But it's 1988 now," I said, trying to remain calm. "January 1988."

"I just fell in." She stood still, listening, but not to me. "I mean it. Angel was cryin' just a couple minutes ago." Her voice floated away, and I knew I'd found much more than I could handle. "I forged that creek," she said as if I'd understand.

I stood, transfixed by her melodrama, and watched as she moved to the edge of her small bed. Grabbing a quilt that looked twenty years old, she rolled it into a ball and cradled it in her arms like a baby. She rocked it back and forth as a yellow puddle grew around her bare feet. The urine smell caused me to gag, and I ran to the sink and waited to vomit. I wiped my mouth as I cried out of guilt. I wanted her to know it was all precious: her matted hair, her flight across the room, her demons, her urine. I cried for the death that was there after all.

"No, it's me," I said then, moving nearer. But she stood frozen, almost catatonic. "I'm here." I wanted to touch her but was afraid she might crumble. Instead, I stepped into her urine puddle. Only then did her empty eyes search mine until I saw a hint of recognition, dark and frosty. "I've finally found you," I said.

"But how did you get here? Who brought you back?" she asked, her face ethereal, as if she wasn't seeing me at all, but rather glimpsing heaven. "Tell me how you got here."

I reached out, but before my arms could surround her, she stomped her foot and urine splattered my legs.

Within seconds, Dr. Angus's breath filled my ear. He whispered that I should go. That it was too much for one day. His hand was on my back.

"But she seems all right," I said, resisting his gentle push. "She knows me. I think she knows me."

"Actually, my concern is for you." His hand went to my shoulder, pushing harder, and feeling as if my whole life had suddenly become too much, I allowed him to lead me away from what I'd thought would be the end of my search. "I'll show you where the bathroom is," he said.

I just want *mother*, I thought.

"She's not gonna respond to you appropriately," Dr. Angus said. "You have to understand that. Remember, schizophrenics have, at the same time, a block and a continual flow in their expression."

"I don't really understand." My head shook too much, and I knew then that it had become a habit.

"She thinks autistically, but not all the time. In other words, she has thought processes not used in conscious, awake minds like yours and mine, but rather the kind of thought found in dreams or in very small children. She sees the world differently than you and I."

I knew about dreams. "But do you think she's happy?"

"She hasn't smiled like that since I've been here. I think that says a lot."

"So you think she really remembered me?"

"She remembers the Angel she met once upon a time, an Angel that made her happy." He squeezed my shoulder like a father would his son's. "She talks about it a lot."

"What did she mean about a creek? She said she forged a creek."

"She's talkin' about blood."

"What blood?" I asked but wasn't sure if I wanted an answer.

He shook his head as if deciding not to tell me. "It's all very complicated."

We stopped and stood outside the ladies' room. "I wanna help her," I said. An orderly dressed in white carried a mop and bucket into Betty Lou's room while someone far away screamed as if dying.

Dr. Angus didn't seem concerned. "Honestly, I think she can help you more than you can help her."

Then I heard her voice. It traveled through the sterile corridor, the voice of a dead woman calling from beyond a grave too shallow to hold her. A strange power, generated by her ability to see things none of us could imagine, carried it past the other voices. "Angel," she screamed. "Angel!" Her voice flooded my brain like the lullaby I'd never heard, multiplied by her absence, magnified by her madness.

I wanted to save her.

Suddenly, I was exhausted. And there he was again. Darwin. From my side of the frozen river between us, I could see his hair waving over his forehead. I wanted to sweep the chunky curls aside so I could see his eyes. But I couldn't reach across. He wanted me to join him on the other side, but every time I considered stepping in, I saw cracks, like wrinkles in the ice, and I was scared shitless. The only time I saw that frozen river with open eyes were the times my father's face had collapsed at the mention of her name. I think Carla had seen it, too. It made her angry, and in those moments, I feared we were all slowly drowning.

Darwin was like my father. Weak. And Carla knew but she stayed.

* * *

I woke in Dr. Angus' arms. Nurses, orderlies, and crazy people with Betty Lou faces surrounded us, creating a mountain range of white garb.

"Are you okay?" he asked, helping me to my feet.

"I have narcolepsy," I said, watching as the orderly carried the bucket containing Betty Lou's urine from her room. I wondered where he'd pour it out. I thought of how my childhood friends sometimes used the bathroom after their mothers and then flushed it all down together, how their mothers changed their diapers.

"Why didn't you tell me? You're well aware of the stress involved in this situation." He grabbed my wrist to check my pulse. "I spent a full hour with you. You should have told me about this."

"It's not life threatenin'," I said. "If you wanna know the truth, I usually try to pretend I don't have it."

He didn't look happy. "You should probably call your father."

"He doesn't know I'm here," I whispered. "Nobody does. They think I'm at Disney World," I said, smoothing down my shirt. I ran my hands over my hips. Within a few months, if Dr. Angus saw me, he'd assume I'd gotten chubby, or he might suddenly decide that I had an odd shape.

Nobody expected me to be pregnant.

"How old are you, Angel?"

I'd told him twice already. "Twenty-one," I said. "Actually, I didn't come all the way here by myself."

"Aren't you on medication?"

"Not anymore," I said, trying not to look him in the eye.

"Well, I'm sorry, but I have very limited knowledge of narcolepsy. It's not my specialty. Betty Lou Duet's my specialty." He winked, and I felt a little better.

The crowd had dispersed with the exception of an odd man who lingered too close. Dr. Angus ignored him, but I couldn't. "Angel, a lot of people seek the truth, but as some get close, they forget their humanity. They turn into animals. They attack or back away or some-times they just stick their head in the sand and expect it to go away. They find out the real truth is that they really didn't want to know that much after all." The odd man began to cry. "Reality isn't always pleasant. But I think you know that already."

Remembering the dried urine splattered across my legs, I suddenly felt dirty. "Why does life have to be so sad?" I asked as I pushed my way through the bathroom door.

☑ umbrella

Dr. Angus walked with me back to Mac's car. It was a long, quiet stroll. Far in the distance, a flock of birds flew toward us. First a gray blur, they darkened, multiplying into hundreds once overhead. Their loyalty struck me as odd. They instinctually stayed together, traveling wherever their current leader wished to go. The leader's motivation wasn't questioned. I wondered if those in the rear even knew where they were headed.

"Will you be back to see us?" Dr. Angus asked.

I couldn't answer. I didn't know. Part of me wanted to stay. I wanted to go back and stay with her as long as it took to find the woman who'd taken the photographs in my father's foyer. I stared up into the belly of the flock. They moved fast and furious above my head as I walked slow and steady to Mac's car, realizing how small and confined my life was going to be. I'd lost my leader. I'd gained the sense to ask where he was headed and why. I didn't want to follow blindly anymore, yet I also knew I needed him. I didn't know how to get anywhere on my own.

I was disabled.

Dr. Angus looked up and chuckled. "I hope they don't get us," he said.

I didn't care if they *got* me. My mother just peed on me. The birds were peanuts. As we approached the car, I said, "I don't understand why my father lied about all this." The birds were gone, again a gray blur in the distance.

"I'm sure he had a good reason. You and your father have a lot of issues to address." He put his hand on my shoulder. "Are you gonna be all right?"

Mac and Tim got out of the car. Tim scurried over to us, asking, "Is she all right?"

"We'll take care of her," Mac said. "I'm a doctor, and we're her friends."

"Are you her neurologist, by any chance?"

"No, just a friend," Mac said, staring off into the bird-infested distance. He was amazed, like me, at how fast they came and went. I think he realized how lucky I was that the shit didn't hit me. He thought I cared. "I'm in emergency medicine, but I'm familiar with her condition."

"Well, that's good," Dr. Angus said, shaking Mac's hand. "It's gonna take her awhile to adjust to all this. It's not easy for anybody."

"We'll take care of her," Tim said, opening the car door. As I got in, I heard him say, "Surely, this doesn't happen too often. How many crazy people do you have stashed in there that nobody knows about?" The door closed. I didn't hear the answer.

I slept on the way back to the hotel. Then I slept in the hotel. I couldn't stop sleeping. "The doctor did say she needed rest," I heard Tim say.

He also said, "Her dad's a dick."

I heard them laughing.

* * *

"Angel?" Mac's voice entered my dreams, sounding like Scarlett. "You've gotta get up and get movin'. We gotta leave tomorrow mornin'." He sat next to me on the edge of the bed, weighing it down. "We cain't stay anymore."

"I cain't," I whined, turning away. "I don't wanna leave." I pulled the hotel blanket over my head, but he pulled it back down, exposing the top half of me. The chemical smell of the blanket followed by the splash of cool air woke me a little more.

"You cain't sleep forever." He leaned over and brushed my coarse hair away from my face. "I know it's temptin', but it won't change anythang."

"But it will," I whispered. "When I sleep . . . in my dreams, I don't have narcolepsy." He leaned down close to my face to hear. His smell reminded me of our nights in his on-call room at the hospital, but then I remembered how it felt lying next to Scarlett. "And Betty Lou's there, in my dreams, and she's not dead and she's not crazy." I was almost awake. "She's just there, in the flesh. She touches me, and I feel it. My dreams are like that, Scarlett," I said, confused. "People touch me and I feel it."

"But it's been two days," he said, his voice sweet. "We cain't stay. We're goin' back to Shreveport. They're expectin' us."

"In my dreams, there's no Shreveport. There's only home, and it doesn't look like that place at all."

"There are worse places to live."

"Your wife's there," I said, realizing again that it was Mac above me, not Scarlett.

"Maybe we *should* stay here." He stroked my forehead. "But that's where we live. You have to go back and deal with your dad, and I have to go back and deal with my wife. Those are the facts."

"My facts are all different now." I wanted him to kiss me. "But I guess yours haven't changed."

"You have to go back," he said, looking as if he wanted to deal with his wife. "It cain't be helped."

"I wanna go somewhere else but I cain't 'cause I'm practically crippled and 'cause I thought Betty Lou was dead and now she's alive and every single thang I knew isn't right." Tears dribbled down my face. "Nothin's right. It's not fair. And don't give me that lecture on not feelin' sorry for myself, because I've got reason." He wiped my face with the edge of the sheet and helped me to sit up. "Where's Tim?" I asked, looking around the room.

"He's in the shower."

I smiled weakly. I wanted him to pull me into that embrace large enough to hold both of us, me *and* his wife. I wanted that kiss. I reached for him, but as he got close, I went stiff. It was a rigidity that came without thought. It came from that smell of urine on her floor and vomit in her sink. Mac felt it and released me. "I'm sorry," I said. "I should be thankful. Shouldn't I be happy she's not dead?"

"Yes, I think you should be happy." He smiled and moved closer. I wondered if he thought we were back together. Did he remember that I was pregnant? "You know, Angel," he said, "I've always thought that bein' a doctor would make me feel better, that it was a way that I could do somethin' right. And I've always known that most of my friends became doctors to make other people feel better, not themselves." He looked away. "I don't know what to do for you now, and I wish I did."

I held his hand. "I don't think there's anythang you can do."

"I think you're wrong. I think my friends who became doctors to help other people would know exactly what to do." He kept wiping my eyes with the sheet, soaking up the tears as they popped out. "I'll always be your friend, if you'll let me." I wondered how he could continue being my friend when his wife was at home waiting for him. "And I'll always be honest. Don't listen to Tim when he says I'm not. He doesn't know me."

"You wanna be more than friends. I know what motivates you. And I don't wanna be a sympathy case," I said, wondering how I could trust him. If I couldn't trust my father, an insidious cheater, how could I trust a man who cheated openly? My father cheated by twisting the love I had for him and my mother to suit his purpose. He'd kept her healthy by killing her. He'd used me to perpetuate his life with her. If he'd cared about me, he would have protected me from this day, this reality, by giving it to me in little doses all along. He would have told me where he was headed.

Mac said, "I cain't believe you're questionin' my motivation. If I just wanted sex, I could get it from anybody. You think I'd risk everythang to bring you here? Trust me, there are others who'd come forward in a heartbeat if they knew I was on the market." His look shifted to smug. "Hell, they come forward anyway." It was true.

"Why would you choose me? Is that what you were gonna say?"

He didn't answer.

"Do you love her?" I asked. "How can you love her and be here with me, even as a friend? She doesn't even know you're here. You're hidin' it from her. You're lyin', and I'm sick of lies."

"I don't know," he said. "I thought I loved her." He lay back across the bed, and I shifted over to make room for him.

"Well, I thought my mother was dead, and she's not. But she's still gone. Don't lie to yourself about your wife *or* me. I still don't have a mother, and my dad . . ." I couldn't finish. My eyes fluttered, tired again.

Mac turned toward me, putting his hand on my hipbone. "I'd be your mother *and* your father if I could. I know you don't believe me, but it's true." He rubbed my stomach as he spoke. I closed my eyes, and he was Scarlett again, because she would say something like that. Scarlett showed me *mother*, I thought. But Mac couldn't possibly be a mother or a father, not for me, anyway. Not yet.

"I gotta wake up," I said, realizing that I was still not functioning, that I was mixing people up, losing track of who was really there, who was telling the truth, who was lying, who was leading, and who was following.

But he was quiet, so I didn't move. I stared at the ceiling, imagining my life was a giant clay pot, filled to the brim with soil. My father watered it with his tears, but nothing grew. I held the soil together as if that was the objective—as if what he'd given me could make something beautiful grow. But I was wrong. The pot was empty. I was empty. Nothing could grow. My father's lie about the death of my mother had poisoned the soil from the start. His sorrow had nothing to do with love, but with shame. "What am I gonna say to him?" I asked. "Maybe I shouldn't tell him. Maybe I should just be like him and lie for the rest of my life. Maybe I should be like you." I stared at the ceiling. I heard

Tim get out of the shower. Even the air around me felt dishonest, thick with Mac's smell. "And Carla . . . how could she know? I don't think she knows." For the first time, I felt sorry for her.

* * *

The only reason I got out of bed was to shower. I felt dirty. I'd slept for thirty-six hours. My hair was flat and itchy, and the sheets were damp with sweat. After I cleaned up, Tim and I decided to take a walk out to the beach while Mac called his wife. It was hot and wet because it had just rained. The rain dried beneath our bare feet as we moved toward the Gulf.

"It sure does dry up fast here," Tim said.

"It does in Shreveport, too."

"Yeah, but it's different here," he said, looking around. "I guess it's less humid. In Shreveport, it looks dry, but it's all around you . . . in the air, you know?"

"I guess," I said, looking out into the rippling tide.

"Don't you wish we could just sail away?" Tim asked. He'd read my mind.

"Why would *you* wanna sail away? I thought you always liked your rut and all that."

He picked up a shell and tossed it into the water. It barely made it in. "I have reasons, but I'm not gonna complain about my family right now, not with what you're goin' through. It wouldn't be right."

"You can tell me. I don't care."

He shook his head and bent down to pick up another shell.

"I'd like to know," I said. "I don't mean to be nosy. It just seems like everybody else's life is perfect right now compared to mine."

He sat down and began burying his feet in the sand. "Well, that's pretty far from the truth. Nobody's life or family is perfect. Not to make light of your current situation." His face looked so sad that I thought he must be right. Then I felt grateful to him for taking Betty Lou off my mind for a moment. I wanted to pretend that she only existed as my father described her and that he was back home crying over the tragedy of her death, not her life.

"Do you think it's possible to be gay and have a fairly perfect life?" I asked. "Is that what you want?"

"I want it, sure, but I don't know if it's possible."

"Because people tease you, is that it?"

"Because my family doesn't know I'm gay."

I was surprised.

"They don't know about Scarlett or Rhett, either," he said. "We only know about each other. The teasin' doesn't bother me. When I was in high school, it bothered me that I couldn't talk to my mom about it. She's so tender-hearted. It was temptin', you know?"

"Then why cain't you tell her? I cain't believe you haven't told your family when it seems like all you do is go around preachin' about bein' truthful." It made me angry, another liar for the flock. "Maybe she already knows, somehow."

"I guess I'm a hypocrite after all." He grabbed the sand in big scoops and poured it over his ankles.

"Well, I guess you cain't *always* be truthful," I said. "Not every second."

"Why not? Why cain't I? Why couldn't your dad? I don't think it's fair. I lie awake in bed at night thinkin' about it."

I sat down in the sand next to him and dug my feet into the beach, but I didn't feel like burying them. Instead, I helped him bury his. "I think maybe you can be truthful about just about anythang, but the time has to be right."

"How can you say that after comin' here? After bein' lied to like that? I truly believe that if you put it out there, right on the table, no matter what time it is, people will be forced to set their clocks by it. You know what I mean?"

"What's your mother really like?" I asked. "If she's so nice, why cain't you talk to her about your feelin's?"

"Well, I don't think a person can realize what's really good and bad about where they came from until they go someplace else. I'm in Shreveport and that ain't too far, but it's enough. In Hope, people are so nice it makes you wanna puke. Their niceness kind of hovers around 'em like a force field or a big box that cain't be penetrated. Even if they see you for who you really are, warts and all, that box keeps 'em at arm's length. Even if they take a person in who doesn't fit their description of proper or appropriate, the kindness they show is for *their* benefit, not the other poor soul's." I thought of Mac and why he'd become a doctor. "Somehow they never let you forget their charity. It's a racket, you know?"

"But the poor soul benefits, right?"

"Not when the poor soul is their son, or when the person knows exactly what's goin' on. None of it's real." His feet were completely buried.

"I understand why you're resentful, but you cain't stick your head in the sand and pretend it's not an issue, right?" I stared at the sand covering his feet. "Isn't that what I'm supposed to be avoidin'?"

"I'm not a frickin' ostrich, and I'm not really resentful, not yet, anyway." He pulled his feet out and flared his toes. He dug the sand out from between them. "One day I'll be so goddamn resentful, my guts will split just hearin' my mother's voice. I can feel it growin'."

I thought of the attic weeds my father created. "But if you see it comin', why don't you stop it? Nobody wants to feel that way." I didn't want to feel that way but decided it was too late for me. I hadn't seen it coming.

"It cain't be stopped. It's psychology." He shrugged his shoulders, so accepting of it that I wondered if he were trapped in some kind of box himself. "That's life."

I could feel my own box tight around me with only my unborn child inside. I put my hand on my belly, glad it was there and that I wasn't alone. The baby was the best thing happening. It didn't matter what people said or what they might say. It gave me hope, blind faith that perhaps I could find a way out of all the lies. I could have my own little family and do it right. "Don't you think people in Shreveport live in boxes, too?" I asked.

"Probably. But at least there's a little more diversity. One day I think I'll move somewhere else. I'll always love certain thangs about Shreveport and Hope, but I don't think I'll wanna be there in the end."

I didn't think he would either. "Well, you're lucky you can make that choice," I said, standing up, ready to go. I reached out to him. He took my hand, and I pulled him up out of the sandy rut he'd created.

"You shouldn't give up," he said. "I'm not. Even if I am a hypocrite right now, I won't always be."

We headed back to the hotel. "Well, it sounds like you've given up on Hope, anyway. You never know, maybe one day your mother will be somewhere else."

"Maybe you'll be somewhere else."

"Some things *are* hopeless," I said.

"Bullshit," he yelled back into the gulf. "Bullshit!"

Just before we reached the hotel, I asked him if he thought I was gay and he said no.

*   *   *

Once inside, I dialed my father's number. Carla answered. "Hello," she said.

Tim sat in the cheap vinyl chair by the window and Mac sat on the bed next to me. "Carla, it's me, Angel."

"I recognize your voice."

"Oh, well, I'm callin' 'cause I didn't go to Disney World. But I *am* in Florida." I paused and Mac put his hand on my shoulder. "I came to find my mother."

Silence.

"Carla, she's alive. Don't tell Dad, but I found her."

☑ vehicle

Back in Shreveport, falling asleep beneath my canopy, I wished I hadn't stuffed my Holly Hobbie bedspread in the trash. I was cold and wished my prairie friends were there, holding me close as if nothing had changed. Of course, not having them didn't keep me from sleeping. I was tired, and it was more than just the narcolepsy. It was the pregnancy and the lies and the truth all weighing me down, pushing me into that shell of a bed.

I managed to make almost all my classes but slept through the rest of my life.

Months passed.

Then one day, as I was sleeping, someone decided to pull me out. Strong hands tugged and nails dug in until I was hanging on the edge. At first I imagined they were Holly's nails. All those tiny girls had come to life, joining forces to drag me out. But then even stronger arms nearly lifted me. Partly, I lifted myself. I should have known it wasn't them. After all, Holly Hobbie isn't real. And even if she had been, she was gone now, gone like the mother I thought I'd lost.

It was Carla, dragging me out of my bed and through the house. But I was in too deep and couldn't wake myself. I struggled to grasp what she was saying and where she was taking me, but the voices of those in my dream overpowered hers. The dream was good, and I didn't want it to end. I wanted to stay and pretend it was real. Betty Lou was there, and Mac, and Darwin. They were all there except my father.

But she continued to pull me out. "Angel?" I heard her call through the tunnel running between my dreams and reality. "Angel!"

"Leave me alone," I whined, though allowing her to drag me toward the front door. "I don't wanna go. I'm tired."

"Wake up!" she hollered in my ear. "Wake up! I'm not gonna let you sleep your goddamn life away."

Startled, I said, "What?" as she shoved me through the door.

It was a warm March day. The sun stung my eyes, and I stopped to rub them, trying to wake up.

"March!" she said, pushing me toward the driveway. "March!"

I lowered myself into her car, still wondering what she was trying to do to me, but it wasn't long before I conked out again, safe in the dream she wanted to kill. But then the car stopped and the horn blasted. "What are you doin'?" I asked, covering my ears. "Are you crazy?"

"I'm honkin' so they'll know we're here. Look, I'll admit I'm pretty tough, but I'm not strong enough to get you up there," she said, referring to the three-story building facing us. It was the sleep clinic. The stairs were outside the large building, looking more like a hotel than a medical facility. "Only in America would they put a sleep clinic on the third story." She rolled her eyes. "Don't they know you people are tired? They're askin' for a lawsuit, if you ask me."

"Why don't you tell 'em, then?"

"Maybe I will," she said, looking smug.

I lowered the visor and peeked in the mirror to see how bad I looked. "Why did you bring me here?" I asked. "Why do you care how much I sleep?" I looked like shit.

"I know you haven't been takin' your medication. It's gonna catch up with you, you know. You've worked pretty hard." She paused and then said, "That Darwin paper you wrote was good, Angel. It was extremely well-written."

"It's none of your business. How many times do I have to say that?" Up on the third floor, two nurses began making their way down the stairs. "I don't need them," I said. "I can walk up myself. I'm not a cripple."

"Yes, you are. You are because you think you are, and I'm sick of it. You know, Angel, a disability does not make a cripple. A cripple is someone who allows their disability to rule their life. You're lettin' your narcolepsy rule. Actually, I'm not so sure that narcolepsy is your biggest disability. There are other kinds of disabilities—aside from physical. You have absolutely no appreciation for the good luck you have."

"So you think I have a 'lack of appreciation' disability?" I asked. "Are you talkin' about me? I'm lucky? My mother is crazy, and my dad's a liar. I have narcolepsy, and it's not goin' away." I looked down. "And I've got other thangs you don't even know about."

"Your life is filled with gifts you cain't even see."

I rolled my eyes.

"Well, okay then," she said, "why don't you tell me the rest of the sob story? What's stoppin' you?"

"It's none of your business." She was larger than me in more ways than one, and I felt cornered. I wondered if I should just get out before our conversation grew deeper, pulling me into something I couldn't escape.

"Look, just stop it right now," she said. "You're my business because your father's my business. He obviously has some thangs to deal with and isn't givin' you what you need. I'm tryin' to help both of you. I've told you, you both gotta relearn your ABCs. I'm not gonna stand by when I know I can teach you, at least to some degree. I know my ABCs, Angel, and I didn't learn 'em the easy way."

A wave of sleepiness washed over me. I struggled, trying not to let it pull me under. The ways in which Carla was so together, so adult, made me tired. They sapped the energy I tried so hard to reserve for trying to be an adult. I didn't buy her story about learning things the hard way. A lot of people say that. Everybody thinks they learned the hard way. Carla was like the blind man who couldn't perceive color.

She was a *mothered* child. I was sure she had no idea what loneliness really felt like . . . that big hole I knew so well, the one that kept growing larger, large enough to house all the crippled and the motherless in the world.

She sat, stone-faced, waiting for a response. I stared back, suddenly wishing she were my mother. I looked away because the thought of it salted my wound. But then I thought of the baby, inside with my wound. I knew it would bring *mother*. The baby was the only one who could shrink the hole.

But I'd still be crippled.

"You're not perfect," I finally said.

"I didn't say that," she replied before opening the door to get out and talk to the approaching nurses. They all three looked at me, slumped down inside the car, and then turned and began the trek back up. When Carla got back in the car, she said, "Now, please just go up and see the doctor. Please get back on your medication and stop actin' like you've got no reason to stay awake."

"You know what I don't get?" I asked. "I don't see how you're even still with him. He's not even divorced. At least, I don't think he is."

"He's not. I checked." She looked pleased with herself, but a little sad, too. "I know how to find out thangs like that."

I turned toward her, thinking that I'd like to see her pain just to know she was human after all. "Well, doesn't that tick you off or hurt you, even just a little?"

She ran her hands over the steering wheel and stared out the window. Then she said, "I stay because I love him. That's what love is. It's taken me a long time to learn that. I was a very lonely, sad person for most of my life, Angel." Her face changed, just for a moment, and I thought of Tim and Scarlett and Kimmy and how they all had something that made them sad.

But they're not like me, I thought.

"It's only been in the last ten years or so that I've been happy," she said. "Nothin' I feel now, nothin' that comes along makes me as lonely or as sad as I once was. This is peanuts. It's real, and it's important, but it's peanuts."

"What got you so happy?" I honestly wanted to know.

Her hands dropped to her lap and she began to tug on a loose thread hanging from her shirt. The thread changed her. She didn't normally have hanging threads or snags or pantyhose runners. It wasn't like her. But then I decided she must have always had them. She was just skilled at keeping others from seeing them—she found them first. "It was just a strange sequence of events that landed me on the upswing, somehow," she finally said. "Somehow I grew up into a different person. It's hard to explain, really."

"Well, that's a little evasive, especially for someone who's tryin' to get me to spill my guts."

"Okay, I'll tell you how I got my wakeup call. I had some personal trouble in law school and didn't handle it quite right because I wanted to finish school. Nothin' was gonna stop me, you know? Then, within a couple of years, I realized I'd made a mistake I couldn't take back."

"What?" I asked. "Did you get pregnant or something?" I asked because, in a way, I wanted to talk about it. I wanted her to know that *I* was pregnant. It wasn't the only hint I'd dropped, but neither she nor my father had noticed. Nobody noticed because nobody expected me to be pregnant. Girls at school joked about the color of pregnant brides' wedding dresses and even a teacher had joked about a girl's father coming after a guy with a rifle because he'd gotten his daughter pregnant. At first I felt sorry for those people. I thought they'd feel bad about what they'd said in front of me once they realized I was an unwed mother. Then I got angry because I knew they'd forget. They'd forget that I'd been there, listening, just like they conveniently forgot about me when I was splayed out on the floor or sitting at a cafeteria table with my face in my food.

Carla finally released the thread, looked up, and said, "You're very smart, Angel. There are some thangs in life that can never be recaptured. You have to be careful about those thangs, like lovin' someone and your health and your youth . . . the choices you make."

I was stunned. I lost my sarcastic edge. We actually had something in common, but it was something I didn't want to share. I was over six months along and still able to hide it, but soon I'd be exposed. "You had an abortion?"

"No, I didn't get the chance. A guy hit me in the stomach. He hit me, and I miscarried. It was just some guy, rollerskatin' down the street . . . on campus. I think the father of the baby hired him to do it, but I couldn't prove anythang. He said it was an accident . . . a roller-skatin' accident." She shifted, clearly uncomfortable. "I learned a lot about myself and other people . . . men, I guess, at that time."

At least Christian wouldn't do that, I thought. "Well, you're lucky you had a mother and an honest father," was all I could think to say. And I meant it. I meant it to make her feel better.

"Oh, get over it," she said, misunderstanding. "You *do* have a mother. Your father just couldn't bear to tell you she was in such bad condition. You're bein' selfish, if you ask me."

"I didn't ask," I said, sarcastic again, but didn't forget what she said. I wouldn't forget.

I wasn't even sure why I was waiting, why I didn't just break down, tell her I was pregnant, and let the two of us have that in common. I wanted things in common but couldn't bring myself to let it happen. But waiting wasn't going to change the facts. Eventually we'd have that thing in common.

I wondered if not telling made me a liar like my father. I opened the door and headed for the clinic. I was ready to tell the doctor. Carla was right. I didn't need to sleep so much. I had plans to make.

* * *

Kimmy's small trailer was still laced with Christmas lights. I was sure that during the holidays, in the dark, they'd made the tiny home bear-able, somehow quaint and inviting, but in the March sun they hung dirty and inappropriate. The trailer was so small it made Kimmy's parents look even bigger. Her mother let me in and then dropped back into her spongy chair. She and Kimmy's father sat, side-by-side, in matching recliners that filled their tiny living room. There wasn't one for Kimmy, and as I walked through, I wondered where she sat. The trailer was dark except for the faint light from the small covered windows. I wasn't surprised that they were the types who sat in the dark during the day. All I could see was their faces, their chairs, and their clutter. Junk was piled everywhere, even on the floor. Again not surprisingly, Kimmy's room was the neatest spot in the trailer.

I almost didn't recognize her. She'd lost at least twenty pounds and her hair was short, practically buzzed. She touched her head as I walked in the door. The tiny room made her seem bigger, too, but not large like she was before. She had changed. The strength she'd gained made her larger. She had catapulted out of her rut. Now, propped up in her bed, she was a new person.

Her light was on.

We were both new but she was better. I was still in the dark stage of my change, like the black of her coma. It was too soon to tell what would happen to me, but I was glad for her. She finally looked twenty-six.

"It's growin'," she said, referring to her chopped hair. "It was all shaved." She smiled, and I wondered how such a bad thing had turned out to be good. Looking at her, seeing her changed, told me it was good.

"I'm sorry, Kimmy," I said, sitting on the end of her bed. It was too soft, and as I sat, she seemed to lift, rising above me, making me feel small in comparison.

"For what?"

"Because I stopped comin' by. My life just got . . . complicated, I guess. Tim kept askin' me to come. He's a good friend." I thought of our trip to Florida and how he'd watched me throw up. "I've never been the greatest friend, but it doesn't mean I haven't thought about you. I have, and I'm sorry."

Magazines were piled around her, and she began to stack them. "Tim thinks it was his fault."

"Do you think it was?"

"No, and I'll still go there again. I'll just be more careful, that's all, more attentive to what's goin' on around me next time. That's how you avoid this kinda thang. If I'd been payin' better attention, I would have seen it comin'."

"You're brave," I said, looking down because I didn't want her to see that I was upset. If I'd paid more attention, I wouldn't be pregnant, I thought.

Before I could change my mind, I told her about it. I told her about Christian and the Ecstasy, about hitting my head on The Blue Flower pavement, and about how he hated me now. I told her everything except the part about finding Betty Lou.

She gave my leg a motherly pat. "What are you gonna do?" she asked, concerned. I wished I could move closer. I wished I could snuggle up next to her and pretend again.

Instead, I said, "I think I'm gonna quit workin' at the hospital. That's the first thang."

"But won't you need your job, especially now?"

"I'll still be livin' with my dad," I said, wishing I didn't have to, or that I had a choice. "He'll help me."

"Did he say that? Did you talk to him? I knew a girl in high school who got pregnant and her parents kicked her out. And she didn't expect it. It was sad. She ended up havin' an abortion just because she didn't seem to have too many other options." She looked at me as if I should consider it, too.

"Well, I cain't do that. I won't," I said as if to defend myself, as if to say that I had plenty of options.

"I didn't mean that *you* should," she said.

I stood up, wanting to walk around, but her room was so small that I just sat back down. "I'll have a degree in a few months, and I'll be able to take care of myself and the baby. I mean, how would it be right to get rid of it when I know I can take care of it?" I shifted away from her, starting to feel trapped in her room and her trailer. "My dad will help."

She looked down. "It is complicated. You're right about that."

"Actually, it's even more complicated, if you can imagine."

She looked up at me, wondering what could be more complicated than being narcoleptic, unwed, and pregnant. I reconsidered telling her about Betty Lou. It had something to do with the new look in her eyes. Before, I'd always had the feeling that although she was older, I knew more. I felt that I had something to offer. Now, she'd suddenly grown older and wiser, and although I needed a friend, I was nervous. I needed to talk but wasn't sure if I knew her anymore.

As soon as I returned from Florida, I'd made an attempt to talk to Carla, but she'd been too upset. She agreed that I should be the one to tell my dad about Betty Lou, but she was angry that I was waiting. She didn't understand.

"Well, what is it?" Kimmy finally asked after an uncomfortably long silence. "Is it the married guy? Is that what it's about?"

"No, it's Betty Lou."

She looked puzzled.

"My mother," I said.

"Your mother?"

"She's alive. My dad lied about her. He lied all these years. She has schizophrenia. She's crazy, that's all."

Her buzzed hair stared. As I waited for her response, I was suddenly confused as to why I'd come to see her after all. People never know what to say when you tell them such things, things like narcolepsy and mothers dead at childbirth. She was speechless like the rest of the ordinary world.

"I told Carla about it. I don't know why," I said, ashamed. "Maybe I wanted to hurt her or maybe I just wanted someone else to know, someone who'd care . . . about her not being dead, I mean."

"That musta been a shock."

"She was speechless," I said, watching Kimmy pat down the blankets around her. She smoothed them out gracefully—not at all like the big, virgin girl who'd awkwardly tackled the cotton field. Watching, I had the feeling she'd become one of those perfect people who always knew the thing to do.

* * *

The next day, I said to my father, "I've decided to quit the hospital." He didn't seem to hear, so I said it again. I told him in the kitchen because he was most receptive there. Surrounded by his eclectic collection of pots and knives, he was creative and more open-minded.

His pots hung from the ceiling like shields. The knives were gathered in numerous wooden blocks on the counter, stiff like soldiers. Each one he purchased inspired a more complicated or exotic dish. Cooking was his only means of moving away from the man he'd been before Betty Lou, before his lie. Other than the cooking and the lying, he was the same. But he'd become dry and barren despite his consistency. Dry because he'd cried all he could and barren because that was how the tears left him.

"I thought you were gonna work there until you're through school," he said.

"It's gettin' to be too much. I need a break," I said, swinging one of his pots. It swayed and wobbled, threatening to crash to the floor.

He grabbed it, holding on until it was perfectly still. While I watched, mesmerized, he said, "Well, now that you're back on track with your meds, don't you think it'll be easier?"

"No, graduate school's gonna be harder. I'm gonna have to do a ton of research."

Just as he let go of the pot, Carla strolled into the room in her usual authoritative style, Bippy in hand. He was cooking for her; she'd asked for duck. I wasn't thrilled about eating it, but figured I'd try. "How's it comin' along?" she asked, weaving her arms around him.

As I stood watching, it struck me that over the last twenty years I'd become trapped in a bubble. Like the boy in the plastic bubble. But they were inside it, too, and the only way I could escape was to tell my father that I'd seen Betty Lou, that I'd seen the flesh and blood of his lie. But there was also the pregnancy. It was too much. I couldn't decide which to tell and which to hang on to. The lies I had to expose were sharp, like pins. I wanted to use them, to bust us all out, but was afraid we wouldn't be able to breathe on the outside.

I'd never been outside.

"Angel's gonna quit her job," he said to Carla.

"Oh, why is that, Angel?" She aimed her sly grin my way as if to remind me that she could blow my cover. It scared me because if any of us could breathe outside the bubble, it was Carla. "I thought you liked your job, or at least when you go. You haven't really made it there in the last few weeks, have you? I'm surprised they haven't fired you, actually. If you worked for me, you'd be fired already."

"She doesn't need that kinda treatment." My father's voice was doughy, sort of uncooked and incomplete. "She's just realizin' she needs to conserve her energy even more. Right, Angel?"

I swung another pot. "Yeah, I've gotta conserve."

"Well, doesn't your medication help at all?" Carla said. "It's good you're takin' it again, anyway." She smiled, a reminder that I should thank her for that.

"Actually, I'm not," I said before I could stop myself.

My father put down the mixing bowl he was holding and turned to face me.

Carla's eyes narrowed.

Bippy pounced from her arms and slid across the floor.

"You mean to tell me that I dragged your ass down there and you're still not doin' what you're supposed to be doin'?" She threw her hands up. "That's it, Frank. You're gonna have to take some control here."

I instinctively grabbed the edge of the counter to catch myself. I was falling like a drunk falls, eyes glazed, hands flying. "I *am* doin' the right thang," I managed to say as my other hand shot up, hitting several pots with enough force to send them all clanking.

Just before I hit the floor, my father grabbed me by the shoulders with one arm and said, "Stop bangin' my pots!"

By the time I woke up, they'd already eaten. The duck was gone. I found them in the kitchen, cleaning the dishes together. I stood in the doorway and said, "Did it ever occur to you that I can take care of myself? I may not always do what *you* think I should, but I don't just haphazardly do thangs, you know. I have reasons. I've put a few holes in the wall, Carla, and if you were a little more observant, you'd see them." I smoothed my shirt down over my belly, exposing its roundness. They both stared, speechless. "I've nailed holes, Carla . . . just like you."

Then, like the suddenness of my falls and my sleep, my father's arms were around me. They were stiff, like always, but they were there. And for a few moments it was if he hadn't lied at all. I forgot about Betty Lou and the bubble she lived in, the one she'd somehow dragged me into. He held me tight, pressing my face against him.

I smelled him.

The *father* smell of him made me cry.

"I'm sorry," I said. "I didn't mean for it to happen, but it did, and I don't know what I'm gonna do. If you help me, I know I can make it work."

"Do you realize the implications of this situation?" Carla asked, intruding on our moment.

I pulled away from my father and seeing his wet eyes, I suddenly hated him. I hated his *father* smell. I hated his lack of *mother*. I hated him for forcing Carla into my life and forcing Betty Lou out. Most of all, I hated needing him so much.

"You people really do live in a dream world, isn't that right, Angel? You both live in a goddamn dream world. It's not right, Frank, and you're the one who has gotta stop it."

"What are you talkin' about?" he asked, wiping his eyes. "Stop what?"

Carla and I exchanged a glance.

"You know exactly what I'm talkin' about and so does Angel." We all stared at each other. Back and forth we stared, wondering. But atop the wondering, my father's face was blank.

"Are you *ever* gonna tell me how Betty Lou died?" I spit the question out into all that wondering, all that blankness. "I'm gonna have a baby. What if it happens to me?" My father's face clouded, and again, if I looked closely, I could see her in his eyes, the letters of her name floating, adrift, out of order, but still there. It was the craziness after all. She'd left a little of it with him and when he thought of her, it surfaced. Right before my eyes, it surfaced every time, but just as they chose to ignore my enlarging belly, I'd chosen to see death. I'd seen it in his eyes, seen an illness so devastating it swallowed both his life and mine, sucking us into the bubble in which we now found ourselves trapped.

I wondered how loud the burst would sound.

"I have no new information on that, Angel," he said rather curtly. "All I can say is that you're gonna be all right." He patted my back. "Everythang will be fine. We'll work this out. God only knows how, but we've weathered worse storms."

Carla winked and said, "I'm sure he's right. You'll be fine. I think that's the least of your worries. So what does Christian have to say for himself? Or is that weird guy responsible? The one who left a different name every time he called."

My face grew hot, and I looked to my father for help. For once, he came through. "Lay off, Carla. What are you tryin' to accomplish anyway? You're embarrassin' her. Don't you think she's got enough to deal with?"

"You bet she does," she said as she bent at the waist and scooped up Bippy. "Look here, Frank Duet," she said on her way back up, "you may not like my tactics. I may not always be the most tactful woman around, but I love you, and believe it or not, I also care about Angel."

"Right, well, this is a family, albeit a small one," he said, stroking her head as she stroked Bippy, "and part of the love found in a family, in this family, is its ability to nurture and protect, not break each other down."

She stepped away from his caress as if hurt. "I'm not tryin' to break anybody down. I'm just tryin' to expose some issues here that aren't being addressed. If you wanna to go about your life pretendin' thangs are fine, that's your choice, but I'm not gonna stand by for long and watch what happens as a result."

I watched my father's face as she spoke, wondering if he was thinking about his lie, wondering if he suspected she knew. I was grateful to her for keeping the secret. It struck me as proof that she did care in her odd sort of pushy way. Maybe she could help me and just maybe we could have something in common after all.

Again, it was one of those times when I was forced to become close. I never chose those people or situations—life just forced them on me. As my father said, "What the hell are you talkin' about?" I wondered if that's how the best relationships form. I wondered if someday it might work that way with a guy, some big meathead maybe. I hoped Scarlett, or someone like her, wouldn't be forced into being my meathead. The notion that I might not be allowed to choose was frightening.

Just then the baby kicked, making me smile despite my fear. Carla left the kitchen, unable to give my father an answer. "Don't worry, you'll be all right. We'll all be all right," he said, his face awash with the threat of bursting bubbles and exploding lies, with straying vines, and love.

I wanted to believe him.

And I wanted to believe in Carla, too, and that someday my life, like hers, would be filled with peanuts.

☑ whale

Scarlett stood motionless like a flame stands. Even still, it moves. Her eyes glowed at the sight of me. As I wondered how she burned so bright, I snuffed something out that I felt welling up. She stood, surrounded by Tim's apartment, in what seemed like a message. She still liked me despite my growing baby. Tim knew, too. We looked at each other as if to agree on the message, as if to say we'd both gotten it.

As the door clicked shut behind me, she said, "Look at you with that cute belly!" She bounced toward me, stopping a little too close. "You look so cute with that little belly."

"It seems huge to me," I said.

Her hands lifted slowly like hands moving toward an insect. They move into position and then they strike. I stood still, wondering where they were going to land. "Can I?" she asked. "Can I feel the baby?"

I stepped back but said, "Okay, I guess." I looked past her at Tim, but only saw his back. He'd turned to leave the room. Her hands moved toward me, inching their way to my belly. Then they rested on either side of the tight mound. Her narrow hands wrapped around me like a belt.

"How far along are you now? Because you don't seem that big."

"A little over seven months," I said.

"Does the baby do a lotta movin' around? I don't feel anythang. I'd love to feel it because I've never really felt a baby movin' before." She stared into my eyes, so close, and I wondered how she could be so smooth, like a guy on the make, with a pregnant belly in her hands.

I felt stricken.

"What do you want from me?" I asked.

She looked surprised. "I just wanna feel the baby. I just love little babies, you know? They're so soft and cute and cuddly and inno-cent." Shirley Temple curls bounced around her face. "I cain't wait to see your cute little baby. I cain't wait until it's born so I can hold it and play with it. I hope you're gonna let me play with it. I'll baby-sit for you and help you with it. Whatever you want me to do. I mean, in case you were wonderin', girls like me still love babies. Right, Tim?"

"I think you're makin' her nervous, Scar," Tim said as he came back into the room. "I don't think Angel wants the baby to have two moms."

Her face suddenly looked a little burnt. Her belted hands unbuck-led. She let go, and I followed her to the couch where we sat, side by side. She said, "Well, you sure do look good pregnant. You really do, and I'm not just sayin' that to make you feel better." Tim sat across from us, sipping tea. "I've never really known anyone who had a baby. I mean . . . not close. I haven't known them much, I mean."

"Can I ask you a question, Angel?" Tim said, cutting her off.

I stared at him, surprised that he'd asked permission. As I looked at his bright white face, I was suddenly glad he was my friend. He'd done a lot of things I knew were wrong. He'd taken me places I wasn't supposed to go and given me things he shouldn't have, but he was still a good friend. I wasn't sure how all that could add up to being a good friend, but it did. "What's the question?" I said.

"Why are you havin' the baby, anyway? I'm happy for you. I mean, if you're happy, I'm happy, but how can it be a good thang?"

I looked at Scarlett, wondering if she had the same question, and then I wondered if the whole world had that question, if they all wanted to ask me why. "Why?" I asked, trying to figure out the answer. "You wanna know why?" I stood up, belly first. "You wanna know why I would put myself in this stupid situation?"

Scarlett said, "I told you what I think. I think you look pretty damn good."

"Look, don't be gettin' all upset," Tim said. "I'm just curious because it doesn't seem like the best situation. That Mr. Borin' is a son-of-a-bitch and you've got the narco shit hangin' over your head."

"Tim, how about givin' her a break? I'm sure she's doin' what she thinks is best, right, Sweetie?" Her hand touched the back of my leg.

I sat back down, primarily to force her hand away. But I didn't move back. I stayed on the edge, keeping my distance. "You know," I said to Tim. "I tried to tell you once that you could never understand my life . . . what my life has been like, even though you're gay and that's hard. I know it's not easy." I looked at Scarlett, whose burnt look was fading. "It's hard to explain and at the same time it's so simple. It's always been just my father and me, and for most of my life, I've watched him cry over my mother. Can you even imagine what it's like to live with a ghost and wanna bring it back to life?" I tried not to cry. Scarlett's hand was on my leg again, pressing harder now, pressing.

"It wasn't meant to be such a complicated question. I was only wonderin'."

"It's okay—I wanna talk about it. My life's been spent tryin' to swim through all that cryin' and find him. I tried to find my dad, and I wanted a mother. I tried to make him happier, to make him not wanna cry anymore." I got up and walked around the room, looking at what made up Tim's life. I quickly realized that it wasn't filled with much. Everything was neat and orderly, but it there wasn't much there, nothing that would challenge his organization skills. He managed very little. "Once I was diagnosed, thangs changed," I continued. "He stopped bein' so sad." I shook my head. "No, I think he just stopped showin' it. He *tried* to stop, I think. Then he was just sad about me, and I couldn't stand that. I just ended up makin' him worse."

"So now you wanna have a cute little baby 'cause it'll cheer up your daddy? Is that it?" Scarlett asked.

"Gimme a break," Tim said, bending at the waist and putting his head between his knees.

"No, I want it to make *me* happy. I wanna have it because I can." Tim sat back up. "It's somethin' of my very own that I can hold in my arms. It's somethin', *someone*, who I can share my life with, and it'll be a *new* life, apart from all that sad, cryin' crap. When that baby comes, when I hold it in my arms, a page will turn and an old book will close. *My* book will start, my very own that nobody can take away. All the choices will be mine and they'll be different. From that moment on, they'll be good. They'll be happy, you know?" I looked at them for understanding, but they only looked bored. Tim was trying to suck a piece of ice out of his tea glass. Scarlett's face looked more scarred than ever. She was listening, but she wasn't hearing me.

Then, as if a buzzer went off, they suddenly turned to each other. "Do you think it's time?" Tim asked Scarlett. "Should we do it now?"

"What time is it?" she asked.

"Six."

"I'm as ready as I'll ever be."

I sat back, feeling spent, wondering what the hell I was doing having a baby. But I didn't want to turn back. I loved it already. And I knew it was a love that would surpass all others. It would be pure. Truthful. I would taste it in my mouth and feel it on my skin. It would settle over my skin, adding a new layer.

"Hang on, Angel. You can finish tellin' us in a minute," Tim said, but I didn't care anymore. I'd told myself and that was all that mattered. "I'll be right back." He went to his bedroom and came back with a fistful of Ecstasy.

Scarlett's eyes twinkled. "I wish you could go out with us tonight. If you want me to, I'll stay here with you. I'll hang out for as long as you want. You can tell me your whole life story because I really do wanna hear about it . . . *all* the details, you know."

As I listened to Scarlett's singsong voice, I watched Tim sort of spring around the room in his girlish way. "Do you think the feelin' it gives will have any lastin' effect?" I asked them both.

"I'm not worried about it," Tim said.

"You mean like side effects and all that kinda stuff?" Scarlett said.

"Not side effects like a headache, *lasting* effects. Look, you wanted to know why I'm havin' a baby. Well, I wanna know why you take drugs all the time."

They looked at each other, but didn't answer.

"We're all takin' chances, aren't we?"

"I'm not worried about that shit," Tim said, looking a little upset.

Scarlett said, "I guess I'm gonna have to think about it. Can I think about the question for a while and get back to you?"

I knew she'd never have an answer. Neither of them would.

We sat listening to Patsy Cline and then Boy George for almost thirty minutes. Tim gave me a snack. They were waiting for the smiles they craved to find their faces. My smile was hidden inside, and it was real this time. I tried to remember that ecstatic feeling, the one I promised myself I wouldn't forget.

As the sun drifted down and the apartment grew darker, Scarlett inched her way closer. She bent down and put her ear to my belly. I didn't stop her. As Tim went to shower, his smiling lips told us he'd soon be ready to leave. Scarlett smiled, too, her eyes bright. Without asking, she lifted my shirt. She pulled my maternity pants down a little to expose my belly and put her ear against it again without asking. I touched her soft hair. It fell between my fingers, gliding through, aching past. And I ached because I longed to touch her, not because she was what I wanted but because she was something I didn't have. Mother dead or mother alive, it didn't matter. Even with the head on my belly, the silky hair, and the scar, *mother* was still missing.

Soon Tim came back. He was gleaming, scrubbed clean, and I tried again to understand how a bad person by many standards could be good after all. I couldn't come up with an answer but I did sense that, in the end, what he'd given me would prove good for me, but not for him.

* * *

On the day I finally faced Mac's wife, getting to the back of the hospital wasn't easy. At eight-and-a-half months pregnant, a slow waddle had replaced my usual bent run. I hadn't seen Mac in months, though he'd called. After we returned from Florida, he continued to call at least once a week. Usually he called himself Steve, and sometimes Johnson because that was his middle name. I didn't ask about his wife and he didn't mention her. Our conversations were brief. I missed him.

When I saw his face through the on-call room window, I knew he missed me, too. He peered through the glass without his usual cocky smirk. I suspected that he lost it somewhere in Florida. The confidence was still there, but he had softened somehow. I stared through the glass, wishing he could be my meathead. We couldn't speak because of the window between us, but it was a close moment. I hadn't chosen it, but it was happening. He missed me, and I missed him. I touched my belly, wishing the baby *was* his, wishing he wasn't married. I wished he could admit his mistake. His face was filled with it. It had washed the smirk away weeks ago. It had deepened the crow's feet around his eyes. It had beaten him. He didn't love her. He couldn't because he loved me.

But I wasn't sure if I loved him. When I thought it possible, visions of Christian and Scarlett flashed through my mind. The feeling of wanting more and knowing what I couldn't have sank in, so I focused on my unborn child.

I didn't believe that I could love more than one person, that the heart was large enough to love countless people. I didn't realize that if you can love a child, a mother, and a father all with the same heart, you can also love other men and women, friends and lovers. I didn't know that love comes in many varieties and that, in the end, you choose your flavor. I thought that love would choose me.

I went around to the door and he pulled me in.

"What the hell are you doin'?" he asked. "Have you totally lost it? Walkin' around like this?"

"But aren't you glad to see me?" I asked, choosing to ignore my puffiness, to forget I looked so fat.

"Of course I am." He looked me over. "Look at you! Holy shit!"

"Stop, you're makin' me feel bad."

"But you look great," he said, almost like a physician. "Actually, quite sexy." He put his arms around me, but the embrace that had once left room to spare was all used up. I knew then that his arms weren't large enough to hold us both anymore.

"What's goin' on with you?" I asked. "How's your wife?" Pregnancy, like the dosage I'd taken during my days in the cotton fields, had increased my nerve. I surprised myself.

He looked surprised, too. "She's okay," he said, looking like a liar. I was getting better and better at spotting them. "Actually," he continued, "thangs aren't that great."

"And that's a surprise?"

"I know. I'm a jerk. And it's not even about you and me after all. It's been awhile, you know?" He took my hand and kissed it. "She doesn't wanna have kids. No kids, period. She likes her job and doesn't wanna have to stop travelin'."

"It's gotta be more than that," I said, pulling my hand away. "Cain't she get another good job?"

"She just got promoted."

"And you wanna have kids."

"Yes, I do. I'd never really thought about it until . . . this happened." He put his hand on my belly, and I moved away. He was making me nervous. He wanted something that I wasn't prepared to give. I was big and fat and pregnant. I had narcolepsy. I didn't even know why I came.

"So it *is* about me in a way," I said, thinking that I should hurry and leave.

He must have sensed my unease and changed the subject. He said, "Why are you out walkin' around?"

"I've been fine. I've only had a couple of problems since I've been pregnant. I've slept a lot, but it's been my choice."

"Well, I don't like it. And I mean that as a physician, not just as a friend." He was still James Bond, but he'd lost his edge. I couldn't decide if I liked him better with or without it. "Angel," he said to get my attention. I must have been daydreaming. I knew I wasn't asleep. "Look, I want you to promise you'll stop after tonight. You're close to your due date. You could go into labor any day. You have to be more careful and keep close to home."

"Why are you always so worried about me?"

"Because I don't wanna lose you."

"But you don't have me," I said, angry that he always assumed we were still together, even when I didn't see him for days or weeks or months. I wondered if he thought I was just one of those women who would strip naked in a heartbeat if he asked. There were a lot of them. I'd seen them: nurses, patients, patients' mothers and even grandmothers. "I'm practically an invalid," I said. "I live with my dad in the house where I grew up. And you cain't even leave your name when you call."

"Maybe that'll change."

"Don't even say that."

"Why not? It's not like I've told you anythang like that before. It's not like I've ever lied to you."

"No, but you're scarin' me, okay?"

"Why does that scare you?" he asked, looking scared. "Do you wanna be with me at all or are we *really* just friends? Because every time I see you, I'm riskin' a hell of a lot."

"What exactly are you riskin'? You don't even love her, do you? You just jumped into marryin' her, didn't you? Why did you do that? People don't do that, do they? How else could you come back here and get involved with me a couple of months afterwards? Are you just a jerk? Did you just wanna have sex with a narcoleptic patient, is that it? Because if that's it, I hope you had fun."

"What the hell is this all about?" he asked. His forehead wrinkled and his eyes sparked. "You didn't require much coaxin', if I recall."

"It's about my life. I deserve more than that. I deserve to be loved. I deserve the option of lovin' the person I wanna love."

"I know you do."

"And you deserve that, too."

"What?" He looked tired, his face worn down by the wrinkled forehead and pained expression.

"Real love."

He lay down on the small hospital bed that always seemed to fill the room. "What is that, anyway?" He raised the head of the bed, propping himself up.

"I don't know. You're the one who's married. Shouldn't you know? I've never been in love." I shrugged my shoulders. "I don't think you realize it, but I've barely been able to date, to go out on one successful date. That's why I liked Christian. I liked bein' with him because for once I was a normal person."

"No you weren't. You were takin' drugs."

"Well, I was doin' that anyway. And the drugs my doctor gave me weren't helpin' that much. What Tim gave me helped."

"It's not the same, Angel. *Prescription* is the key word. You were under a doctor's care, and you basically said, 'Screw you.' You were treadin' on extremely dangerous ground. And I didn't like those queers you were pallin' around with."

I had to sit down. My swollen legs ached. "How are they any worse than you?"

"I don't do drugs."

"No, you just do it to women who aren't your wife."

"Why are you so mad at me all of a sudden?"

"I'm not mad at you. I'm mad at myself. I'm twenty-two years old, I'm gettin' ready to have a baby, and I don't even know what love is. Is it what we have? Is it what I feel for Scarlett?"

"Scarlett?" He rolled his eyes. "Look, Angel, you're not gay, if that's what's botherin' you."

"How do you know? If I don't even know, how could you know?" He got up and walked over to the chair I was sitting in. It was a short walk, but it reminded me of the time I walked toward Christian, how I thought the moment so important, so critical. Mac walked and walked and walked. Then he was standing next to me and the moment was over. He held out his hand. His fingers were long and large, his palm round like an offering plate. I wanted to take it. I wanted to accept what he had to offer, but then realized that the only times I'd seen an offering plate were the times I'd been expected to fill it.

"I'm sure it was just healthy curiosity," he said. "A lot of people go through that . . . a lot of women, anyway."

I didn't take his hand, instead standing up. He put his arms around me, and I tried to get close. He held me tight, but I felt far away, my pregnancy between us like a rock. I struggled to get closer, stretching my arms as far around him as I could, but my belly was hard and immovable. And my arms could only stretch so far.

"Have you?" I asked.

"Hell no, but that's beside the point," he said as the door opened and the screeching began.

In the midst of my desperate, humiliating grope, I heard the door open.

His wife's yelp was like the screech of his whistling, yet it pierced in a whole new way. As much as I wanted to remain in his arms, as much as I wanted to *be* her and have some claim on him, I understood her pain, and it made me sad. I didn't know if I should let him go or hold on and hope for safety. Finally, as if in slow motion, my arms dropped, and I turned to face her, to finally see the woman I'd imagined.

Her face was beautiful, smooth, and although older than mine, relatively young. Her long, thin hair was dark, her face extremely narrow. She had a birdlike look that was opposite to my full, freckled one. I wondered why he would want me, a virtual Raggedy Ann, when he could have such a pale, delicate creature.

Her yelp turned to shrieking, and I froze, waiting to conk out, waiting for what I was programmed to expect. I wrapped my arms around my middle, hoping to protect the baby. But nothing happened. I remained standing, facing her, unable to avoid the situation. I wished I could fall. I closed my eyes, wishing. But when I opened them I was still standing, face-to-face with the screeching bird.

Carla was right. Narcolepsy *was* my escape, an excuse to leave. I looked around the room, searching for another focus, as if to somehow run away when I couldn't.

A deep ache shook me. But I still didn't fall. Instead, I stared at Mac's wife, unable to breathe. There was nothing else on which to focus. It was as if a magnificent, regal bird had flown into my cage and shown me that there was a cage. I didn't know about the cage until I saw her in it. Narcolepsy formed its bars, but I knew then that I'd fashioned the cage out of my disability. And I was stuck inside, next to him, next to her, in a space too small to house us all.

It was too small now for me.

She continued screaming, her words indistinct. Then she suddenly focused on me, on my belly. She fell silent, perhaps trying to decide if my pregnancy meant there was hope for an explanation or if the baby was his.

"It's not what you think," I managed to say, which was partly true. I felt like a fool, like one of a million with whom he could have been sleeping. I felt cheap.

"Shut up," she said, her beaklike mouth ready to peck. "You just shut up!"

"Don't talk to her like that," Mac said. "She's pregnant."

"You're takin' up for *her*, you son-of-a-bitch?" She pointed at him, shaking her finger. "How can you do that?"

"She's pregnant, and it's not what you think. She's a friend of mine. She works here. She did work here."

"Why don't I believe you?" she asked, shaking her head. She lost her momentum. She looked tired. "Why aren't you the kind of husband I can believe? You've never been that for me. And that's what I wanted, Mac. That's what I want." Her eyes filled, and red blotches spread across her pale face.

He said, "I'm sorry," and I wondered if it was meant to be an admission. She looked at him and then at me. She stared at my belly and then walked out.

I didn't move but rather shook in place.

Mac went to the door and watched his wife of a little more than a year walk away. "Don't be upset," he said without looking at me.

"How can you expect me to be calm?" I asked, surprised at his nonchalance.

"I don't expect anythang. I just don't want you to be upset." He paused. "It's not good for the baby."

"Aren't you gonna run after her? Isn't that what you're supposed to do?"

I watched as he realized he wanted to stay. "No, it's not," he finally said.

"But I thought you loved her." I went and stood next to him. "Don't you love her?"

He finally said, "I thought I did." He stepped back into the room and looked around as if assessing his life. "Actually, now I'm not even sure about that. I don't know if I ever really believed that I loved her."

I could feel my blood pressure rising. "Well, why did you marry her, then?" My arms and legs felt thick with the extra blood I'd produced for the baby. The anger I'd been carrying around for months was churning such that I wanted to strike out. I wanted to shake him, to beat him down, to say he was an ass for cheating on his wife. He was an ass for marrying her in the first place.

But I didn't say anything.

"I don't know," he said. "She was dyin' to get married. We were drinkin' the night before. It all just happened so fast." He walked away and then began to pace back and forth across the small room. "I don't know the answer. I really don't know. It seemed like a good idea at the time." The sweat on his forehead beaded and rolled down the side of his face. "I didn't think it through."

"How can you *not* know the answer to such an important question? You're a grown man. You're supposed to have answers to questions like that. At the very least, you're supposed to know why the hell you do thangs, aren't you?"

He stopped. "What makes you think that? You think that once you reach a certain age, you're gonna suddenly have all the answers? That all the answers are gonna fall down from the sky? I forget how young you are," he said, as if something were wrong with me, as if it were a curse to be young.

Now I know that being young *is* a curse, and also a blessing. It's a joke God plays.

"Well, see, you go and say thangs like that, implyin' that once I'm older, I'll know more. So how am I supposed to believe that older people *don't* know more? It makes sense that they would, right?"

"You're misunderstandin' me. The older you get, the more you realize that you *don't* know all the answers. When you're young, you *think* you know all the answers. I'm just beginnin' to realize that I don't know shit." He paused and then said, "It's kinda liberatin', actually."

"Why are we even talkin' about this?" I asked. "What are we doin' here? I don't even know why I came."

"See, you cain't necessarily explain all your actions, either."

He had a point.

"I don't know," he said. "I don't know what the hell we're doin', what the hell we ever do." He went into the small bathroom without shutting the door behind him. Then he asked, "Whatever happened with Christian, anyway?"

"Why do you ask that all of a sudden?" I spoke louder so he could hear.

"Another question I don't know the answer to," he said. "Just humor me, okay?"

I walked over to the bathroom, wondering how long he was going to comb his hair or whatever it was he was doing. He was holding on to the sink with both hands. His head hung down as if his neck were broken. "I'm so confused," he said. "I don't usually get confused."

I wondered if he'd been trying to get away from me. "I'm not talkin' to Christian these days," I said, feeling a little sorry for him. "Dad and Carla talked me into askin' him for child support, and Carla's handlin' the legal stuff. She talks to him. He's got a new girlfriend." I didn't know why, but it still hurt. Seeing Mac with his head dangling and thinking of Christian with his head held high despite his irresponsibility hurt. I felt the crush of their mutual failure and my own boiling blood. My head hurt.

My heart would hurt much longer. The pain would slither through me like love for my child. Intertwined, the sorrow and love would create the rope of reality that would finally run through my life, grounding me. With each passing year, with each day that my child's life unfolded, the sorrow of Christian's face and name would grow. The lack of details, the faded memories would sting. That pain and the joy of my child would grow together, forever entwined. And to escape the grief, I would think of Christian less and less until finally even to say his name would be nearly impossible.

"That baby should have been mine."

"But it's not," I said, thinking of Christian's freckled face.

Mac turned to look at me, and for the first time, I saw through his windows clearly. I saw something broken and strong. "But it should be," he said again.

The magnificent bird had flown. She was flying away, down the corridor, down the road, away from Mac. She left the cage open and dirty but somehow honest. The shit was on the floor. Mac was standing in it despite the open door. And I was left standing, too, amazed to find that the cage Carla warned me about *did* exist. I knew then that somehow I'd find the way out.

☑ xanadu

"I've been closed up, but that's all changed now," my father said. I studied his graying temples and dark eyes, and thought of the residents of Hope. I thought about how they were closed up, boxed in by their self-serving kindness, about how it was cultivated all around them. "Carla's done that for me," he said. "She changed everythang. And I think that now—with the baby here—we're a family. We should be one. You, Carla, me, and the baby."

"We're not a family," I said, disappointed that the birth of my child had not wiped out the resentment I felt toward him. "She's my new family, not you and Carla."

"But you need us now more than ever." He sat down next to me on the bed. "You know that."

I looked away from him, down at the thin blanket covering me, and wished I had my Holly Hobbie bedspread. "I don't want to, though." I wondered when they were bringing the baby back.

"I should have been monitorin' your activities more." He picked at the fuzz on his plaid shirt. "This is all my fault, really. I haven't been takin' care of you like I should. I know you're an adult now, but you have a disability."

"That's ridiculous. It's not your fault," I said, shaking my head. "I'm grown now, and besides, I'm happy."

"That may be, but a blind man doesn't go walkin' where he knows there's a cliff nearby."

"You sure are grown up," Carla said as she strolled into the hospital room. "You're a mother now. That baby is the cutest little thang I've seen in a long time. I knew she'd be cute. You two are pretty cute yourselves, especially you," she said, giving my father a kiss. She talked as if she really were part of our family. Part of me wanted her to be around forever. I liked having her there to explain things like nailing holes into walls and relearning ABCs. But another part wanted to be the only mother now. I was ready but knew I couldn't handle it on my own. I needed her but didn't want a stepmother. I was confused.

My father said, "Carla and I have been discussin' marriage." He picked harder at the fuzz all around him. Now that he was *opened up*, he was noticing things like fuzz and dirt and clutter. "I guess it's a good time to tell you that now. We don't want you to worry about how you're gonna care for the baby. And despite what you say, I know you're concerned."

"She has a name," I said.

"And it's a beautiful name," Carla said.

"Claudia is gonna be well taken care of by the three of us," he said. "We'll all pitch in and make this work."

"Are you sure you're ready for marriage?" I asked my father while looking at Carla.

She winked and said, "He's closer than he knows."

"What's that supposed to mean?" he asked.

Carla ignored him. Instead she turned to me again. "Angel," she said, sitting on the edge of the bed, "you better promise me that you'll be a good mother. You promise and don't ever forget. I doubt I'll ever have one of my own," she glanced at my father, "so I'll be damned if this one doesn't have the best."

"You think I cain't do it?"

"I think you're more capable than most. You'll be a great mother. I know you will because I'll make sure of it."

"What's that supposed to mean?" I asked, sounding like my father.

"Well, your dad and I, we've just been talkin' about it a lot, and I'm gonna help you, that's all. You can depend on me is what I'm tellin' you. You're gonna need some help. You're gonna have to face that reality, sooner than later."

My father sat silently, probably thinking about his divorce from Betty Lou and his marriage to Carla. A baby cried outside the door, and I knew it was time. Claudia had made me a mother, had given me *mother*, and I wasn't going to ruin the day by allowing him to continue lying. "I know about Betty Lou," I said suddenly. The words came out of the blue, out of the clouds floating through the sky we'd stared into all those years. "I know." The wide, blue sky, those clouds, would never look the same.

My father froze as if shot in the center of his forehead. Then, slowly, I saw the blood, the death. It streamed off his head in giant beads of sweat. It flooded his eyes until dark no longer described them. There was no name for the color they turned. He was silent. I had silenced him. Carla was silenced, too. She waited, so I waited. The three of us sat silently together as he realized the bullet had struck him between the eyes and the life he'd known was over.

It felt good to give and take life in the same day. I'd managed to kill a dead man, I thought, but then remembered that he'd been in the process of rising. Carla had been busy teaching him the alphabet. She'd taken him back to Sesame Street. She'd been showing him a place where the air was clear.

He finally said, "What?" It was nearly a whisper.

"I know about her. I've seen her . . . in Florida."

He looked at Carla.

"I know, too, Frank," she said with a tender voice. "We both know she isn't dead. What we don't know is why you chose to lie about it. How did you think we were ever gonna get married when you're already married?" When he didn't respond, she said, "You're still married, Frank."

"I wanna know why you lied to me," I said. "That's all I wanna know, right now."

"Considerin' your condition, I don't think this is the best time," he said. "You've just had a baby." He tried to smile, but it didn't work. "Let's not ruin such a special day."

"My condition is fine. I think you're tryin' to protect *your* condition. This day will only be ruined if you're still lyin' to me when it's over. I've decided my life is gonna change. Today."

"It was never supposed to go this far," he said.

"A bigger man would have stopped it sooner."

His head jerked as if taking another bullet.

Carla said, "Frank, you're a good man. I'm sure you had reasons, but now it's time to clarify thangs, to explain. Angel's an adult now. She deserves that."

"You saw her?" he asked, ignoring Carla. "You saw Betty Lou . . . in Florida . . . in that place?"

"Yes, I saw my mother. She peed on me. You put me in that situation, among others."

His face suddenly closed, the window shades drawn and the river dry. "I don't know what you're talkin' about," he said, and walked out of the room.

"He'll be back," Carla said, her eyes shining as if a plan she'd made was playing out. "You know, he's probably right that this isn't the best time. This is a great day for you." She touched my leg. "You're a mother now." Every time she alluded to the birth of my child, to my becoming a mother, it was almost as if she were talking about herself.

I began to cry. "How am I supposed to be a mother?"

She didn't answer but she kept her hand on my leg. All I could feel was her hand. I didn't want her to go.

* * *

As soon as Kimmy entered my hospital room, I knew we would not remain friends. It wasn't that I didn't want to be her friend, but rather that I couldn't anymore. Her hair was short but chic now that it had grown several inches. Attached to her by way of holding hands was a boring-looking guy in his early thirties. She didn't look at all like the girl who'd worked at the Piggly Wiggly. She didn't look like herself.

I wondered if I looked different, if *mother* had changed me already.

I kept telling myself that the new Kimmy was better than the girl who prayed, ripping napkins, crying. I'd been sure of it that day in her parents' trailer. Staring at her sweaty palm clasped tight around the hand of her new boyfriend, I wondered if a person can improve so much that they move too far to the other side of the invisible pendulum monitoring our normalcy. I was sure that the day I'd gone to see her at her parents' trailer was Kimmy's one perfect straight-as-an-arrow day.

And I wondered if that day, for me, was the birthday of Claudia. I felt arrow-straight holding her in my arms.

Kimmy's time to be my friend had passed. There was a time when I would have been glad, but now I wasn't glad at all. I wanted the old Kimmy back.

Her boyfriend called her Kim.

"Angel, we saw the baby in the nursery. She's so adorable." I'd never heard Kimmy use the word *adorable*. "This is Glen," she said, remembering her manners. "We met at the drugstore. I was gettin' my prescriptions filled. He's a pharmacist."

"Nice to meet you," I said, thinking that he looked like a pharmacist.

He smiled but didn't say anything.

"He's kinda shy," Kimmy said, nudging him. His eyes twinkled, and I knew that he loved her. He seemed like a nice guy, a guy who would name his daughter Nicole and hang a bird feeder in the front yard for Kimmy. "So how was it?" Kimmy asked. "Was it bad?"

Glen finally spoke. "Excuse me, Kim, but I'm gonna run down to the pharmacy to see if I can locate a friend of mine. If you don't mind." He looked at me.

"No, you go ahead. Angel and I have a lot to talk about."

"It wasn't that bad," I said. "They gave me an epidural, and I fell asleep."

"You slept through it?"

"Mostly, but I was awake enough. I mean, enough to experience it, you know? It was amazin'. It's weird. The whole time you're pregnant, you know a baby's in there. You know it has to come out. But when it does and you see that little tiny human, that person, it blows your mind. I screamed when she came out. The epidural wore off about an hour before she was born."

"That sounds terrible."

"But it wasn't. It was as if I could hear someone else screamin'. They told me to push. I was pushin', and it was so hard, and the scream just came out with the push. It was an involuntary scream. If you can imagine."

"I cain't wait to have babies. Glen and I have only been datin' for two months but I really think he's the one. I really do." She'd gained some edges; her face was thinner now.

"How do you know?"

"I just do. I cain't explain it. I just have this feelin' that my life has finally fallen onto the right path. I've finally hit that sequence, you know, the way thangs are supposed to happen. I'm finishin' school. I'll have a college education. I met a nice guy. I'll get married, buy a house, and have children. Boom, boom, boom, just like that, just how it's supposed to be."

"Are you sure it's always supposed to work out like that?" I asked, thinking of my fatherless child.

"Of course. I've always known that. I just couldn't afford to go to college right after high school, so I had to get a job. And then I was on my way, just like you told me, but I got stuck in a rut. And Tim was right. The thangs we did," she lowered her voice, "the thangs we tried broke me out of it. If it wasn't for him, I would never have met Glen."

"But, Kimmy, if it's supposed to happen that way, what about people like Tim? How could it happen that way for him? What about me?"

"Well, I'm not gonna judge other people and the choices they make, but the right way, the way thangs are supposed to happen, is A, you go to college, B, you get married, and C, you have children."

I wondered if she'd join the Junior League. "Then what? What happens in the end?"

"Well, I don't know. You live your life. You work. You go to church. You become a grandmother. Then you die, I guess."

"What if you get divorced?"

"I won't."

"How can you be so sure? And what about me? I just had a baby. I just graduated. I don't see myself gettin' married anytime soon. I may have to live with my dad and Carla for the rest of my life."

"You won't."

"How did you get so sure about everythang all of a sudden?"

"I've always known this stuff. I just never had the confidence to say it or show it. After the accident, I realized that I don't have time to sit around worryin' about everythang. I'm not afraid anymore."

Glen walked back into the room. I barely heard him. I didn't realize he was back until I saw him standing there, holding Kimmy's hand again. As I studied them, I realized Kimmy's life would probably turn out the way she thought it should. I knew I should be happy for her, but I wasn't. I was glad my life wasn't on the same path as hers. Her path was so mapped out, so final. The end so clear and the journey boring. And then I remembered what Tim had said about Kimmy being ordinary, how she might die one day in the same spot in which she stood.

I didn't want to be ordinary—Kimmy showed me that.

* * *

Later, Carla stood next to me while the nurse gave me breastfeeding pointers. I was glad my father had stepped out of the room. The moment they laid Claudia in my arms, I loved her. She turned her tiny face toward mine and stuck out her bottom lip. I'd been waiting for her. It was as if I recognized her, as if I'd known all along what she looked like. Claudia Duet was a new person, one that I'd created. I knew then that we were not missing anything by Christian's absence. He was the one missing out. I would never forget that. Through the years, I would even feel sorry for him. I'd feel sad that he was so unfortunate, that he never knew her. She would prove to be an extraordinary person.

I was thinking of him when Tim and Scarlett came through the door with outstretched arms and Ecstasy smiles. I shuffled to cover my breasts. Carla stared at them as if she knew they were *on* something.

Then she watched me to see if I knew. As they came closer to the bed, to my child, they seemed to become caricatures of what they'd been.

☑ yarn

I stood in my father's foyer, looking at the last photograph—a car. I wrote the word *car* next to the number twenty-two on my notepad. Then I wrote "vehicle." I still couldn't figure out where the big picture fit, the one Carla forgot to check before reframing it. I didn't hear my father come in. He touched my shoulder, and I spun around, wondering why he'd come home so early.

"I've gotta talk to you," he said. His suit was wrinkled and his tie loose.

I held the notepad out toward him. "Look, I figured out what Betty Lou was doing. What she was tryin' to do."

He took the notepad from me but didn't look at it. "Where's the baby?" he asked, looking around. He looked as if he hadn't slept for days. He'd been avoiding me since Claudia's birth.

"She's upstairs—asleep. She's fine. Aren't you even gonna look at that?" I asked, motioning to my notepad. He stared down at it as if illiterate. "What's the matter with you? Why'd you come home so early anyway?"

Silence.

"Are you ready to talk to me?" I asked, sensing he finally had something to say.

He pulled at his tie. "I thought I'd come home and try and cut down that dead tree out back. It hasn't had a leaf on it in years." He handed me the notepad and headed for the back yard.

"But it's gonna rain," I said, looking outside to see how close the storm was.

He didn't seem to care. "I just need to get rid of it."

"Wait," I said, and he stopped. "Didn't you say you wanted to talk? I know this isn't easy for you. It's not easy for me either. I told you about Florida, about Betty Lou, because I wanna live an honest life. I still don't understand why you didn't tell me the truth, but I'm not gonna turn into a zombie."

He still hadn't turned around. "Like me? Is that what you mean?" he said. I didn't answer. "What are you gonna tell Claudia when she grows up? What are you gonna tell her about her father?" He walked over to the window and stared out at the dead tree.

"That I was young and stupid. That I was in love."

"Were you?" His head turned. I thought he was going to face me, but instead he studied Betty Lou's clouds.

"I thought I was. Doesn't that count for somethin'?"

"Did you really think you were? 'Cause I didn't get that impression."

"Well, I *wanted* to be."

He finally turned around. "Are you gonna tell her that you met her father at a bar and that you only dated him for a few months?"

"Eventually, if I have to. Why are you turnin' this around on me? I'm not gonna lie, if that's what you're askin'. I'm never gonna lie, 'cause I'm not ashamed. She's the best thang that ever happened to me, even though it didn't happen the right way, the normal way."

"And you were the best thang that happened to me," he said, as if he really meant it. "Don't you realize that? You were *my* miracle, Angel."

"I thought Betty Lou was the miracle."

"I loved her, but now that all these years have passed, I see that she wasn't the best thang." He took a deep breath and held it. "The most tragic, maybe . . ."

"Her life was tragic, not yours. Your life's not over, you know."

Thunder boomed and Claudia began to cry. "I'll be back," I said, handing him the notepad again. "Look at this and see if you can figure it out."

When I came back, he was sitting at the bottom of the stairs, staring down at my notepad. "She was obsessed with this. It was somethin' she'd started workin' on before I met her. She'd gotten pretty far. She was incredibly methodical about it, but after . . . but once she started goin' downhill, she became obsessed."

"You knew about this?"

He shook his head.

"You knew and didn't tell me? I don't understand you at all."

"There's a lot you don't understand."

"Maybe I could if you'd give me a chance." I yanked the notepad from him, angry. "I'm sick of hearin' that from you."

"Tell her the truth, Frank." Carla stood in the doorway, soaked from the rain. Her normally perfect makeup streamed down her face, and matted hair stuck to her head. She pulled a tissue out of her purse and dabbed her eyes.

"Whatever it is, I can handle it."

"I don't think you wanna know." He stroked my head with his large palm. "I hope you know how much I love you. I hope you'll always remember that," he said.

"Tell me, please," I said, and put my hand on his.

"Before you were born . . . Betty Lou was raped by two men. They said the trauma triggered her schizophrenia."

"That's what you couldn't tell me?" I asked. "It's very sad, but I could have handled knowin' that years ago. I'm stronger than you think, Dad."

He stared at me, his eyes blank now. "It was my fault. We had a fight that night. We were visitin' her parents in Florida. She ran out, and I didn't go after her."

I thought about Mac and how he'd let his wife leave.

"These two guys were just out roamin' around, lookin' for someone to abuse." He began to choke up. "They broke her spirit." He wiped his eyes. "It never came back."

I sat down and grabbed a pillow from the sofa. I thought about the blood she'd talked about.

"They beat her up. I cain't stand to think of it," he said. "I've tried to forget for so long. It was brutal," he said. He stared at her photographs. "They basically killed her."

Carla said, "Frank, tell her the rest." She was sitting next to me now, close, as if she were my mother.

"Why cain't we just leave it at that?" he asked, but Carla's lawyer eyes would not let him go.

I thought of my mother's storm photographs and how the clouds she once loved had turned black and ugly.

"Her family blamed me. They'd always thought I was too old for her. I'd finished law school, and she was barely out of high school."

"Frank, tell her the rest," Carla said again, like a broken record. It was the technique we used in the ER to force people to do what they should when they couldn't think for themselves.

I stared at him, thirsting to hear more.

"Frank," Carla said.

I stood up, not completely sure what was going on.

If there is a specific moment in which the relationship between parent and child changes, in which it crosses from love due to admiration to love born of pity, it was that moment in which we floated. I feared the thing he'd tell me next. I was beginning to understand that perhaps there were secrets I didn't want to know. I stood up and walked toward the door, trying to somehow escape the truth like Dr. Angus told me people do. But it was too late. I heard him say that he wasn't my father at all.

My knees buckled. Numbness overtook me, a muting of Angel Duet, the girl I knew. She was distant from me, floating outside, beyond me in that tragic moment, drifting away. I stared straight ahead, caught in a cataplectic nightmare, the first to strike since Claudia's birth.

The baby, I thought. Where's the baby? I vaguely recalled that she was not in my arms, but sleeping upstairs. I knew then that I would only fall on my own face. Because my knees had bent, I would fall on my face and only hurt myself. It would bruise, yellow and purple, ugly like always. I mentally prepared myself for the pain, but instead of hitting the floor, I landed on something soft but strong . . . *someone* strong and warm. She caught me in her arms, and I realized how fast she must have swooped down. I couldn't comprehend who it was until I heard her speak.

"We knew this might happen," Carla said to my father.

When I heard her voice, it all made sense. It made sense that in the end she should be the one to catch me. I was dying after all, I thought. The Angel Duet was gone who'd evolved in the shadow of Betty Lou's clouds, the one with the long horsetail who'd stood by her father's side as he cried beneath those same clouds as if they could rain solace. Her last breath escaped seconds after my father finished speaking, after he uttered the last shocking truth.

Perhaps, at last, I'd found *mother*, but I'd lost my father. It was a death that changed me permanently. Left with the flawed man towering above me, I could not foresee redemption, perhaps forgiveness, in time, but no forgetting, no retrieving what once was. What never existed cannot be retrieved.

Once the blind man sees, he cannot continue living in his imagined world.

As I lay powerless in Carla's embrace, I wondered if it was worse to be one parent short or to be raised at the center of a lie by the one you thought you had.

"Frank, where are you goin'?" Carla asked. "Come back!" Her words bolted past my ear in a shot of hot *mother* breath. His footsteps were loud and frantic. "Please don't go, Frank," she said. "She'll be all right. We'll all talk this out. She needs that from you, Frank!" She hollered through the open door, "Tornados are comin'," but it was too late.

As the door slammed, I decided that the lying was worse. Replacing a parent you never had is easier than erasing a lifetime. "He didn't take an umbrella," said Carla. A tear dropped onto my cheek. I felt it roll until she wiped it away.

Like a mother, she stroked my face.

* * *

"I need your help," Carla said as she finally pulled me up off the floor.

A pillow and blanket lay at my feet. "How long was I sleepin'?" I asked, wiping my mouth.

"You were conked out for about ten minutes and then you fell asleep for an hour or so." She looked at her watch. "I guess you're gonna have to start back on your medication."

"Where is he? Did he come back?" I moved slowly to the kitchen and sat down at the table. "Is Claudia still sleepin'?"

"She's fine. Newborns sleep a lot, don't they? I wish I could sleep that much."

"No, you don't."

She looked sorry. Her short hair had dried into an odd shape. "Listen, Angel, your father didn't come back, and I'm really worried. He never acts like this."

"Well, not in the last ten or so years."

"You've gotta try to forgive him, Angel. No matter what, you *are* his daughter and he loves you."

"I'm not his daughter."

"You really have no choice but to forgive. You don't have a lot of options. You need your father and he needs you."

"So I'm supposed to sympathize with him? I'm supposed to feel sorry for him because he bore a self-inflicted burden all these years? What about me, Carla? What about me?"

"This is not the time to be selfish, Angel. He virtually devoted his life to bein' your father. Your father gave you everythang he could."

"Everythang but what I needed."

"But he believed the truth would hurt you. Don't you understand?"

"Sometimes the truth does hurt, but it's still the best thang. The part that hurts is just reality slappin' you in the face. I could have used that slap, you know. I grew up in a frickin' dream world. Nothin' was even close to what I thought it was." I knew I should be cryin', but I couldn't.

"Even if you'd known about your mother, your father would still have grieved. He would have suffered even more knowin' that you knew. He *wanted* to be a good father, a *real* father."

"I understand that. Don't *you* think that if I fall in love and get married one day, I'll wanna pretend my husband is Claudia's real father? Don't you think I'll wanna believe that? Well, I will. I know that already, after three weeks of bein' a mother. No matter how much my husband loves her, I'll always feel the pain of knowin' there's somethin' precious, priceless actually, that I cain't share completely. But I will never consider lyin'."

"We all live in different worlds, Angel. It's somethin' you'll learn in time. I see it every day in my work."

"But there has to be a common thread, a rope of truth runnin' through all these worlds you're always talkin' about. Isn't that what we're supposed to hang on to?" She stared at me as if I were making sense, as if she agreed. "Well, that's *not* the rope I grew up clingin' to," I said. "And I could have had it."

She wiped her forehead, trying to decide what to do.

The weight of my father's grief finally struck me. I felt heavy in a new way . . . like Kimmy. Heavy but not fat, weighed down by those around me, smothered by their facts and their memories. I suddenly wanted to call Kimmy and say that her parents weren't so bad after all. I wanted to say that she's lucky they live in a world in which the rope of reality stretches thick and bristly between their flop-flopped feet. Perhaps she would never like their world—perhaps she'd choose a different one—but they'd provided that rope, and when she found her own place, it would be there. It was within her reach. And that's what made us different.

"We should go look for him," she said, shaking her head. "When you were sleepin', I called the office and some of our friends, but nobody's seen him. The weather's gettin' worse, and I don't know where he could have gone. I thought maybe you might know." Without her makeup, she looked older. She looked desperate.

"Don't you realize that everythang about my life—my dreams, my personality, my choices—are all based on the lies he told? How do I forgive somebody for that? Even if I wanted to, it's not that easy."

She reached across the kitchen table, taking my hand in hers. "Please," she said.

I stood up and headed back toward the stairs. "I cain't leave Claudia."

"We can take her in the car with us."

"You've obviously never been a parent," I said, but then remembered that she'd had the chance once. "I'm sorry," I said, "but it's stormin' out, and she's only three weeks old. She might get sick."

"Don't you have any friends you can call?"

I thought of Kimmy. "No."

"What about Tim? Maybe he'll come over and watch her."

"He might," I said but wondered if I could trust him.

"Please, Angel, just call him."

"Okay, but then I want you to look at somethin'."

Tim agreed to come, although he was uncomfortable about taking care of an infant.

Carla followed me back out into the foyer. "What is this?" she said, looking at the notepad I'd shoved in her face.

"Look at the photographs. Look at the clouds. I wrote down all the words that were on the back."

She looked back and forth between the clouds and the notepad, trying to figure it out.

"Do you see it?" I went to each photograph and pointed as I said the words, "Angel, baby, candy, decoy . . . they're in alphabetical order. She was trying to find and photograph clouds in the shapes of these . . . these thangs," I said, pointing again to the photographs one by one. "She was movin' through the alphabet."

"I think you're right." Her face brightened, and I knew she was thinking about our plans to get them published. We both sat down at the bottom of the stairs. She asked, "Do you think your father knew about this?"

I shrugged my shoulders as if I didn't care.

"I don't see the significance," she said, "besides it makin' for a more interestin' collection."

"Well, that *is* the point. It was her creative idea. I think it's fantastic. It's interestin' and she knew it. She had a vision. Just like you, Carla, she had a plan. And it was ambitious. Do you realize how hard this would be?"

"Your father told me she spent hours and hours waitin' for the right clouds."

"Maybe that's what drove her crazy," I said, but knew it wasn't true.

"It's creative, Angel, but it really doesn't mean anythang."

"How can you say that? It tells us somethin' about her—it tells me about her personality."

"You already knew she was creative."

"Yeah, but this is different."

"I don't see how, that's all."

I grabbed my notepad from her and stood up. "How can you be so cruel, especially now? She's my mother. She's all I've got . . . except for Claudia. "

"You're wrong, Angel. You've got your father and . . . you've got me," she said, standing up. "I love you, Angel."

"How could you love me?"

"I do," she said, moving closer.

"You've always hated me. You didn't even want me around."

"No," she said. "I love you."

I felt a crack somewhere. "Please don't say that," I said, my heart breaking.

"I love you, Angel," she said again, reaching out to touch my arm. Her hand was warm and small like Scarlett's, but bony and veined like Betty Lou's. "First of all, I've never hated you, and secondly, I may not have found it easy to relate in the beginnin', but relationships grow, feelin's change." She stepped closer, causing me to move toward the wall on which Betty Lou's clouds hung.

I was trapped between Carla's love and my mother's clouds.
The doorbell rang.
My father was gone.
My child was crying.
I said, "I think I know where he might be."

☑ zipper

The thundering sky drowned out the boards creaking beneath Carla's feet as she bolted across the planked floor. "Frank, what are you doin' in here?" she yelled above the roar of rain and wind. My father remained crouched in the corner of the tiny one-room house. From the doorway, I could barely see him, huddled like a small child banished to the corner. The day was dark and angry like those in Betty Lou's attic stash of photographs. Rain splattered my back.

"Leave me alone," was all he said. He shoved his head between his knees like a dog's tail.

Carla didn't listen. Instead, she sat down beside him on the dirty floor while I remained in the doorway, remembering the old house. After fifteen years it remained unchanged. All those years ago, my father told me it was once the home of slaves, kin to the numerous shacks here and there throughout Shreveport. Gray squares with tiny porches, they were all in various stages of decay. This one resided, as if planted in the soil, at the far end of one of the fields my father and I had frequented for a time. According to my father, it was Betty Lou's favorite.

He cried deep, dark man cries I could barely hear. I *wanted* to feel sorry for him. I searched for love, but couldn't find it. The thunder grew louder. Light shot through the dilapidated home, stripping it of its charm, illuminating its flaws, forcing us to face each other in the light. My eyes ached, and I squeezed them shut. The house shook, and I feared its walls would crumble. Carla and my father seemed unaware, but I feared it would trap us beneath its hundred-year-old weight—its boards would close in like fingers. Trapped in the palm of its splintery hand, we'd share the fate of the slaves who suffered within its walls. Their cries traveled with the wind's howl, creating a score for our fractured scene. Then the wails of Betty Lou permeated the tiny shack, rattling it uncontrollably. I was sure that hers was the wail my father struggled to block by covering his ears.

Carla assumed he was trying to escape her own steady voice.

Only my father and I heard Betty Lou.

I pictured my mother's varicose veins and matted hair. I smelled her pee on the floor.

"Frank," Carla said, trying to pry his large hands away from his ears. "Please stop. This is insane! And no, I'm not gonna apologize for sayin' it. Everythang that's happened—none of it's your fault. The only thang you're guilty of is love—for a child—and that's that. You've just gotta get up and move on." She looked at me. "You both gotta move forward."

"Well, I don't see it that way," I said above the storm. "He's not my father anymore as far as I'm concerned." I walked closer, staring at him through the musty air. "You stole the truth from me 'cause you were a coward. And don't try and tell me that I can just move on like it's simple," I said to Carla. "Nothin' in my life's the same as it was last week."

My father wiped his nose and cleared his throat. "You're right," he said. "I cain't understand *exactly* how you feel, but you cain't understand my feelin's either, or my decisions." He finally looked up. "This storm was the type she'd run out in." He took a deep breath. "And when I'd try and stop her, she'd scream so loud and horrible you'd think I was killin' her. A couple of times, she got hold of you and ran out before I could catch her. She held you up into the storm like a lightin' rod."

"My God," Carla said, rubbing his back as best she could without splintering her hands on the slave-built wall.

"She tried to kill you."

"No," I yelled. "She loved me!" I didn't know if I wanted to move closer to them or back out into the storm. Moving in seemed limiting while the storm, although frightening, seemed like the best escape, the only route to somewhere else.

"You have no idea what it's like to live with a mentally ill person," he said, "to watch 'em slowly lose their mind. At first she didn't think she was crazy. She thought everyone else had the problem. She thought the world was collapsin' around her. She thought she was the only person standing upright. The pressure was killin' her."

"I understand, Frank. I do," Carla said, trying to ease his pain.

"Why did you keep me? Why did you even want me?"

"Because she loved you and wanted you more than anythang."

"But you said she tried to kill me."

"She was sick, that's all, Angel," he cried. "The schizophrenia got worse and worse as her pregnancy progressed. She insisted that the baby was ours, but I knew it wasn't. Everyone knew."

I thought of the pork rinds in Florida. "Her parents, you mean?"

"They knew it wasn't mine because we'd tried to have a baby for two years. I'd been tested—it was my fault." His words came like a flood he'd held back for years. "I tried to tell her. I tried to explain that the baby wasn't mine but she wouldn't listen. Finally when you were about one and a half, she couldn't fight anymore."

"I don't want to know anymore," I screamed. "Stop!"

"Angel, you hear your father out, goddamn it," Carla ordered.

"She cut your tiny arms," he sobbed. "She took you outside, and I couldn't find you, either of you. I just kept runnin' and runnin' until I realized I was runnin' in circles. I had to call the police. Finally, I heard her screamin'. She screamed and screamed and screamed."

I slapped my hands on my ears. I could hear her screaming my name through the mental hospital. I sank down onto the floor and curled into a ball like Bippy. I closed my eyes and tried to sleep, to shut out the pain.

"This is what you wanted, Angel. It hurts, but you have to listen."
It was Carla. I reached up and clung to her like a child clings to its
mother. I cried into her chest and swore I would never let go.

My father continued, "I couldn't protect her anymore. They took
her away. They arrested her, screamin' like that, and I couldn't save
her. I watched her go, and all I could think about was that sweet eigh-
teen-year-old girl with blond curls who loved the clouds and fields and
me. She was gone. Don't you see you were all I had left? It didn't matter that you weren't my biological child. Her parents didn't want you.
They couldn't bear to look at either of us. We were freaks to 'em."

I could hear myself crying. I wished I could sleep, but remembered
that Mac's wife had shown me the cage I hid inside. I held Carla
tighter, knowing she'd been right all along.

"Frank," she said. "All that matters is that you loved her. That's
what makes a father."

"But he's weak. He lied," I cried. "He said she was so special and
that she died. But I remembered her. I wondered my whole life how I
could remember."

"Angel, I didn't know what to do. It was a horrible situation. For
over two years, I tried to take care of her myself, but she sank deeper
and deeper until there was nothin' left."

* * *

When we finally got back to the house, my father and I both walked
past all twenty-two photographs like zombies, afraid to turn our heads
and look. I wondered if they could retain their meaning. It pained me
to think that I might look at them and only remember this night.

"Where's Claudia?" I asked Tim, who was standing in the foyer
looking as if he wanted to leave. "Is she sleepin'?"

"She's in the livin' room," he said, "with Mac."

"Who's Mac?" Carla asked.

"He's a doctor," Tim said, smiling. "He knows about babies."

My father walked upstairs to lie down. As I watched him go, head
still hanging, I knew he'd relearned all he needed to know.

Mac was sitting in the living room with Claudia in his arms. He
looked like a new father, his eyes open and bright with wonder.

I knew then that he was the one true thing I could believe in.

I sat down next to him expecting to take her, but he held her close. Her eyes peeked open; she was content to stay. I asked, "What are you doin' here?"

"Tim said you needed me." He looked down at Claudia. "He said you both need me."

"I'll take her," Carla said, as if she understood. My father was right about her. She was strong and good. "Tim," she said, "I have a few questions for you. Angel said you were the only witness to Kimmy's assault?"

"Yeah," he said as they left the room.

I leaned back into the sofa and took a deep breath. "Did he tell you everythang?"

"Pretty much," Mac said, putting his hand on my knee. "How are you?"

"I cried all the way home."

He wiped my damp hair away from my face. "Angel, you know, in the end bein' a father is more than genetics."

"I cain't forgive him," I said, shaking my head. "He's not the person I thought he was. I don't know if I'll be able to forgive him."

He stared at the fireplace. "Can you forgive me?"

"For what?" I asked, new tears surfacing.

"For cheatin' on my wife, for marryin' her in the first place, and for being a total ass."

"Where is she?"

"I don't know. She's gone, and it's okay," he said, turning to look at me. "Do you remember when we were in Florida and I told you that I didn't know what to do to make thangs better for you? Do you remember how I said that all my friends who became doctors to help people would know exactly what to do? I said I became a doctor to make *myself* feel better."

I stared at him.

"You're the only one who made me forget myself."

I shook my head, trying one last time to resist a moment that would pull me close and make me feel loved.

He held my head still and pressed his cheek against mine. "You made me forget all the shit," he whispered. As his words registered, his clean-shaven skin became *mother* soft. It hadn't been before, and I realized I was finally feeling what was inside, beneath his skin, feeling something soft and warm, accepting and positive.

I pulled away. "Maybe it's just 'cause I have enough for both of us."

"No . . . I love you, Angel."

"Why are you doin' this to me now?"

"Because now I know what to do to make thangs better for you, and for Claudia."

"But I don't wanna be your patient. I wanna be loved for who I am, not for my weakness. I'm so tired, Mac," I cried. "I'm just so tired."

"But you gave me strength," he said, pulling me into the strong embrace that, in the end, was big enough for me . . . and for my child. I fell limp against him, not from narcolepsy but from the knowledge that I could finally relax, that I was exactly where I should be. "How can I ever forgive him?" I cried into his shoulder.

"I don't know, but I know it's possible. I also know that I could love Claudia, if you'll let me. I understand how your dad loved you because he loved your mother. All these years, he was tryin' to protect you. He just didn't realize it was the kind of situation you cain't hide from. It finds you in the end."

"But someone else is my father, someone horrible. Someone who drove my mother crazy and ruined everythang."

"Your mother has schizophrenia. It would have surfaced in time, no matter what. It was just waitin' for a trigger. That's how it works."

"But why did it all happen?" I closed my eyes, wishing I knew the answer.

"Your father gave you a gift," Mac said.

I clung to him and felt the storm clouds, the circus clowns, and the shit clearing away. In time it would all be replaced. I opened my eyes and saw my mother's clouds stretched across the wall, stretching across my life, making me feel as if I could actually fly.

NEWS ABOUT TOWN

SHREVEPORT—A local resident has obtained a publishing contract for a collection of unique photographs. The set includes twenty-six cloud formations, each in the shape of an object beginning with the letters A through Z. Some of the objects found and photographed by the tenacious cloud-watchers responsible for the inspiring collection are a snake, a nail, and an umbrella. One particularly unusual photograph, aptly titled "Xanadu," captures an entire city skyline hidden in the clouds. The photographer, Angel Boyd, completed the collection begun by her mother, Betty Lou Duet. Duet took twenty-two of the twenty-six photographs over a seven-year period in the 1950s and '60s before succumbing to severe mental illness. Duet now resides in an institution in Sarasota, Fla. While Boyd does not have plans to pursue a photography career, she is working on a novel based on the events that led to publication of the photographs. Boyd is an associate professor of history at Louisiana State University. She and her husband, a local physician, and their two children reside in North Shreveport.

Aberrations by Penelope Przekop

BOOK CLUB QUESTIONS

1. *Aberrations* is a probing emotional drama that explores a number of themes—parent-child relationship, love, friendship, self-image, mental illness—but at the heart of the story is this undercurrent about truth. Do we really know what's true in our lives? How do we handle the truth once we uncover it?

2. The main character, a college student named Angel, suffers from narcolepsy. How does Przekop shed light on such a complex dysfunction?

3. It seems the other characters also go in and out of a sleep, so to speak, as they live not fully in reality. For instance, it seems each character is troubled by what they see as their own flaw or issue and is so blinded by their perceived deficiency that they fail to fully awaken to the fact that others have their own dysfunctions and their own fears or insecurities about them. Why is it so hard for us to look past things that certainly may seem like baggage but in the end make us who we really are?

4. One character is gay but hasn't told his mom. Another is a 26-year-old virgin who is adopted and lives in a trailer with her white-trash parents. Another loses his wife to a tragedy. Another has the burden of a miscarriage. What do they each have in common?

5. Przekop writes of mental illness, including schizophrenia. It's hard for the loved ones closest to the mentally ill to see them so weak, so helpless, so utterly in pain. How do the innocent standbys deal with that?

6. *Aberrations* takes place in the late 80s in Shreveport, Louisiana. What did you learn about this place and time, and how does life there compare and contrast with where you grew up?

7. Many of the characters live with lies or secrets and yet it seems these lies eventually are exposed. Why do we tend to burden ourselves with secrets that we know deep down will one day be revealed?

8. Angel grows up without a mother and she seems to always be looking for someone to be that mother for her. Why does she think she's found the touch of her mother when she has a one-night experimental fling with a lesbian?

9. *Aberrations* is also clearly about the choices we make—and the sacrifices we volunteer to undergo. But sometimes we make the wrong choice and our life is never the same. How does one live with their mistakes or regrets?

10. Przekop says that sometimes the gifts we receive are not what we want and that only in time do we see their worth. What does this mean to you?

11. One of the characters is an adulterer. Why does he stay in a marriage that he shouldn't have entered in the first place and why would someone want to date a married guy?

12. Angel is resistant to accepting a woman as her step-mom whom her dad has been dating for a long time. Why can't she embrace this woman who wants nothing more than to love and help her?

13. Angel discovers she'd been lied to her whole life about some very serious things. How does one confront that their life is not at all what it had appeared to be?

14. Przekop's story redefines what it means to be a parent. What is it truly all about to raise a child, especially if the child isn't a blood relative?

15. One of the characters asks: "Is it bad to want more than what you have?" Is it?

16. One character says: "The smallest thang can change somebody's world. We all live in different worlds. You didn't think we all lived in the same one, did you?" What does this mean?

17. Przekop writes about overstepping boundaries. Who sets these boundaries and should we break past them if we want to grow or change?

18. How does *Aberrations* show the danger of idolizing someone, as Angel does her mother?

19. Why do we think or assume the lives of others are perfect compared to our own?

20. Is holding back the truth from another a lie?

21. One character says she was guilty of "the need for someone else to make me perfect simply by thinking it was true." Why do we act this way?